T0199105

Cold, hard facts are what make or break a case for the FBI. But when there's evidence that one of their own has been turned, there's more on the line than the truth. There are personal bonds that can be stretched to the limit...

After blacking out, a discharged weapon and hazy memories put FBI profiler Cynthia Deming at the scene of a crime: the execution of six federal witnesses against the mob. The one and only person she can turn to for help is her best friend, Boston forensic pathologist Charlie Foulkes. It's a relationship that no one on her team knows about—and it's about to be tested by danger and desire...

Charlie knows that Cynthia is no killer. But as they embark on a shadow investigation to clear her name, evidence surfaces implicating him. With the conviction of a mob boss hanging in the balance, they'll have to uncover who's framing them to take the fall, and what lines they're willing to cross—in their professional and personal lives—to prove that nothing will tear them apart.

Books by Kris Rafferty

Secret Agents Series:

CAUGHT BY YOU
CATCH A KILLER
DEADLY PAST

Deadly Past

Secret Agents Series

Kris Rafferty

LYRICAL PRESS
Kensington Publishing Corp.
www.kensingtonbooks.com

LYRICAL PRESS BOOKS are published by

Kensington Publishing Corp.
119 West 40th Street
New York, NY 10018

All Kensington titles, imprints, and distributed lines are available at special quantity discounts for bulk purchases for sales promotion, premiums, fundraising, educational, or institutional use.

Special book excerpts or customized printings can also be created to fit specific needs. For details, write or phone the office of the Kensington Sales Manager: Kensington Publishing Corp., 119 West 40th Street, New York, NY 10018. Attn. Sales Department. Phone: 1-800-221-2647.

Lyrical Underground and Lyrical Underground logo Reg. US Pat. & TM Off.

First Electronic Edition: December 2018
eISBN-13: 978-1-5161-0815-2
eISBN-10: 1-5161-0815-9

First Print Edition: December 2018
ISBN-13: 978-1-5161-0818-3
ISBN-10: 1-5161-0818-3

Printed in the United States of America

For my smart, handsome, funny father. I love you, Dad.

Chapter One

Searing pain had Special Agent Cynthia Deming's blue eyes opened and wide as she bolted upright in bed, her blond hair draped over half her face. Heart racing, vision blurred, she threw her legs over the mattress's edge, suffering nausea and a headache that left her gasping. She touched the back of her head and felt matted, sticky hair around a clotted cut. When her vision cleared, she studied the resultant blood smears on her manicured fingertips, on her expensive gray pantsuit, on the worn and ugly bedspread.

Wait. Not her bed, or her bedroom.

"Well, this can't be good." Her voice came out raspy. *What the hell happened last night?* Fully dressed, injured, in a stranger's bed? This was an unwelcome first.

The stale air did seem familiar, however, as did the brown drapes pulled closed over windows. The bedroom was innocuous, its furnishings dated and worn. Maybe a cheap motel? Bare beige walls, fragrance of carpet cleaner, and a television against the wall did hint at a rented room, but there was no desk, phone, or tiny refrigerator—things that would indicate a motel.

She struggled to her feet, swayed, and felt dizzy. A heavy object fell to the floor. A gun. Cynthia's hand palmed her hip holster and found it empty. No small beans. She didn't remember removing it from her holster. *Definitely* not good. Cynthia retrieved it from the floor too quickly, inviting more nausea and spiking head pain, forcing her to sit again as panic teased the edges of her composure.

She couldn't remember. Not how she'd arrived here, or even where *here* was.

Pulling back the gun's slide, she noted the bullet chambered, checked the magazine, counted rounds, and found six missing. A sniff told her it had been discharged recently.

"Well, shit." Bad news was piling up, and it was beginning to feel personal.

Cynthia struggled to her feet. She had to take a moment to find her balance, so it felt like an accomplishment when she'd made her way to the heavily draped window. She nudged aside the curtain, winced as morning sunlight irritated her eyes, and felt relieved to recognize the view.

Chinatown, Boston. She was at a federal safe house she'd used three weeks prior for a case now closed. Why was she here? Injured, with gun drawn, red flags flapping in the breeze. From her vantage point, she could see her black Lexus parked at the curb across the street, indicating she'd driven here. A quick press of her palm to her pants pocket and she found her car keys, which eased her mind enough to holster her gun. There was no sign of her iPhone, or wallet, suggesting she'd been robbed. But then what?

She couldn't remember.

Whatever had happened had prompted her to seek shelter at the safe house. Not the worst decision she'd ever made. An active safe house had on-site personnel who could help her, and *fill in some blanks.* Hope spiked as she hurried out of the room, and it grew as she continued to recognize familiar wall-to-wall rugs, worn to the backing in places, dingy beige drywall, the dark hallway, the smell of cigarettes and air freshener. She might have lost time, but she remembered these details.

The safe house had a hollow feel, and it surrounded her in silence. Calling out, searching every room, she continued to hope *someone* was there, until the last room was searched. Nothing and nobody. Not unusual, just damned inconvenient. When not staffed, the safe house was locked up tighter than a tick, heavily alarmed to protect its expensive surveillance tech. So how'd she get in?

The security cameras would have the video. Cynthia hurried back to the surveillance room on the first floor, in the back near the kitchen. It was hard to focus past the stabbing pain in her head and the accompanying nausea, but she did, punching in the door's code with trembling fingers. Afraid the code might have been changed since she'd last been here, she waited nervously, and then enjoyed a wave of relief when the door clicked open. She stepped inside to view a wall-to-wall display of monitors, each screen dedicated to a different live security camera: the building's two entrances, all abutting streets, and the roof. A long desk in the middle of the room was covered with electronics, hard drives, and keyboards.

Cynthia sat at the desk, logged in using her FBI security clearance, and pulled up archived digital video, searching for last night's time stamp.

The desk's phone caught her eye as she scrolled through the video, keeping her finger on the keyboard's down arrow button. It nudged her conscience. Her team leader, FBI Special Agent Jack Benton, would be wondering why she hadn't arrived at work yet. Eight AM. He'd want her absence explained. He'd have questions, deserved answers, and she'd have none.

She'd look like a fool.

Cynthia's heart sank as she thought of the many ways her team would spank her over this bizarre turn of events, but when she factored in the safe house's phone protocols—three levels of security on all incoming and outgoing calls—it had her hesitating to broaden the scope of who knew of her troubles. Staff, rightly, would require explanations regarding a federal agent's unauthorized use of a secret safe house, and her blackout would produce incomplete answers, suspicion, and be noted in her personnel file—a high cost for a potentially benign reason for waking, injured, in a Chinatown safe house.

"Ugh." A lifetime of following rules could not be ignored. She grabbed the phone, and then her image appeared on the monitor's screen, distracting her enough to place the receiver back on its cradle. Digital time stamp: 10:30 PM. Cynthia's image staggered down the center of the street, just outside of the safe house, gun drawn and hanging at her side. Drunk? Cynthia refused to believe her eyes. Then her image moved and a streetlight illuminated her face. She froze the image, zoomed in, and recognized pain—not inebriation—contorting her face.

She'd arrived at the safe house injured. Good to know.

Rummaging in a desk drawer, she found a flash drive, inserted it into the computer's port, and watched as her image progressed past her parked Lexus to the safe house's stairs, and then its stoop. Whatever her level of impaired cognition last night, she'd been clear-headed enough to punch in the door's security code, but not clear-headed enough to drive. Cynthia paused the video, clicking appropriate pulldown menus, and copied, then downloaded, the time-stamped video footage.

Benton would have questions, and this video was all Cynthia had to offer.

She clicked "copy," and flinched as pain flared behind her eyes. It blinded her for a moment, forcing her to breathe through the nausea. Her stomach lurched without warning, forcing Cynthia to lean over a waste bin as she emptied her stomach. Shaken, blinking past watering eyes, she struggled to read the screen, clicking a message panel she assumed said "download complete." Tucking the flash drive into her pocket, she managed to breathe past the worst of her stomach's spasms, and finally her vision cleared.

The screen's pop-up message box stated, "File deleted."

"No!" Cynthia hit the computer's power button, hoping to hard boot the system, maybe activate an auto-recovery program. The computer didn't respond. The screens remained unchanged as the words "File deleted" stared back at her. She hit the power button again. Still nothing. In full panic mode, Cynthia yanked the wires from the hard drive's ports, front and back. All monitors went dark, and the hard drive's motor fell silent. Heart racing, her breathing labored, Cynthia stared in horror at the wall of now *blank* monitors. What had she done?

She'd fucked up.

This computer system didn't respond like her personal laptop. Where were the fail-safes? High tech *federal* security hardware should have fail-safes, but tech hated her, so maybe she'd found a way to make them fail. Cynthia couldn't keep a watch more than six months before it died, and had long since given up wearing them. Even her iPhone hated her, always freezing, never working correctly. Why had she assumed she could finesse these computers? Cynthia groaned, realizing there was nothing she could do now but cut her losses. Tech support would clean up this mess as they'd cleaned up her other messes in the past.

She pushed away from the desk, spared a glance for the soiled waste bin, and then remembered the sheets and comforter that she'd bloodied upstairs. Ten minutes later, she tossed them in the dumpster out back and headed across the street toward her car. Clicking her Lexus's key fob, she opened the driver's side door and slid behind the wheel, instantly relieved to see her pink Kate Spade pocketbook in the backseat. Her gym bag was open on the passenger seat. Resting her hand on the clothes, she realized they were still slightly damp, and it triggered a memory. The gym last night. A couple blocks down. It might have security cameras, too, so maybe video there could fill in her memory gaps. Her iPhone lay on top of the soiled gym clothes—battery dead, big surprise—next to a small container of peppermint gum, which she fell on like a starving child. Her wallet was in her Kate Spade bag.

"Hm." Cynthia's anxiety had her chewing the gum frenetically. "Curiouser and curiouser." Finding her phone and wallet ruled out robbery, so what was left? Abduction by aliens?

Fifteen minutes later, she parked at the curb of her Back Bay Gloucester Street apartment, impatient to call Benton from her landline phone. The peppermint gum had settled her stomach and her headache was under control, but she was panicking. Memories were flooding back…of men on their knees, bags over their heads, hands tied behind their backs. A brick wall. Blood. Lots and lots of blood. So…definitely not aliens.

Cynthia dropped her keys twice as she worked the front lock to her apartment. Once inside, she hurried down the hall to her landline phone in the living room. In her rush, she dropped her pocketbook, and didn't see him until she flipped on the overhead light. Cynthia lashed out with a punch, shrieking as fear suffused her. He twisted his upper body upon impact, stripping her blow of power, but by then her fright had turned to anger.

"Charlie!" If looks could kill, she'd be planning a funeral.

Charlie Foulkes. The center of her universe, her past, her present, her best friend. He stood between her and the phone, arms folded over his chest, and he was glowering. Totally pissed. Almost as pissed as she was with him. Cynthia had been avoiding Charlie for months, and just looking at him now made her cringe with embarrassment.

"Damn, Charlie!" She holstered her gun, only then noticing she'd even pulled it, and that her living room was a mess. Among other things, an empty carton of mango sorbet with an accompanying dirty spoon littered the side table. Clean laundry waited to be folded on the ottoman, and four pair of heels were underfoot, scattered over her rose-colored Persian rug. Fighting back mortification, she gathered the shoes and tossed them behind the leather couch, pretending not to hear the loud clatter as they bounced off the oak wainscoting. "I almost shot you!" she said.

Charlie—Boston Police Department's forensic pathologist—didn't seem all that impressed with his close call. Sexy as hell, his red hair disheveled, Charlie wore his usual jeans, boots, and short-sleeved shirt. His big blue eyes were hooded by furrowed brows, his full lips thinned with anger, and the sight was impressive. Intimidating, even.

Lifting the laundry basket, she gave Charlie a wide berth as she set it next to the grandfather clock, out of his line of sight. After a last scan of the room, she decided the rug didn't need vacuuming, and the books and newspapers on her antique side tables weren't technically clutter, so she mirrored Charlie's posture—arms folded over her chest, scowling. Cynthia hated when Charlie got mad at her. Other people? She could give a damn. But Charlie? It *really* bothered her, *and he knew it*. He'd weaponize himself, and her one defense was being angry back, because it *really* bothered Charlie when she was angry at him.

They were best friends; it didn't have to make sense. They'd known each other since she was twelve, and up until a few months ago they'd been as close to inseparable as friends could be. Friends. Just friends. Whatever had prompted his drive to her apartment—at nearly the crack of dawn—had him upset enough to interrupt his morning routine. He'd foregone his shave. Cynthia hadn't seen him unshaven since…well, since the accident, and that was ten years back. The scruff was a menacing layer to his full-bodied frown. Boots braced shoulder width apart, Charlie towered over Cynthia's five-feet, six inches, intimidating her, though he'd be the last person to admit that was his endgame.

"You look like shit," he said. His biceps twitched as he rolled his shoulders, as if working out a kink.

"Kiss my ass." She nudged a matted lock of hair behind her ear, hating that he was right. Hating that he looked sexy and fit in his dishevelment, while she not only felt like hell, he'd assured her that she looked like it, too. She walked to the couch, peeled off her ruined suit jacket, and then sat, using her jacket to protect the leather from her disgusting hair.

"Where have you been?" Charlie lived for his job and his family, and not in that order. He was taking her absence personally. She wanted to throw a denial in his face, to tell him he had no right to worry about her, but she knew it wasn't true. They didn't share so much as a DNA strand, but Cynthia was family by default. Terrance's little sister. Terrance, who'd died ten years ago, after wrapping his new roadster around a tree with his best friend, Charlie, in the passenger seat. "I've been waiting here since eleven last night," he said.

"Who asked you to?" Cynthia hated the guilt he easily summoned. "Since when do you show up unannounced at my apartment, using a key I gave you *only for emergencies*, by the way, and question my whereabouts?"

"Cynthia—" Her name left his lips on a growl.

"No, really, Charlie." She felt at a disadvantage—sitting, while he towered over her—so she flavored her tone with belligerence to hide her weakness. "What if I'd pulled an all-nighter last night with a strange man I picked up in a bar? Then I find you here when I return home, making things all awkward. I could lie to you, of course, and pretend it didn't happen. That I wasn't doing the nasty between the sheets with some dude named Jeff. Should I? Should I lie?"

She hated that he'd just assumed she'd be here when he showed up last night, as if she had no personal life. Odds were nil she'd do the nasty with a stranger, named Jeff or otherwise, but *damn*. A woman had her pride and he had no right to assume her sex life was dull as dishwater. That was Cynthia's sad little secret. She wasn't even sure he was listening, because he seemed fascinated by her hair, his anger expanding his chest and widening his eyes.

On a sharp exhale, he said, "Your head is bleeding."

"Huh?" She pressed her palm to the top of her head, instinctively trying to hide the evidence, which was stupid. No hiding that she'd been roughed up.

He finally met her gaze, and looked ready to explode. "Are you telling me *Jeff* did this to you? *You had sex with a 'Jeff,' who did this to you?*" Shock nudged aside irritation, and now that she thought on it, it wasn't unreasonable for Charlie to draw that horrible conclusion from her hypothetical social life with the nonexistent Jeff.

"No." She bit her lip, recoiling from the thought. There it was again: guilt, guilt, guilt. There seemed to be guilt connected with every damn interaction they'd had lately. "No, Charlie. I'm sorry. Forget I said anything." Yada yada yada. Her head hurt. She didn't have any more energy to wade through another emotional quagmire. When would she learn to just shut her mouth?

"So Jeff," he said, allowing his words to hang as he waited for more information.

Cynthia waved him off. "Doesn't exist. Forget it." Flushed, she felt stupid now that her Jeff example had blown up, especially since it seemed like a clinical example of a blatant cry for attention. Almost as if she'd wanted to make Charlie jealous. She peeked at him from behind a lock of hair hanging over her right eye, wondering if he was...*but that would be insane*, because they were just friends. She wanted to change the subject. Not easy, under the pall of Charlie's dark frowns and him looming over her, making it hard to think.

Especially since the last time they'd talked, *really* talked, she'd been quite drunk on tequila and had kissed him: a full-throttle, moan-inducing, tongue-thrusting, hips-grinding kiss. Just thinking about it mortified her. Well, not the kiss so much as what had happened afterward. The damn man pushed her away, and the kiss had gotten off to such a great start, too. Hot. Sexy. Bone-meltingly arousing. She could tell he'd liked it, too, because when her hips ground against his rock-hard erection, he'd moaned, too. It was the sexiest, most arousing sound she'd ever heard in her life. *Then* he rejected her.

Rejected her kiss, and more importantly, rejected everything the kiss would have preceded. She'd been drunk, so she'd respected his integrity and everything, but Cynthia's pride still stung. And *despite* all attempts to avoid him since, Charlie kept pushing, pushing, and pushing past every roadblock she'd erected between them. The guy refused to give her privacy to lick her wounds and move past his rejection, and insisted on hovering, worrying, trying to gentle them back into the comfortable "friendship" they'd enjoyed since the accident.

But she wasn't ready. Every time she looked at him, she remembered how she'd revealed herself. She'd been emotionally naked, and he'd pushed her away. How did a woman move past something like that? She didn't.

Cynthia went so far as to decline invitations to his parents' house to protect her pride. Even that backfired. Delia and Paul Foulkes, his parents, kept sending Charlie to her house, demanding to know why she was avoiding everyone with the last name of Foulkes. Well, Charlie knew. Actions had consequences. Rejecting her kisses had consequences. And the man had to learn.

"What do you want, Charlie?" His deep blue eyes bored into hers and narrowed, telling her he was irritated with her tone. Well, duh. That had been the point of her tone.

"*You* called *me*," he said.

Charlie's shirtsleeves strained as he adjusted his arms, folding them more firmly over his chest, making his biceps pop. His thigh muscles stretched the fabric of his jeans also, and his waistband rode low on his hips, revealing a strip of muscled lower abdomen, that tasty bit of belly that separated the "six-pack" from "the package." Cynthia loved that strip.

Charlie was large, mere inches from being "too muscular," though she'd yet to hear a woman complain. No, women didn't complain about Charlie, but they talked. Lots of talk. If Cynthia had to hear one more woman at the precinct swoon over the sexy Boston Police Department forensic pathologist, Cynthia was going to spit, because she knew any one of them had more of a shot with Charlie than she did.

"I called you?" When Cynthia found her cell in her car, it had been predictably dead.

"Last night." He stepped close, his boots between her shoes, trapping her on the couch, forcing her knees to widen or risk touching his legs with her inner thighs. A glance told her he was examining her for damage, noting every tear in her suit, every smudge on her face. "What's with the blood?" He pulled her head forward and none too gently examined her laceration.

"Hey!" Cynthia slapped at his hands, but he easily maintained control of her head, poking at her scalp.

"Stop it. Let me see," he said. She felt him pick aside her blood-matted hair. "It's not bleeding anymore, but you still might need a stitch or two to help it heal correctly." He palpated the rest of her scalp, then drew his warm fingers down her neck and checked her pulse with one hand as his other moved to her shoulder, stopping her from squirming. His touch felt like a caress, and his nearness made her feel all weak inside, and vulnerable. "You hurt anywhere else?" He lifted her hands, his touch gentle, almost reverent, as he studied them. She leaned back in the couch, needing to put distance between them. He was making her feel things she didn't want to feel.

"What are you doing?" she said, loving how his strong hands enveloped hers.

"You look like you had one hell of a brawl last night, but I see no knuckle abrasions or bruising, so what happened?"

She had no idea. Not fully, anyway.

Cynthia pulled her hands from his strong grip. "I...I'm fine."

"You're clearly not." He walked away, leaving the room, and it felt like a reprieve. From Charlie's alarmed expression, she feared her head laceration was worse than she'd supposed. He returned moments later, a bag of frozen peas in hand. When he pressed it to her head, her pain spiked, taking her breath away. She gasped, batting at him.

"Hold still." He took her hand and pressed it to the frozen bag before releasing it. "Keep that in place. The cut can't be stitched if the wound is too swollen." Head bent, she stared at his boots, focusing on the sensation of the cold bag against her overheated hand.

"Stop treating me like a child." The bag slipped from her grip, forcing her to use both hands to adjust it back in place. "I'm all grown." He sat next to her, doing the whole "manspread" thing, and the heat of his thigh pressed against hers made it hard to concentrate, especially since she suspected her stringy, matted hair, and hunched back from holding the bag to her wound, made her look like a crone.

"I've noticed." His smile confused the hell out of her, until he raised his brows suggestively. Her heart curdled with embarrassment. Leave it to Charlie to think *now* was a good time to talk about the-kiss-that-shall-not-be-mentioned.

"Listen, Romeo." She swatted his thigh and scooted away from him on the couch. Cynthia didn't do humiliation well, so she defaulted to anger. "Yes, I kissed you, it was a disaster—"

"A disaster?" His smile was kind, and playful. She would have preferred a swift kick.

"I've kissed loads of guys, and sometimes it's good, and sometimes, yes, it's a disaster, but not one of them acted—*months later*—as if the sky was falling."

His cheek kicked up. "It sure felt like the sky was falling. Or maybe that was the earth moving."

"*Stop*." They both knew he'd rejected her. Why was he acting as if he hadn't? "I don't appreciate you embarrassing me."

"I'm not." His eyes widened as he shook his head.

"Yes, you are! Can you just leave it alone? The kiss was a mistake. I didn't like it either—"

"You didn't like it?" His brows lifted again, skeptically this time.

"No, I didn't, and please do us both a favor and pretend it never happened. I had too much tequila. We both know what happens when I drink tequila."

"We've drunk plenty of tequila and you've never stuck your tongue down my throat before."

"But—" He had her there, and as she struggled to piece together a suitable comeback, she found herself studying his features. He was enjoying himself, and here she was *injured, bleeding, for heaven's sake,* and he was torturing her.

"Yes?" he prompted, giving her his complete attention.

"As I said, I didn't like it. So…just stop, will you?"

He sighed, and then finally averted his intense stare, only to give her the side eye. "One disastrous kiss shouldn't ruin a friendship."

The very idea was ludicrous on both counts. "I never said that!"

"We kiss. You think it's a disaster, and then you avoid me like the plague. If I were a better kisser, would you still have cut me and my parents off?"

"*I didn't.*" A bald-faced lie. She did. She really did.

"And I'll have you know, *plenty* of women think I'm a good kisser."

Plenty? She didn't want to think about it. Struggling to say the right thing and keep her pride, she floundered. "I'm sure you're a good kisser with…well, with someone else. Or…I don't know." Who was she kidding? Their kiss had been fabulous, and try as she might, she couldn't get it out of her head. "It's just—" His eyes narrowed and Cynthia gave up, groaning as she leaned her head back on the couch, squeezing her eyes shut.

"What? Talk to me." He took her hand and gave it a squeeze.

She'd kissed him. Took a chance, and now it was time to suffer the consequences. She'd earned this comeuppance, and it was only right that she take it like a…well, a woman.

"Go ahead. Have at it," she said, allowing her head to loll to the side so she was forced to see the male arrogance on his face as he declared his superiority. For Charlie didn't want Cynthia as she wanted him, and that put her at a disadvantage. They both knew it. "Say what you will." Only she didn't see male arrogance radiating off him. She saw kindness.

"Okay." Charlie tugged her to his side, and when she was comfortably enfolded in his embrace, he gave her a brotherly squeeze. "I've been worried since ten last night, after you called, and I've been checking police scanners ever since, fearing they'd find your body on the side of the road."

Guilt, guilt, guilt. Her bottom lip pushed out. "I'm sorry. I don't remember calling you." His long silence, coupled with his body tensing, told Cynthia he was going to make a big deal out of this, and she wasn't sure she had the energy to argue with him.

"Explain," he said.

"I blacked out. What did I say on the call?"

"Nothing," he said. "I answered, and the line went dead. When I hit redial, it went straight to voice mail. I called your landline. No answer. I called Benton, Gilroy, O'Grady—"

"Dammit!" She groaned. He'd called her supervisor, and her teammates, so they'd been worrying since last night, too. "Who *didn't* you call? Now they'll—"

His arm around her shoulders squeezed, making his embrace more restraint than comfort. "I was trying to track you down. I was worried. Tell me about this blackout you suffered." His protective tendencies had been triggered, and Charlie had slipped into big brother mode. He'd spent the last ten years—even the year he'd been flat on his back after the accident—worrying, doing his best to be a big brother because of a misguided belief he could have stopped her brother from driving drunk and dying. Cynthia knew better. Everyone who had ever known her brother knew there was no controlling Terrance.

"I'm sorry." Cynthia pressed the frozen bag to her head again, feeling the weight of those familiar words. *Sorry* she'd made him worry. *Sorry* he felt responsible for her, for Terrance's death. *Sorry.* Guilt, guilt, guilt. Their tragic history linked them forever, and couldn't be ignored, because it'd shaped their identities, and now their lives were a mutual tapestry of obligation. Pull one thread, risk unraveling it all.

Kissing Charlie had pulled a thread.

"I'm such an ass," she whispered, and then pressed her face to his chest, resting there, finding comfort in the beat of his heart, so steady and strong. She couldn't hold the frozen bag anymore. It was too cold, so she dropped it on the cushion next to her and warmed her hand against Charlie's bare arm. "Why do you put up with me?"

It was a rhetorical question. They both knew why, but Cynthia felt it was important to ask once in a while, just on the off chance Charlie might start asking that question himself. He deserved to cut bait and live his life out from under the obligation of Cynthia, the little sister he never asked for.

"Who hurt you?" He picked up the bag, gently pressing it to her injury. "Where were you last night?" His scruffy chin abraded her forehead as his lower lip pressed against her skin. It felt like a kiss, but was simply his lips moving, asking questions.

"I don't know. I mean, I know bits, but"—she shrugged—"not everything."

"Tell me." He didn't bother hiding his worry.

"I told you," she said. "I blacked out."

"Last night," he said, "Benton said you'd left work with plans to go to the gym. I called there first, and the front desk said you'd left around ten." He gave her a little squeeze. "You called me at ten on the nose." Cynthia pushed off his chest, digging into her pocket to access the flash drive. She held it up, showing him.

"Security footage placing me at a federal safe house in Chinatown at ten-thirty last night." Charlie frowned as he took it from her hand. "I don't remember leaving the gym, Charlie. Just a scattering of weird memories. Horrible memories."

"What do you remember? Exactly."

"A brick wall. Men on their knees, bags over their heads, tied. Screaming. Begging for their lives."

"Bags?" His gaze lowered and lost focus as if she'd triggered a memory for him. Pulling her gun from its holster, she handed it to him. He sniffed the gun's slide, studying it from all angles. "It's been discharged," he said.

"Recently." They both knew that Cynthia would have cleaned it after practicing at the range. "I have to call Benton and tell him what's happened."

Charlie stood and lifted the television remote off a side table, then turned on the set. Local news appeared on the screen, broadcasting live. It was a media circus, and the station's chyron spelled out, "The Chinatown Massacre." Special Agents Benton, Gilroy, and Modena—three black-suited, white-shirted, black-tied FBI task force members—were on screen, working behind yellow crime scene tape against the backdrop of a brick building.

"Benton knows," Charlie said. Cynthia's heart pounded as she carefully stood, eyes focused on the screen.

"That's the place…from last night!" She pivoted toward the living room entrance, where she'd dropped her pocketbook, and made quick work digging out her phone and plugging it into the wall charger. "They must have been calling—"

"Since an hour ago." He stepped to her side. "Six dead. Executed, wrists zip tied, cloth bags on their heads, affixed by duct tape circling their necks." He tilted his head toward the television screen. "Why didn't you call it in last night? You called me at ten. Shots were reported around then. That's a half hour unaccounted for, if the video recorded you entering the safe house at ten-thirty."

"I know." She bit her lower lip. "A half hour after the murders, on foot, blocks from the crime scene, holding a recently discharged weapon."

"A half hour where you didn't call for backup." He spoke with slow, measured tones, but she understood the context. *Why?* Damned if she knew, but she understood her behavior looked sketchy as hell.

"My phone must have died." She'd left it in the car, in her pocketbook. "I don't know, Charlie, what more do you want me to say? I don't know." He tossed the remote on the couch and took her by the upper arms, forcing her to meet his gaze. Whatever he saw there had him pulling her close, holding on. Evidence shuffled in her head like a pack of cards until the facts lined up. *Cynthia looked guilty as sin.* He wasn't saying it, but they were both thinking it. "I'm afraid," she said. His fingers curled into her back as he more completely formed his body to surround hers, even resting his chin on the top of her head. He was her shield against the world.

"I've got you," he said. "I've got you."

She believed him. Cynthia had a target on her back, so Charlie would protect her. It made her feel safer, but it was no comfort. Instead, it just filled her with guilt, guilt, guilt.

Chapter Two

Charlie held her close, hating how she trembled. They both knew she was in trouble. The only questions seemed to be: to what degree, and how could he help. Both he and Cynthia were supposed to be at the crime scene, although his instinct told him neither should be within a mile of it. Just showing up had the potential to taint an evidentiary hearing, thus creating liability for the District Attorney when it came time to prosecute. *If* Cynthia was the "unknown subject." The unsub. Which she wasn't, couldn't be, but that didn't mean a judge or jury of her peers would not see it otherwise.

"Why did you come to my house last night?" he said.

Cynthia tilted her chin back, meeting his gaze, but her grip remained strong, as if she feared he'd leave her. "Excuse me?"

"Last night, sometime around nine PM." Her confusion had him second-guessing himself. "I saw someone in my driveway and thought it was you. No?" Her expression grew stricken.

"Charlie...*I don't remember.*"

"I'm sorry." He gave her a comforting squeeze, and then became distracted by her curves, and how they pressed against his length. He shut that down real quick. Had to, or he wouldn't be capable of much thought. "I heard something outside last night, looked out the window, and thought I saw you." He adjusted his stance to subtly put distance between their bodies...just a bit, enough to prevent himself from embarrassing either one of them. "When I stepped onto the porch to check, you were gone and my car trunk was ajar. That's when I found the duct tape, zip ties, and brown cloth."

"Huh?" She searched his expression. "You found them in your trunk?"

He nodded. "Then you called at ten. I thought you were calling to explain, but then the line disconnected. When you didn't answer your phone, I became worried and headed over to your apartment. I've been here since eleven last night."

"Show me the stuff I put in your car." She stepped out of his arms completely, and Charlie had to stop himself from reaching for her again. What was wrong with him? He clenched his fists, blaming his behavior on his unease. Circumstances were out of control, and instinct told him to hold on, to control Cynthia.

"It's still in my car." He led the way through her living room and then out of her apartment to his black Charger, parked at the curb. Popping the trunk, he indicated the items in question with a tilt of his head. Cynthia went over to the driver's side, reached inside, and unclipped a pen from one of his notepads. She used its tip to lift one of the cloth pieces. Two-ply, a foot square, he noted three of its edges were sewn together, creating a pouch of sorts.

"Charlie, these are—" She dropped everything back into the trunk, pressing her palm against her chest. He looked at the cloth more closely and then immediately saw what had upset her. Yup. They were hoods. "And I put these here?" she said.

"You don't remember." It implied brain trauma. He looked more closely at her pupils, and was relieved to see they weren't dilated. "Like I said, last night around nine, nine-thirty maybe, I saw... I thought it was you." She turned from him, looking down the street, but he'd have been surprised if she saw anything, because her eyes were unfocused. Cynthia seemed on the verge of a full-on panic attack. "Come on." He didn't want her losing it in a public place. He closed the trunk and led her back inside. Soon he had her back on her dark leather couch, frozen peas on her head, clutching one of her fringed green throw pillows.

"I don't remember, Charlie, and this is upsetting me. I can't even remember going to the gym," she said. "Though I know I did. My gym clothes were still damp this morning. What if—" She compressed her lips, seeming on the cusp of crying.

He hovered, trying to catch her gaze. "Let's go to the hospital." She needed an x-ray, maybe a CAT scan.

"This is crazy," she said. "If I was at your house last night, I wouldn't have broken into your trunk and put evidence inside." She squeezed the pillow tighter to her chest. "Not without talking to you first." Maybe. Cynthia was forgetting her recent and dogged attempts to cut Charlie from her life. *Because of that damn kiss.*

He sat next to her, but was careful not to touch her again. Lately, when she was near, everything had a way of being about what happened after she'd kissed him. The kiss was never far from either of their thoughts, apparently, but for very different reasons. She regretted it, and he couldn't seem to stop reliving it in detail: how she'd felt in his arms, how she'd smelled, and... Right now, those memories were counterproductive. Charlie needed to focus, and to do that he needed to maintain a physical and emotional distance from Cynthia. Not that he knew how to do that. Not with Cynthia, anyway. He'd never learned.

"All I know is I saw a blond woman," he said. Of her size and coloring, who looked a hell of a lot like Cynthia, but now he couldn't be certain. They both knew there was no such thing as witness infallibility. He'd *assumed* it was Cynthia when he saw the blond hair, so his imagination could have filled in the blanks with what he'd supposed should be there. Her expression settled into a scowl, directed at him, and he had no idea what he'd done to deserve it.

"How many blondes do you know?" she asked. When he didn't immediately answer, she swung the pillow at him, as if he'd done something wrong. It bounced off his chest and fell to the floor. "I mean, blond women who come to your house?" He retrieved the pillow and returned it to her. By then, Cynthia's eyes had widened, her outrage stoked, as if he'd compounded a sin. What sin? "Charlie!"

"Do you want me to list them?" It wouldn't take long. It was her and his mother.

Cynthia's scowl hardened as she sunk deeper into the couch cushions. "Forget it."

Her behavior confused him. After months of being ghosted, Charlie hadn't taken Cynthia's unexpected call lightly last night. In truth, he'd hoped the call had meant she'd finally moved beyond her embarrassment, and that she'd called him because she knew their friendship mattered more. Now, he didn't know what to think.

"Two blondes. You and my mom," he said.

"I *said* forget it."

"Listen, you called me at least a half an hour after I saw the blonde in my driveway, and then you hung up. Why wouldn't I assume the blonde had been you? It was an *assumption*. Shoot me. All that matters is that I have no idea who she is, or why those items are in my trunk." She narrowed her eyes, as if he were talking around an issue. It told him she wanted to continue arguing about blondes. Charlie had other plans. He stood, using a tilt of his head to indicate the door. "Shower first, or go to the ER now. You choose."

He feared her blackout was symptomatic of traumatic brain injury, something that contributed to about thirty percent of all injury deaths in the United States. Her confusion seemed normal given the circumstances, and other than lost time, her cognitive abilities hadn't suffered. That didn't mean she was safe. A cerebral hematoma could build slowly. Even as they spoke, Cynthia could be bleeding out, blood exerting pressure on brain tissue, killing cells. She needed an x-ray, or, better yet, the more informative CAT scan.

Cynthia lowered her face to the pillow, ignoring his concern. "Leave me alone. I'm fine." Her words were muffled by the pillow, and she was clearly not fine.

"You can't remember," he said, staring down at her. "Come on. Let's go."

Cynthia lifted her head, and seemed on the verge of crying. "Why can't I remember?" she asked in a little voice.

"Let's talk about it on our way to the ER," he said, holding out his hand to help her up. She shook her head, dismissing his hand. "Please, Cynthia."

"Last night. Did you see my car, or me driving off? Because my Lexus was parked across the street from the safe house when I woke this morning."

Frustration urged him to act the caveman and drag her ass to the car, but he didn't want to instigate a fight, because Cynthia would fight back, and probably reinjure herself. He needed to think of some other way to convince her to seek medical attention. He sat next to her again, grimacing.

"When I walked out to the porch last night, your car was gone." He stopped himself, regretting his words. "Sorry. I mean, whoever it was in my driveway was gone." He silently replayed what he'd said, and wasn't sure he'd been clear. "I mean, when I looked, the person was gone and there was no indication your car was, or had been, in the area. I don't know if it was you...." He shrugged. "Basically." Clear as mud. He wondered if he should give explaining another shot, but Cynthia looked as if she'd moved on already.

"And you didn't think that was odd? Me, showing up and not coming in?"

No. Charlie schooled his features to give nothing away. In fact, he shifted his body on the couch, so she only had access to his profile. She was touching the third rail here, inching closer to broaching the topic of their kiss again, and Charlie knew if that happened, somehow, she'd find a way to make it his fault. She nudged his arm, but he wouldn't meet her gaze, suspecting the question was a trap.

"Charlie? Didn't you think my behavior was odd?"

Her behavior was more of the same, continuing fallout for a drunken kiss *she* gave *him,* one more frustration layered on the rest. But how to tell that to Cynthia? Not possible. She didn't want to hear it.

"A bit," he temporized. "But then you called, and I figured..." *Trap*, his mind asserted. Dropping truth bombs now would be a mistake. "I don't know what I thought."

"You thought I was in trouble and came to the rescue, but I was nowhere to be found." Cynthia slumped back as she moved her crumbled suit jacket behind her head again to protect the couch leather.

To Charlie, her gloomy attitude contradicted her words. Wasn't being rescued a good thing? And he'd hunted her down despite her ghosting him ever since *she'd* kissed *him*. That should have earned him points. Why didn't it? Nothing about that night, or what happened since, made sense to Charlie. He'd resisted Cynthia's kiss because she'd been drunk. He was supposed to resist.

And he had, at first, anyway. Was that what bothered her? That he'd been weak, and gave into pleasure? Circumstances had long ago dictated he take on the role of big brother, and with her two tequila shots past sober, stopping their kiss had been the right thing to do. Her reaction was proof positive of that, because apparently, his *briefly* kissing her back had put their friendship on the rocks.

"You'd do the same for me," he said, and was relieved to see her nod.

She'd rescue him, because they were best friends, had history. He'd be damned if he allowed his moment of weakness to take that from them. He just hadn't found the right way to muscle through the awkwardness, and suspected it was because the moment still felt so raw. It'd happened months ago, but his instant arousal at her touch was fresh in his mind: her hands roaming his body, clutching his ass, and her lips on his. The kiss had hit him with the speed and effect of a mule kick, so there was no wonder why the memory refused to fade.

He blamed her moan. It had triggered his breakdown of reason, and had him ignoring the booze in her bloodstream, and the surety that she'd never have kissed him sober. It had him ignoring their friendship, and his obligation to protect her. That night, months ago, Charlie had ignored everything but his need to kiss Cynthia back.

Truth was, he couldn't help himself.

He'd lingered, and drunk her arousal as if it were intended for him, not caring about anything but finally tasting her, feeding his hunger. When he *couldn't* stop, his helplessness had hit him like a cold bath of reason, clearing his mind enough to thrust Cynthia away and end their kiss, if not his panic. He'd lost control, and knew his desire for Cynthia wasn't going away. Willpower in tatters, was it any wonder he feared revealing his feelings? She'd cut him from her life with surgical precision over a kiss *she'd* instigated. She'd called it a "disaster," and said she "didn't like it."

Telling her he loved her would be insane.

"Let's go to the ER," he said, shifting to face her more squarely on the couch. "You could have a concussion."

"That would be the least of my problems." She gave no indication she was willing to move from her slumped position on the couch. "I'm in a ton of trouble, and I don't know what to do."

He told himself to be patient, to reason with her. "I'm a doctor giving you sound medical advice. Let's go." He nudged her shoulder, but she just rolled her eyes and slapped his hand away.

"You work with dead people. When I'm dead, I'll listen."

As a forensic pathologist, Charlie had a medical degree, was qualified to determine the time, manner, and cause of a death, perform autopsies, and collect medical and trace evidence from bodies for analysis. He was also trained in toxicology, firearms and ballistics, trace evidence, blood analysis, DNA technology, and procedures regarding evidence collection to coordinate with law enforcement operations. A beating heart didn't disqualify him from understanding the medical implications of a knock to the head. She was not being reasonable.

He narrowed his eyes. "Do you really want me working on your dead, *naked* body? Taking pictures?"

Cynthia gave him a sidelong glance. "Perv."

"Stop arguing. We need to go."

Cynthia pulled her gun from its holster and held it out to him grip side forward. "I think... I think there is a chance I'm the shooter, Charlie, and you should take my gun and run tests on it." He studied her eyes and saw she was totally serious. His shock rendered him silent. "I remember the vics alive, and now they're dead, but I have no idea who they are, or why I'd kill them." She dropped her gaze to the gun, still holding it out to him. Charlie refused to take it, because he understood taking it fed this wackadoodle fantasy. "We need to test it against any shell casings found at the scene." Charlie folded his arms over his chest, shaking his head. No way he was taking that damn gun.

"Cynthia, if you shot someone it would be in self-defense or in defense of another. Lost time doesn't change a person's character. My team has been in contact with me twice since they arrived on scene. Those men were executed. You didn't do it."

"Things happen. *You can't know.*" Her tone was fierce, but her expression betrayed her hesitancy. "Take the gun. Evidence doesn't lie," she said. "The safe house video doesn't lie. I put hoods, duct tape, and zip ties in your trunk prior to the murders. We both know that reeks of premeditation." She took a deep breath, then released it slowly, struggling to regain her composure. "Take the gun, Charlie." Her eyes narrowed, daring him to deny her.

"No." He reassessed his caveman plan and decided kicking and screaming might do her some good. "We're going to the ER now," he said.

"*Fine.*" Openly rebellious, she nonetheless followed him, shrugging into her destroyed suit jacket. "I'm telling you, I'm... I'm remembering." Clearly upset, Cynthia's face crumbled as she paused in the hallway, as if hit by a wave of emotion. "The hooded victims." She pressed her hand against the wall, leaning. "Their screams. They were on their knees, bound, all lined up. I was there, Charlie. What if..." A hitch in her breath stopped her words. "What if..." Charlie couldn't take it anymore. He pulled her into his embrace, not knowing what to expect. Would she fight his touch? Sob? Crap, he hoped not.

Cynthia's fingers clutched his shirt's collar, then she did something she'd never done before. Standing on tiptoes, she pressed her face to his neck, burrowing close. Charlie froze, super aware of her warm lips against his skin. It took a moment, or two, to move past the shock and relax his body, to *act* as if it were one of their usual, brotherly hugs, though it was something new.

"It's the same memories on a loop." Her lips brushed his neck as she spoke, sending tingles clear down to his thighs. She clung to him as he held her close, admonishing himself to focus on her needs, rather than how she was making him feel. "Then nothing," she said, shuddering, as if a chill assaulted her. "I woke this morning at the safe house, and I've been struggling to remember since." She tilted her head back, sniffing, searching his eyes. "There's no denying my gun was fired six times, and six people are dead."

"But they were alive when you last saw them. That's important. Maybe the most important thing." He felt gutted by her fear, and it convinced him that she truly didn't know she was innocent. "You didn't kill them. Trust me on this, okay? We'll figure this out." He blamed her reaction on her head injury, and told himself not to worry about her behavior, but then she wiped a stray tear and brought his attention to her bloodstained fingertips.

He was beyond worried. He was afraid for her.

"Benton needs to know," she said, lowering her head to his chest, releasing a short groan. "Why didn't I call him last night?" she whispered. "Or any one of the team?"

"You called me." He gave her a little squeeze, prompting her to look at him again.

"You're right." She forced a little smile. "And you're practically an honorary FBI agent. You're definitely one of the team." When he shook his head, dismissing her words, her expression grew earnest. "No, really, Charlie. You've helped the task force for nearly a year now. You might not be FBI, but without you, we wouldn't have taken down the Coppola syndicate. Dante Coppola, arguably the most powerful crime lord on the east coast, is now behind bars because of your willingness to step up and be our forensic expert witness." She was referring to the time Dante Coppola's attorneys were granted a change of venue for his racketeering trial, and it was moved from New Jersey to Boston. She sighed, threading her fingers through her hair and grimacing. "I'm a mess."

"It doesn't matter. We need to get you checked out," he said. "Take a shower after we run the tests."

Cynthia stepped out of his arms, smoothing her suit jacket with little success. "I said I would. Didn't I? I really need to call Benton, first, though. He'll be worried." She gingerly dabbed at the back of her head with her fingers, and then pivoted back to the living room. "As far as he's concerned, you're not involved, though. Okay?"

No. It was not okay. He turned to argue and knocked a photo off the wall, catching it before it hit the floor. Suddenly, he was staring at a picture of Cynthia's long-dead childhood cat, Darth Vader. He replaced it on its nail, and then hurried after her. He caught up with her in the living room, reaching for her phone attached to the wall charger.

"You're not thinking straight." He grabbed her, tossed her over his shoulder, and she landed with a *whoosh* as air left her lungs. She didn't regain her breath until he was back in the hall, walking to the front door again. "We're going to the ER. Benton can wait, and I am involved, Cynthia. There's evidence in my trunk that links me to these murders."

"Evidence I most likely put there!" She slapped his back hard. "Put me down."

"Doesn't mean you're a killer. Give me a general profile on a person who'd execute six bound, hooded men, all begging for mercy." He reached for the doorknob as Cynthia hit his kidneys with two mid-knuckle strikes. "Oomph." He put her down, grabbing where it hurt.

"I don't feel guilty about hitting you, Charlie!" Her expression told Charlie she did, so he took it as apology enough. "You deserved it."

"Let's go." He opened the front door. She pressed her palm to the door, and he allowed her to slam it shut again, because forcing the issue might have landed her on her ass.

"Stop it!" she snapped. "I have to call Benton and tell him what happened last night."

They both knew Cynthia had no idea what happened. That was the problem. And earlier, Charlie had been speaking rhetorically about the profile, but now realized Cynthia needed to work through it herself. Her priority would be a call to Benton, instead of medical attention, until she believed she hadn't gone insane and become a mass murderer.

"A profile. Do it." He folded his arms over his chest, standing in front of her, glowering.

She poked his chest. "Six rounds are missing from my magazine, Charlie. Six dead and my gun is the murder weapon."

"You don't know that." He took a step closer, pinning her against the door. "Humor me. Profile the unsub." Then they could get the hell out of there. She leaned against the front door, frowning up at him.

"It's not that easy. The stats are all over the place, because a mass murderer is… They usually don't commit mass murder more than once." Whatever she saw on his face had her grimacing, but she finally complied. "They're angry, dissatisfied, have poor social skills or few friends, and then they're triggered." He could see she was irritated rather than relieved that she didn't fit a profile for the unsub, and that made no sense to Charlie. No surprise, Cynthia rarely did. "Ninety-six point five percent of mass murderers are male, and a majority suffer from paranoia and often acute behavioral or personality disorders."

"So, not you."

"No," she admitted, grudgingly. "Not me."

"And this wasn't just any mass murder."

"No." Her eyes lost focus. "The victims… It was a hit, done for money, not excitement." He grabbed the doorknob again, leaning closer. Close enough to feel her heat.

"Can we dispense with your worries now?" He purposefully lowered his tone, attempting to ratchet down the intensity. "You did not execute those men." His whispered words seemed to jolt Cynthia from her thoughts. Now, she noticed his closeness, but made no attempt to scoot away. Instead, she studied him as if logging *his* reactions. She was a profiler, and he knew reading people was what she did, but her searching gaze felt peculiar nonetheless. As a forensic pathologist, Charlie wasn't used to his patients studying him back.

"No," she said. "I don't think I killed them, but it sure as shit looks like I did." She sniffed, then sniffed her sleeve, grimacing. "I smell."

He nodded. She did, indeed. His gaze roamed over her ruined suit, and up close and personal he could see all the dirt and abrasion tears in the cloth. Charlie did his best to appear clinical in his appraisal, but he was unabashedly admiring her body. "You look as if you were thrown from a moving vehicle."

She blinked a few times before stepping to the side, careful not to touch him as she moved away from the door. "Thanks." She didn't sound thankful.

"Did you want me to lie?" He rested his head on the door, doing his best to rein in his frustration. Then he turned and leaned against the door as he contemplated her.

"No." Cynthia kept her gaze averted. "I forgot my pocketbook and phone. I'll get them, and then we can go." She hurried back to the living room and came back with her pink pocketbook, dropping her iPhone into her suit jacket pocket.

"Don't tell Benton anything until we know more," he said. Her look of horror had him shaking his head. "It's only obstruction if you're guilty. And, anyway, the Fifth Amendment protects you. I'm just saying." He shrugged. "Wait."

"Failure-to-report laws, Charlie." She shook her head. "You can't pick and choose which laws to follow."

"We're in Massachusetts. It's not against the law to fail to report a felony here. Just wait to tell Benton anything."

"For what?" Her eyes narrowed, and now it was her reaching for the doorknob, and Charlie keeping his hand on the door. "To be charged with accessory after the fact?"

"We're not concealing anything, least of all a crime. It's on the news. We don't know who did it, so we're not aiding and abetting."

"You know that's not true! And stop with the *we*. I don't want you involved." She used her shoulder, attempting to move him, but quickly gave up when he didn't budge an inch. "I'm giving the flash drive to Benton, along with the evidence in your trunk, and then I'll confess everything."

"I'm involved," Charlie said. "There's no way to keep me out of this without lying, so just wait. Until we know more."

Her shoulders sagged. "You're right. And I can't lie. Look what I've done." She pressed a palm to her forehead, looking ready to cry. "I've dragged you into this. After all you've been put through by my family..."

Her words had Charlie's teeth grinding. Would she ever look at him without thinking of the accident?

Her cell phone rang. She retrieved it from her pocket and they both looked at it. "Benton," she said, sounding worried.

Charlie tilted her chin up with his fingers, forcing her to meet his gaze. "Just wait. Until we know more."

Cynthia hit "accept" and then put it on speakerphone. "Hi, Benton. I'm here with Charlie Foulkes. Sorry, I've been—"

"I've got six executed Coppola syndicate WITSEC snitches on my hands," Special Agent Jack Benton said. Charlie and Cynthia exchanged horrified looks. The vics were Coppola syndicate witnesses for the prosecution of a tightly closed case. This would reopen it. "And the U.S. Marshals are riding me, looking to cover their asses."

"On my way." Cynthia had grown pale, and her hand holding the phone shook. Charlie understood why. The vics weren't randomly killed. Their identities threatened the careers of everyone who had worked on the Coppola case, and this made Cynthia appear even guiltier than before.

"No, Benton," Charlie said, ignoring Cynthia's instant glare. His patience was gone. "Charlie here. Sorry, but Cynthia isn't going anywhere but to the emergency room. She's got a head injury. You caught us on our way there."

Benton's angry tone mellowed to worry. "She okay?"

"Hopefully. We'll know more after a CAT scan," Charlie said. "She's fighting me."

"Cynthia, get the test, and then get your ass to the crime scene," Benton said. "You've both seen the news?"

"Yes, but they said nothing about the victims being Coppola syndicate," she said.

"We're keeping that quiet for now," Benton said. "Your team of techs are here, Charlie."

"I called them as soon as I got your voice message," he said. "They've kept me updated best they can, but I'm assuming they don't know this is a syndicate hit, or they would have said something." Like asked for hazard pay. "We'll be there, too, just as soon as we get Cynthia sorted out."

"Be quick about it. This is no time for the B team." Benton disconnected the line.

Cynthia slipped her phone into her suit jacket pocket. "And so it begins."

"If you *must*," Charlie sighed, resolved to the unavoidable delay, "take a quick shower, but try not to get the wound wet. Then we'll head to the ER. If you check out fine, we'll go straight to the crime scene afterward, but no matter what you decide, you must change. Arriving at the crime scene in this condition will create too many questions."

"You're so bossy." She said it with no heat, and just stood there, as if frozen with indecision. Charlie cupped her cheek.

"Don't think, Cynthia. Just do. You know there's nothing I wouldn't do to keep you safe, right?" She covered his hand, pressing her cheek more fully into his palm. He could tell his words saddened her rather than comforted her, which had been his intent.

"That's what I'm afraid of," she whispered.

Then she left him, tugging her shirt from her pants as she walked down the hall toward her bedroom. He was so distracted by what she'd said that for a second or two, he'd forgotten he'd told her to change, so the image of her unbuttoning her shirt confused him, even as it sent his imagination to uncharted places... Taboo places. When she'd disappeared from sight, he no longer needed visuals to feed his active imagination. It ran free. By the time Charlie heard the shower turn on, he needed one, too. A cold one.

Chapter Three

Why was Cynthia surprised to discover Charlie had friends in high places? Moments after arriving at Massachusetts General Hospital, her ass landed on a trauma room exam table. While others waited hours to be seen, Cynthia shot to the head of the line. Lucky her. The power of Charlie.

She'd balked, of course, at the order to don a hospital johnny, and no perky, freckle-faced, hyper-kinetic nurse in moon and star designer scrubs was going to intimidate her into changing her mind. Charlie was *never* seeing Cynthia in a johnny. Just the idea of him in the room while she was practically naked on the exam table sent waves of mortification through her. Cynthia's rebellion earned her a hostile preliminary exam, and by the time Nurse Ratched left—having poked, measured, and grimaced through Cynthia's vital signs—it was clear she'd won the nurse's "most difficult patient of the shift" award.

Whatever. Charlie acted as if nothing was amiss, so Cynthia just went with it and didn't complain. Though she'd wanted to. She'd wanted to complain a lot, because she was here, and every instinct she had told her to be at the crime scene, finding answers.

Just back from radiology, having received her CAT scan from a handsome, flirting, brown-eyed technician, they awaited the test results. Charlie sat in the corner on a tiny chair, grimacing. He'd been grimacing ever since she'd flirted back with that sexy tech, but she couldn't prove causation. His discontent could be from sitting on that tiny chair. It made him look like a G.I. Joe crammed into a dollhouse. He didn't fit.

Whatever had his panties in a bunch, he was ignoring her, so Cynthia pulled her iPhone from her suit jacket pocket. Charge was at twenty percent. Too much was going on to risk it dying again, so wasting it on Instagram didn't seem sensible. She slipped it back in her pocket and then leaned for another entertainment magazine, grabbing it from the wall rack without falling off the table. No small feat. She pretended to read as she studiously did not swing her feet, despite an overwhelming urge to do just that.

"This is such a colossal waste of time." Cynthia flipped a page, unable to concentrate on the photos of lavishly dressed actresses attending red carpet events, while Charlie sat there, all silent, huge, sexy, and disgruntled. He was perfect, it was distracting, and he had a full charge on his phone. The man was carelessly scrolling, swiping up, looking at who knows what.

Not for the first time, she wished she didn't want him so much, but just looking at him made her girly parts clench. He was the smartest, bravest, kindest person she knew, and he made her laugh. He was her best friend, and wanting more from him was selfish and greedy.

Wanting more would kill their friendship.

In relationships, when one of the people involved feels indebted to the other, that debt colors everything. Even a kiss. She had no idea how far Charlie might go to appease his sense of obligation, and she had no intentions of exploring his limits, because when she kissed a man, she liked to know his tongue was in her mouth because he couldn't help himself, instead of wondering if it was there because he didn't want to hurt her feelings.

He wasn't her type, anyway. Slap a kilt on him and he looked ripped from the pages of *Outlander*. No, one of the later books, *after* the Battle of Culloden. Battle worn, with scars to prove it, he was more fierce than pretty, and her tastes usually ran toward the pretty: like Benton or Modena, members of her FBI task force. Now, *they* were seriously good-looking men. Though Charlie's size was a turn-on, and his pale blue eyes were dreamy…. Still, not her type. So why was she squirming, feeling aflutter just looking at him?

The exam table paper ripped beneath her butt. She peeked at Charlie, wondering if he'd noticed. Of course he'd noticed. He'd noticed she was acting weird, too.

"You're not human," she said. "You should be nervous thinking about what we'll find at the crime scene." Like evidence that could land her in jail.

He compressed his lips, averted his gaze. "I'm more concerned with the CAT scan. Stop being nervous. I'll tell you when it's time to be nervous."

"Don't tell me—" Her back straightened and her jaw jutted out. "Who said I'm nervous?" His calm patience was pissing her off.

"Are you human?" he said.

His cheek kicked up when it took her a moment to realize he'd thrown her words back at her. His cleverness earned him a scowl. Then her shoulders sagged under the weight of her fears. "Yes, I'm…" She glanced at him. "I'm human." She slapped the magazine closed and set it on the table next to her. "What if we find something at the crime scene that points to me? I could lose my career over this."

"Did you kill anyone?" His expression and tone suggested he'd already answered that question for himself, and he'd judged her innocent.

"Not yet." She narrowed her eyes, throwing out that threat. "I didn't kill anyone. Probably. Are you suggesting no innocent person has ever been convicted?" His impatience was marked, yet Cynthia thought the question pertinent.

Grabbing the edge of the exam table, she found herself rhythmically tapping her pale pink, manicured fingernails on the wood underneath the table's cushion-top. She calculated the odds of her falling on her face if she hopped off the table, and then calculated them again on a sliding scale with three-inch heels added to the equation. She was getting antsy.

"Try to be patient," Charlie said, scrolling on his annoyingly charged phone.

She hated sitting there, looking like a little girl who might, at any moment, begin to swing her feet. FBI special agents with degrees in criminal psychology do not swing their feet while sitting on exam tables. In fact, it was impossible to project confident, capable, and professional while atop this plastic cushion with crinkly paper, swinging feet or not. The very act of sitting there put her at a disadvantage. Unfortunately, Charlie occupied the only other seat in the room. His tiny seat.

"I have every reason to be nervous. Blind justice, and all." She studied the aseptic room with its waxed shiny floor, its high-gloss white walls. Everything had the look and smell of something that was bleached frequently. "Our criminal justice system runs on evidence, Charlie."

His smile barely touched his lips, but it was there when he glanced up from his phone. "Yeah? Do tell." Charlie's world revolved around evidence, and Cynthia was caught preaching to the choir.

"It's only a matter of time before they find my blood at the scene," she said, "or my prints on bullet casings."

His brow furrowed for a moment, and then cleared just as quickly. "I'll figure it out."

The way he said that had her worrying. Terrance's death had a grip on him, even now, ten years later. She had no doubt he'd go to extraordinary lengths to repay the debt he felt he owed for "allowing" Terrance to drive drunk. Cynthia, for her part, would make sure Charlie never got that chance. She wanted no part of his risking his career to "figure it out."

"If evidence can clear me," she said, "Benton will find it. I trust him to do his job."

"I trust him, too." He returned his attention to his phone, but he no longer scrolled, or seemed to be reading, which meant he was just avoiding her gaze.

"Is there a but implied there? I mean, it sounds a lot like you're implying a but."

"No buts. I trust him." He finally looked at her, and then slipped his phone into his back pocket. "I learned to trust him during the Coppola trial. The syndicate is dead, Coppola is in jail, and that's because Benton knows what he's doing."

"True." She glared at the shiny tile flooring again, allowing her hair to fall in damp, loose waves over her face. It took forever to air dry after a shower if she didn't take the time to blow dry it. There hadn't been time this morning, what with both her and Charlie impatient to get out of the house, so it was unruly. Cynthia preferred her hair pencil straight, sliding over her shoulders like silk, swaying when she walked, with not a wisp, not a stray hair moving out of alignment. Yet, here she sat, on an exam table, with unruly hair. Not aligned. "Six Coppola syndicate WITSEC witnesses. I can't keep silent, Charlie."

"You will. We follow the evidence, as always, and it will lead to the real unsubs. As always." He folded his arms over his chest. "You open your mouth before we can clear you, we're off the case. Or do you have an alternate idea? I mean, one that doesn't require you to confess to murders you didn't commit?"

She hopped off the table, unable to sit there any longer, and *boom!* Her heel zigged when it should have zagged. Her knees buckled and forced her to grab the cushion-top to regain her balance. Charlie shot forward, intense, like a parent hovering over a toddler: hands out, poised to catch.

"I'm fine," she said. Charlie was *really* close, and chose to remain so, though he'd dropped his hands.

"Get back on the table before you fall on your face," he said. Cynthia waved him off, then felt guilty when he compressed his lips and scrubbed his face with his hands. He looked exhausted, and it reminded her that he'd been up most of the night, worried because she hadn't answered her phone. Guilt, guilt, guilt.

"Not telling Benton where I was last night gives cover to the killer," she said.

He returned to his tiny chair. "We'll contact your gym when we leave here," he said. "They'll have records of you checking in and out last night.

Maybe security video to fill in the time gaps prior to the safe house security feeds of you coming and going. It will help solidify your alibi."

"Alibi? I *remember* being at the crime scene when the vics were *alive*, and—" Cynthia cringed, knowing she had to fess up. "I didn't tell you, because I didn't want to deal with your reaction—"

He groaned, shifting in his chair as if he couldn't get comfortable. "How bad is it? No, go ahead. I'm fine. It's okay, you can tell me, but first, will you get back on the table? You look like you're about to fall down."

She shook her head. "I accidentally deleted the surveillance video on the safe house main server. The only video that survived is on the flash drive."

Charlie blinked a few times, frowning. "Excuse me?"

"Get that look off your face. I didn't do it on purpose. I—" She tucked her hair behind her ears and felt it pouf out, which is what it always did when she didn't take the time to dry it properly. To align it right. The expression on his face was making her nervous, so she paced the small eight-foot cubby of a room to release some energy, and every time she glimpsed Charlie's shocked expression, her heart did a little skip. "You know I'm not good with tech. *You know it.* It's like I'm allergic to the stuff, and tech knows it. Not my fault." He shook his head, clearly stunned, and she supposed it was to be expected. Charlie was a forensic guy. Hearing she'd destroyed evidence had to offend him on a visceral level.

"You deleted it." His tone suggested he still had trouble processing her confession.

"*Accidentally.* But I took a copy first."

"But they have video of you *leaving* the safe house. Yes?" His gaze locked with hers, and suddenly she didn't want to pace anymore. She wanted to sit down.

"No." She cringed at his shocked reaction. "I'd turned it off, thinking to activate a fail-safe—"

"No." He stood up, and his hands reached for her as if he wanted to shake her, but when she stepped back, he sat down so quickly the chair squeaked and she thought it would break.

"I was afraid what would happen if I touched the machine again, so I kept it off, leaving it for the experts. I thought it was for the best."

His jaw muscles twitched. "If those experts recover the video, they'll see what was deleted. Copied. They'll wonder why it happened, why that timeframe. They'll wonder who did it, blocks away from a mass execution of WITSEC witnesses."

Her heart sank. "I'll explain."

"It reeks of intent, Cynthia."

"I know."

"You fucked up," he growled.

"*I know!*" Did he have to keep rubbing it in? Leaning a hip against the exam table, she avoided Charlie's gaze.

"What did you have for supper last night?" he said.

"Hmm?" Now that he'd mentioned it, she *was* hungry. "Falafel truck parked outside the precinct house."

"We'll take a statement from the falafel guy. Get it on the record when you left work." He nodded once, leaning forward, his elbows on his knees. "You remember leaving work. That's good."

"Yeah." She did. "And though I can't remember going to the gym, the workout clothes in my bag were still sweaty, and gym member cards are used, so there'll be proof." She struggled to remember. "After the falafel, though, the next thing I remember is waking up at the safe house."

He studied her features. "But you said you remembered images."

"Just flashes of memory. The vics lined up against a brick wall. Alive."

"That's a lot. We can work with that." He pinned her with a stare. "I presume you'd remember planning a mass execution, gathering the vics up, binding them, transporting them to the scene."

She nodded. "Yeah. Didn't do that." She had a bruise on her hip from last night, and leaning on the table irritated it. She shifted her stance, attempting to get comfortable.

"So, no premeditation," he said. "Do you remember coming to my house? Dumping those items in my trunk?" She shook her head. "Nine o'clock, so you couldn't have anyway. Your gym member card will give you an alibi for that, at least."

Her shoe slipped, and she had to catch herself. She was feeling shaky. "So, me at the scene was wrong place at the wrong time?"

His brow furrowed briefly, as a rebuke, as if she'd slipped on the floor just to piss him off. "Your phone was in your car when you found it, and you called me at ten. It must have died then, and you heard shots fired. Then you ran to the crime scene."

"No. I remember them alive. I remember screams." She shook her head, glancing at the exam table and wondering how undignified she'd look if she crawled back on it. "I don't remember anything, really. I remember the falafel. The rest is a blank."

"You don't have to remember. We can deduce." He shifted on his chair, looking uncomfortable. It made her play with the idea of asking him to change places with her. "You drove and parked the Lexus across the street from the safe house. We know that. You had to have walked to the gym, got back to your car at ten, called me, phone dies"—he shrugged—"you hear screams and run three blocks to the crime scene. You see vics alive, blackout, and you have video of you walking to the safe house, gun drawn, injured. That about right?"

"Sure. Whatever." She still didn't remember anything after eating a falafel, which had been amazing, and thoughts of food were making her stomach rumble.

"That's what we tell Benton." He stood and stepped in front of her, towering over her. "First, we'll go to the crime scene and check it out. Tell Benton *after* we see the evidence to make sure it supports our story."

"And if it doesn't?" she said. He stepped closer, forcing her to lean against the exam table or risk touching him.

"Don't borrow trouble." He took another step closer, his voice dropping to a whisper, his eyes focusing on her lips. "We'll tell Benton after I give the all-clear. You understand?"

Cynthia had to tilt her head back to catch his gaze, because he'd trapped her between him and the table. "Benton has...has my...back," she stuttered. "My team—"

"Will have conflicting loyalties. I won't."

Charlie lifted her by the waist, sitting her ass back on the padded exam table. It was a relief, because now she didn't have to crane her neck to meet his gaze, but her thighs had automatically spread to accommodate his body. Now, with him so close, his hands touching her, all sorts of naughty thoughts popped into her head. Instead of pivoting back to his tiny chair, Charlie's fingers dug into her waist and his eyes narrowed. He seemed to see something in her expression that pissed him off. Then his gaze dropped to her lips and her confusion cleared. She knew exactly what he was seeing. What she'd not thought to hide.

Her desire. She wanted him, was fighting it, and... He knew.

What he couldn't know was his nearness was dredging up every arousing dream she'd suffered through since their kiss months ago. In those dreams, she didn't have to wonder what would have happened if Charlie hadn't rejected her kiss. Her dreams were full of wonderful, happily-ever-afters, but inevitably she'd wake frustrated, because they were only dreams, and she knew Charlie's rejection had been for the best. Those months ago, he'd broken the kiss off, but she should never have kissed him in the first place. And as much as Cynthia hated to admit it, *that's* why Cynthia was truly embarrassed.

Now Charlie stood so close she could feel the heat of his body, and that made it impossible to hide her flushed cheeks, her rapid breathing and hungry eyes. Though Charlie's demeanor shouted rejection, he didn't step away, didn't attempt in any way to dissipate the trigger prompting her arousal. His nearness.

He was too close, her mind shouted. Too male. Too fucking attractive to pretend she didn't want him. *Why was he doing this to her?* Fearing he was moments away from forcing her to admit her attraction, she panicked. She tilted her chin up, putting her lips mere inches from his, thinking he'd panic, too, and step back.

"We kissing now?" she said, her tone dripping with belligerence. The only reaction she received was a miniscule tightening of the skin around his eyes. And...a flicker of hurt?

"Do you want me to kiss you?" It sounded like a threat, and for the first time ever, she saw resentment in his gaze...directed at her. He cupped her cheek and drew his thumb pad over her lower lip. "There was a time I *couldn't* kiss you even if I'd wanted to. Couldn't speak, lift a finger, or even wiggle a toe. Couldn't hold you when you'd cried." He dropped his hand to hers, gripping it. "Or squeeze your hand as you cried at my hospital bedside." Charlie's gaze moved from her lips to her eyes, and she saw his resentment fade. He was back to looking like the man she'd come to rely on. Just Charlie. Supportive, kind, strong Charlie. "I'm not that person anymore, Cynthia. Stop pushing me away." After a last glance at her lips, he turned and sat in the corner again, leaving her breathless and confused.

Pushing him away? Is that what he thought she was doing? She was trying to save their friendship.

If she'd been alone in the room, she'd be clutching her chest, trying to settle her skipping heart. The man had a way of devastating her without even trying. *There was a time*, he'd said. Yes, she remembered it well. Watching her grieving parents struggle though burying a son, consoling a daughter, moving on with their lives. And Charlie. Sitting with him as he fought his paralysis and emotional hell as he suffered in a body that had become a prison of pain.

She remembered hours of resting her cheek on his hand, clutching his fingers, because they were the only part of him not bruised or abraded. She'd read aloud the complete works of Edgar Rice Burroughs in his hospital room. It took the whole *Tarzan* series and the *John Carter of Mars* series for Charlie to regain control of his limbs. They'd celebrated by starting Tolkien's *The Hobbit*, and Charlie was sitting up by the time she'd reached Smaug hoarding treasures in the Lonely Mountain. Then her mother died of a heart attack almost a year to the day Terrance died, and her father stroked out two days later, leaving Cynthia alone.

Charlie became her security blanket. She'd become his burden. She owed him an apology, but couldn't go there. So she settled on a less explosive olive branch. "Thank you," she said, squeezing his hand back. The paper crinkled under her butt, reminding her that they were back in a hospital again, holding hands.

Charlie's cheek kicked up, but his eyes were sad. "Yeah? For what?"

"For always being there for me," she said. He winked, and that was all it took to make her feel weepy.

A discreet knock on the door was a welcome distraction, and prompted Charlie to move away from Cynthia. Dr. Josephine Kepler stepped inside, making the small room feel even smaller. She was young, with dark hair twisted into a messy bun. Her white smock's lapel was adorned with multiple ribbon pins.

"Good news," Dr. Kepler said, her gaze directed at her clipboard. "CAT scan results indicate no concussion. No thrombosis, no fluid retention beyond what would be considered normal for minimal bruising. There's swelling around the laceration, but it's to be expected. It should remain tender for about a week, but scabbing indicates you're healing quickly. You're young, healthy." She glanced up from the clipboard and flashed her brown eyes at Cynthia. "How exactly did this happen?" The doctor glanced at Charlie, as if maybe she was about to ask him to leave the room for privacy's sake.

"The gym last night. Sparring." Cynthia put up her fists and jabbed, illustrating sucker punches. "Ironic, right? Every injury I've ever had resulted from training, rather than using my skills to thwart bad guys."

"Bad guys, huh?" Dr. Kepler smiled. "You were doing weapons training?"

"What?" Cynthia said. Dr. Kepler's smile faded, and then she exchanged glances with Charlie again.

Charlie cleared his throat. "Cynthia, your laceration, and the bruising around it, is consistent with a pistol-whipping."

"Ah. Yeah. That's what I get for training with a newbie." Cynthia donned a sheepish grin as she visualized a few more sucker punches…at Charlie's jaw. *Why had he kept that from her?*

The doctor handed Cynthia a CD in a clear plastic case. "A copy of your CAT scan. I've written the name of a specialist on the disc, just in case you develop further symptoms."

Good news dispensed, the doctor left, and moments later Cynthia hooked her Kate Spade pocketbook over her elbow, intent on getting the hell out of there. When she and Charlie stepped through the ER's automatic glass doors into the parking lot, she threw him a glare.

"Pistol-whipped?" she said, not slowing her gait. "I was pistol-whipped, and you didn't think I'd be interested? I thought I'd fallen and hit my head."

"You had dirt all over you. You did fall." When they'd reached his black Charger, he opened the passenger side door and waited for her to slide inside before closing it again.

When he was behind the wheel, she threw her hands in the air and then let them drop. "I was pistol-whipped. Someone got the jump on me. Don't you think that's something you should have told me?"

"I needed you at the ER. If I'd told you that, you'd have fought even harder to skip it."

She tugged at her seat belt and buckled in. "You're so damn controlling, you drive me crazy. *This is good news.* Someone else was at the crime scene with me, and probably killed those men."

"We already knew that. The killer hit you over your head—"

"I didn't know, because *someone* failed to tell me I was pistol-whipped." She compressed her lips as he slipped the key into the ignition. "Maybe with my gun, too. We should dust it for prints."

"No blood on the grip, so unlikely," he said, putting the car into gear. "I looked when you tried to hand it over. Remember? When you thought you were a murderer?" He grimaced, looking all *I told you so*, as he checked his mirrors.

"It was discharged. Maybe someone other than me shot it. There could be prints. We need to check, access IAFIS. Charlie, we have to try." He nodded, keeping his foot on the brake, holding her gaze as he waited for an opportunity to merge into traffic. "The vics were Coppola snitches," she said. "Benton won't lack suspects."

"I'll do it myself so we don't flag anyone's attention." He drove, turning the wheel. "What are you thinking? Revenge killings?"

"Maybe, but the Coppola syndicate is as much a family as a business, and Dante Coppola turned state's evidence, so why kill his underlings for doing the same?"

He glanced at her. "Call Benton and tell him we're on our way. *And nothing else.*"

"You are so bossy. Tell me to breathe. I dare you." She pulled her seriously charge-deprived iPhone from her pocket, plugged it into his car charger, and dialed. "People will wonder why we're arriving together."

"Benton already knows I brought you to the ER."

"Exactly," she said. "People will wonder." Charlie shook his head. He wasn't saying it, but she knew he was thinking *Who cares?* "No one knows we know each other, Charlie. Everyone believes we're acquaintances. And work acquaintances, at that."

He kept his eyes on the road. "Whose fault is that?"

"I'm not assigning blame." Benton wasn't picking up.

"I am." He glanced at her, before shifting lanes.

"Don't be like that," she said. The call went to Benton's voice mail. She disconnected the line. "I keep my private life private for a reason. It's nobody's business, and I don't want to talk about Terrance." He grimaced, keeping his eyes on the heavy traffic, which had bogged down. It was forcing him to brake repeatedly, and all the stops and starts were making Cynthia's stomach queasy.

"I'm not Terrance," he said.

No, but they both knew there was no explaining Charlie without delving into what happened ten years ago. Her late brother and Charlie were intertwined forever in her head, and every decision she'd made since the accident somehow could be tracked back to that day. "You know what I mean," she said.

"Yeah, I do." And his grimace told her he wasn't happy about it. The traffic began to move again, thankfully.

"You have to admit that suddenly informing everyone we're best friends will put us in the spotlight, and prompt questions," she said. "I'm on the cusp of being implicated in a murder case, Charlie, and you're the department's forensic pathologist. It will look suspicious."

"But I *am* your best friend, Cynthia. It's the truth." He shook his head, grimacing. "I shouldn't be touching this case with a ten-foot pole, and neither should you. Why don't you take a medical leave? Your head injury is perfect cover. I'll take some time off, hand this off to a substitute M.E. Benton and the team can field this case without us. Sooner or later we'll be kicked to the curb anyway. They'll find your prints, your DNA, and even a half decent prosecutor will use that to crucify you during evidentiary proceedings. Add suspected tampering with evidence? They'll fry you."

"You're right," she said. The right thing to do was to leave this case, her future, her freedom, in the hands of Benton and the team.

He glanced at her. "But that's not what we're going to do, is it?" he said. No, because she was innocent, and she needed to know what happened last night. That didn't mean Charlie had to be involved. In fact, his idea of taking time off and leaving town sounded perfect. "Our involvement could kill whatever case Benton builds," he said. "We're officially radioactive."

"I know." *If* she was guilty. Which she wasn't. Hello? Wasn't it his job as best friend to keep pointing that out?

"So, we help Benton. Make sure we don't ruin his case." There he went using that "we" word again.

"Not *we*, Charlie. That would mean putting your career on the line," she said. "I can't allow it. Why don't you take some—"

"Your *life* is on the line." He glanced at her, his eyes intense. "You witnessed murders. There is no scenario that doesn't include me watching your back."

"I blacked out. I don't know anything."

"The killer doesn't know that." His hands gripped the wheel like he was strangling it, though his speed stayed steady, and his eyes were firmly on the road.

"Then why did he leave me alive if he thought I could ID him?"

"*I don't know.* Believe me, I wish I did." He visibly reined in his jacked emotions, inhaling sharply. "And until I do, I need you protected, or I can't function." He glanced at her. "Let's make a deal. When you're not buddied up with one of your FBI team members, you're with me."

"I can't—" She ran her fingers through her drying hair, feeling the flyaway strands, feeling harassed.

"Your instinct is always to push me away. I'm protecting you, even if you don't want it."

"Of course I want you!" As soon as the words left her mouth, she cringed, because *yeah*, she did want him, more than she'd ever wanted a man in her life. "I meant to say *it*." She sank deep in her seat, folding her arms over her chest. "I want *it*."

The silence in the car pressed down on her until she couldn't resist glancing at him, only to see that a calm had settled over his features. His shoulders were relaxed, and when he took the turn at the stoplight, Charlie almost seemed his old self again as their car approached the hustle and bustle of the crime scene. He seemed confident, indomitable.

"We tell Benton nothing until we clear you, solidify your alibi best we can. Hopefully we can get that done today," he said. "And then we work the case. You stay with me or with one of your team at all times. We clear?" He glanced at her until she nodded.

She'd nodded, because she was afraid, and he'd convinced her his way was the safest way to protect Charlie and the FBI task force's careers.

"We work the case," she said. "Find this killer."

"Yeah. That means we need to protect ourselves," he said, glancing between her and the road. "Do this right." She arched a brow, having lost the thread of his point. "This." He used his right hand to indicate her and then him. "Technically, this is collusion, and that's an avenue the DA can pursue to create a conspiracy case against us, maybe even implicate Benton and the team. Not good." His expression gave her no indication of where his mind was at.

"What are you saying?"

"We need to get married, Cynthia."

Chapter Four

"Huh?" Cynthia was surprised. No, shocked was more like it. That, more than anything else, told Charlie she *really* hadn't thought things through. The streetlight turned red, forcing him to brake a block from the crime scene. He could see the center of the chaos, where the media and local law enforcement converged. Before he and Cynthia stepped into the glare of that attention, they needed to be on the same page.

"We need spousal privilege," he said. The testimonial and communication privilege of proof of law. "Otherwise, everything we say or do from this morning on can potentially be held against us in court."

She kept shaking her head. "If I'm guilty."

"Which is determined by rules of law, and spousal privilege would prevent them from forcing us to implicate or testify against each other. If we don't marry, Cynthia—" Now it was him shaking his head. It was almost as if she had no sense of self-preservation.

"I'm vulnerable," she said. "*No*. We're vulnerable. I get it." She bit her lip, her expression stricken. "You've thought this through."

He had. In fact, ever since she'd told him that she'd erased the tapes at the safe house, he'd suspected this was where they'd end up. The only reason he'd delayed telling her was because he knew she'd argue. Well, he could no longer justify factoring in her feelings. This was happening. If some part of him suspected he'd jumped to this solution with more speed and enthusiasm than circumstances warranted, well, that was an opinion best kept to himself.

The light changed, and soon he was pulling up to the curb inside the sectioned-off crime scene perimeter. The noise pollution was loud, even inside the car. Hundreds of voices, shouting directions, or simply talking over the fray. It was also comfortingly familiar, so a calm settled over Charlie. This was where he belonged.

"Will you look at that?" she said, pointing to the gaggle of news outlets waving microphones and aiming cameras as they lined the curb in front of police cruisers, ambulances, and the forensic van. "They act as if it's a red-carpet event. People were murdered here, for heaven's sake."

Cars honked, pedestrians jaywalked around them. Ahead, uniformed policemen directed traffic. Through the windshield, and the spaces between passersby and cops, Charlie could see flashes of white hazmat suits. His team was working the scene, and he glimpsed the FBI task force off to the right, a gaggle of black suits against the backdrop of the tall brick building. Special Agents Benton, Gilroy, and Modena hadn't noticed he and Cynthia had arrived. They seemed deep in discussion, somber and intense.

"Let's shelve this topic until—" Cynthia gave him side eye, but didn't finish her sentence. Charlie grimaced, knowing that meant she'd shelve it and label it "never." He understood her resistance. She didn't want to marry him. Well, tough.

"I don't think so." Charlie shifted his body in his seat until he faced her, determined to have this out.

Cynthia opened the door, and slammed it behind her before Charlie could protest. He got out, too, also slamming his door. Glaring at her over the car's roof, he saw she'd donned her FBI persona, so her expression gave nothing away. No panic. No arguments locked and loaded. That, more than anything else, was telling. He suspected she had no arguments, knew marrying him was necessary, but still wouldn't agree to it. Then he saw a flicker of hesitation in her eyes and suspected he might not be reading her motives clearly. His track record was abysmal. Over the years, he'd relied on Cynthia to be his interpreter for Cynthia. It was easier to ask what she was thinking than guess; it had saved time and misunderstandings. In this case, however, she had incentive not to be forthcoming. Charlie *suspected* she believed them marrying wasn't in his interest, but he *feared* she just didn't want to marry him.

Either way, she'd miscalculated his resolve. She'd be Mrs. Foulkes by end of day.

"I could go old school on your ass," he said. "Toss you over my shoulder. Get a shotgun."

"That's not old school. That's a hostage situation." Her eyes narrowed, staring back at him across the car's roof. "And I have a gun and a badge."

He arched a brow. "You think either of those will stop me?"

She glanced toward the hubbub at the crime scene. "No. But a JP wouldn't marry you to a fiancée who's throwing punches, and if you *dare* toss me over your shoulder again, there's another mid-knuckle to the kidneys in your future."

She was being difficult. He rested his forearms on the car's roof, his attention fully on her, making her see reason. "Shotgun it is then."

"Not at my wedding." She walked away, showing him her back as she headed toward the crime scene tape. Charlie sighed, not surprised, and then pushed off the car to catch up with her. He never thought Cynthia would welcome his plan, but he'd thought he could convince her of its necessity. Now, he wasn't so sure.

"Anything look familiar?" he said, gesturing toward the area behind the crime scene tape.

Masked by the confusion on the street and sidewalk, they still hadn't been seen by anyone, but that wouldn't last long. It was reckless of Cynthia to meet up with the team without agreeing to his plan. She needed to take his proposal seriously and do the right thing.

Marry him.

"Everything's familiar," she said, navigating through the passing crowds. "Not informative." She swallowed hard. "Mostly, it's like remembering a nightmare."

He grabbed her hand, stopping her before they got too close to the ring of media and uniformed policemen surrounding the crime scene tape. Once they were seen, they'd be on the clock, and questions would be asked. Their stories needed to sync. She tried to pull away and walk on, but he wouldn't allow it.

"What are you going to tell the team?" Charlie willed her to say "nothing." It worried him that she hadn't called her team last night. None of them. And it seemed a strange oversight for her to make, which made him fear it wasn't. Not calling them could have been a conscious decision. Her blackout made it impossible to know one way or the other, and his fears had Charlie hesitating to trust *anyone*. It was probably nothing. Maybe her phone had died and the opportunity to call didn't appear until after her blackout, but what if there was another explanation that wasn't so innocent? For safety's sake, he wanted her trusting only him.

She pulled at her hand, looking around, as if fearing people would see their intimacy. Charlie held on tight, tugging her closer. He could smell her floral shampoo, and it triggered a wave of longing that hit him hard, making him want to bury his face in her hair and feel it against his skin.

"We agreed I'd say nothing," she said. "So, I'll say nothing." His relief was real, but he'd hold off celebrating until she'd agreed to the big ask. When she tugged on her hand again, he still didn't release it.

"Do you want to announce our engagement, or should I?" he said. Cynthia scowled, and hit a pressure point on his hand until his thumb released and she was free from his grip. Instead of walking on, she shook her hand out and surreptitiously scanned the bustling scene ahead.

"You drive me crazy," she said under her breath. So, no colossal fight, just whispered annoyance, because in her eyes, his fears weren't credible, and didn't warrant a confrontation. He blamed her miscalculation on stress, and residual confusion from a head wound.

"We're getting married," he said.

"We're friends," she said, finally meeting his gaze. "And we're staying that way. If evidence points to me, I'll deal with it. You will not so much as sneeze to help me. Got that, Charlie? As for spousal privilege, we won't need it, because I have no intention of breaking the law, or even bending it." Her eyes narrowed, and then she poked his chest. "And neither will you."

His suspicions were right. Cynthia was protecting him. She was willing to risk her career and freedom with this stubbornness, because she feared embroiling Charlie in her legal jeopardy. And...she was walking away again.

"Cynthia," he said, chasing after her. She, of course, ignored him, so he slipped off his MIT college ring, wishing he'd had his grandmother's emerald on hand. When he caught up with her, he said, "I'm sorry."

Then he took her left hand again, and slid his MIT ring onto Cynthia's left ring finger.

She gasped, her wide eyes trained on their joined hands. They'd been spotted by the news people, and uniformed officers who recognized them. Interest creeped into their expressions. And now, even the FBI special agents were focusing on them.

"What are you doing?" Cynthia's cheeks had flushed.

"What's necessary."

"*No.*" If glares could kill, he'd be dead.

"If you fight this," he said, "I'll find a different way to protect you, and believe me, you won't like it. Take this easy route. Smile. Say you'll marry me."

"You think *you're* easy?" Her eyes lost focus as she peeked to her right, aware of the growing crowd of witnesses. "I won't allow you to do this."

"Don't you understand?" He nudged her chin up, forcing her to hold his gaze, and he felt her tremble, saw her hesitancy, her unease. He did not, however, see rejection. "There is *nothing* I won't do to keep you safe."

He dropped to one knee. She gasped, pressing her right palm to her chest. *No way* Cynthia would leave him hanging this way. He knew her. Knew what she couldn't allow. She was far too protective of him to allow people to think he was proposing and she was rejecting him.

"*You'll pay for this.*" Her smile stretched her lips, but didn't lessen the ire he saw in her eyes. She was being silly. Spousal privilege would allow him to withhold the damning information he knew about her whereabouts last night. It might be the only thing that kept her out of jail if her prints were found at the scene. She knew it, and should be happy this legal loophole existed.

"Everyone's watching," he said, "and they believe I'm baring my heart and soul to you." He pressed a kiss to the back of her left hand. "They think I'm telling you I want to spend the rest of my life making you happy, building a family, a home, a life." His cheek kicked up as he spoke behind cover of her hand. "They think we're in love. Don't ruin it for the romantics in the crowd." Tenderness softened the edges of his amusement, because he was self-aware enough to know he envied that fantasy version of events.

"Get up." She bit her lip, stepping to the side, presumably attempting to hide that a six-foot, three-inch, one hundred and ninety-pound redheaded bruiser was bending a knee. It wasn't an accident that he'd created this romantic tableau, and Cynthia, whether she realized it or not, was doing a convincing turn at "lover overcome by emotion." She blinked, eyes wide. "I can't—" *And he believed her.* Cynthia couldn't imagine marriage to Charlie.

It suddenly occurred to him that this must be how Teresa Johnson, his forensic tech, must feel. She'd had an unrequited crush on Charlie for months, unbeknownst to Charlie until his other tech, Kevin Hilliard, accidently outed her.

Like Teresa, Charlie was barking up the wrong tree. Cynthia had no interest in Charlie, despite their tequila-induced kiss, and she was acting much like Charlie would act if he was suddenly faced with having to tie the knot with Teresa. He almost felt sorry for Cynthia. Almost.

"I know I'm not what you want," he said, "but I'm what you need." Still hiding behind her hand, his lips against her knuckles, he watched as his words failed to mollify her. "Oh, for fuck's sake, Cynthia. Divorce me later, but smile now." He adjusted his weight, easing a pebble out from under his knee.

"*No.*" She'd become pale, her hand shook, and her smile had become a mere baring of her teeth. "I won't marry you."

He dropped her hand from his mouth and clasped her hand between his. "There is a killer on the loose, and he's targeted you once already. I need you safe, which means I'm working this case. That makes us both legally vulnerable." His argument seemed flawless, and yet Cynthia refused to buckle to his demands.

"I'll handle it," she whispered furiously. "*Alone.*"

"You'll go into protective custody then." It was the only alternative. "If the killer didn't know who you were last night, after your face is on TV, they'll know. They could come for you."

Her strained smile faltered. "I won't marry you. Even Terrance wouldn't ask that." As soon as she said it, she flinched, as if she understood she'd been unkind. "Get off your knee. When I marry, it won't be to stay out of jail."

"You will agree to marry me," he snapped, "or I'm not getting up." Though he wanted to. His knee hurt, and he wasn't a big fan of garnering attention.

She squeezed his hand, glancing at the gathering crowd. "Fine," she whispered. "I'll say...*maybe.*"

He smiled and stood, grateful that the ordeal was over. "Ah...the smell of abject surrender in the morning."

"*Let go of my hand.*"

"Get ready," he said, licking his lips, pulling her against his chest.

"For what?" she squeaked.

"A kiss will be expected." He wrapped his arms around her, embracing her as a lover would. News cameras swiveled toward Charlie and Cynthia, and suddenly they were awash with flashes. "She said yes!" Charlie yelled for the people in the back, then cupped the back of her head, careful to avoid her laceration. "Here we go," he whispered, moving his face closer to hers. "I'm going to kiss you now." He felt her breath on his face. "Don't punch me. Make it look good for the cameras." He smothered her response with a kiss.

And told himself not to enjoy it. He told himself the hunger in her eyes was his imagination. He didn't expect her to wrap her arms around his neck, or for her mouth to open under his. When his tongue instinctively swept into her mouth, and the kiss became less about a show, and more about...*damn*, she was a good kisser, lots of wet heat, tongue. Its only flaw was its audience.

Charlie broke their kiss, shaken by his instant arousal. Multiple flashes lit Cynthia's face. It took a moment to realize the occasion was being recorded for posterity.

She trembled in his arms. "I will not marry you, Charlie Foulkes." Each word felt like a stab to his heart, so he kissed her again, only releasing her when she sagged against his chest, sighing.

A particularly bright flash caught Charlie's attention, and he turned to see a phalanx of smiling faces. Then it was Charlie's face flushing as he hustled Cynthia forward. Forcing smiles, they flashed credentials to the amused uniformed officers and ducked under the crime scene tape. Charlie caught the attention of one photographer. She was young, and nearly dwarfed by her camera.

"I'll buy the rights to those pictures," he said. "It's not every day a man becomes engaged." A few reporters laughed. "Contact my office, and we'll get it done." The woman laughed and nodded, making her brunette curls bob, and then there was a round of applause as he and Cynthia hustled toward the FBI task force team, who greeted them with frowns.

Special Agent Vincent Modena spoke first, his green eyes flashing irritation. Tall, his brown hair newly clipped short, the sheer force of the agent's personality had them stopping a few yards in front of him. "What the hell, Deming?" Modena said.

Special Agent Gilroy was shorter than Modena, but wider and bulkier, with well-earned, sculpted muscle; Charlie had seen Gilroy press three hundred at the gym. He was powerful. Blond hair clipped to his scalp, Gilroy had a habit of rubbing his head when uncomfortable, and he was doing it now. Not a big talker, the agent's lips were compressed, which had the effect of highlighting his large, crooked nose.

Cynthia's boss, Special Agent Jack Benton, looked as if he couldn't choose between shock or dismay. Black hair, neatly clipped, and his blue eyes flashing, Benton settled on a glare. "Deming?"

She rested her fists on her hips, glaring back at her team. Then she turned to Charlie and punched his shoulder. "This is Charlie's fault. Don't blame me."

Charlie remained unrepentant. "A man's got to do—"

"Charlie." Benton said. "You proposed at a crime scene. Not cool." He tilted his head, indicating the bodies and blood behind him.

Modena never took his gaze off Cynthia's face. "You two... You know each other?" He tucked his hands in his black suit's pants pockets, leaning on his heels, seemingly unconvinced.

"No, Modena," Cynthia narrowed her eyes. "We're strangers. That's why we got engaged."

Charlie forced himself not to sigh in relief, but he did feel a calmness infuse his system. She was speaking out of both sides of her mouth, sure, but she was also holding the line when it came to appearances. It gave him another lever to force her to commit to his plan.

Modena ignored Cynthia's sarcasm and turned to Charlie. "I didn't even know you two were dating." Cynthia grew beet red. Time for Charlie to save her.

"Sorry the ER took so long," he said. "Cynthia's fine, by the way. Doctor says no concussion."

"Yeah, yeah. So…engaged?" Modena's steely-eyed stare told Charlie he didn't believe them.

"Enough, Modena," Benton said.

Gilroy cleared his throat. "She looks pissed." Yes. Charlie couldn't fail to notice also. That wasn't a normal response to being newly engaged.

"Understandable." Benton grimaced, glancing at Charlie. "She deserved better than a crime scene proposal." Gratitude had Charlie smiling at Benton. His excuse was perfect cover for Cynthia.

"Yes," Cynthia said. "She did deserve better, and she'd prefer that people stop talking about her as if she wasn't present."

"What did the doctor say?" Benton said.

"You heard Charlie," she said. "I'm fine. Can we work the case, please? What do we have?"

"Forensic techs have been here for a while." Gilroy didn't hide his relief to change the subject as they all, as a group, moved toward the bodies draped with white cloths.

Reporters shouted questions as they passed, and the team ignored them, per usual, and Charlie, per usual, found it difficult to tune them out. He understood leaked intel tampered with prosecuting cases, and that "answers" were proprietary, but he was a scientist who lived for questions, and questions, by their nature, begged an answer. Never felt right to leave the reporters hanging.

When they'd approached the first victim, Charlie could see Cynthia struggling to keep her emotions in check. Her behavior would have been telling, maybe even suspicious, if the crime scene didn't give her cover. It was particularly horrific, and aptly named "The Chinatown Massacre." The cause of death due to GSW to the head, with a relatively intact cranium, was usually due to blood loss. A bullet hits a blood vessels, the vic bleeds out. Charlie calculated eight pints of blood per victim, six victims. Even assuming they'd only discharged half after hypovolemic shock set in, this crime scene was covered with at least three gallons of blood pooling and spatter. Didn't sound like much, until you saw three gallons spattered by six .22 bullets with a muzzle velocity of 700 feet per second.

Blood was everywhere.

Cynthia seemed faint. He wondered if it was from the scene, or the fear that evidence might turn up that might ruin her career. She cleared her throat, indicating the six bodies with a tilt of her head. "What do the marshals have to say about six Coppola WITSEC informants executed in Chinatown?"

"They're scrambling," Benton said, "officially saying nothing. Unofficially?" He frowned at the body at his feet.

"They're swearing a lot," Gilroy said.

"Vics had their wallets, phones," Modena said. "No attempt to hide their identities."

"The killer wanted us to know who he killed." Cynthia glanced at the media. "Wants someone to know, anyway. These men testified already. Why bother killing them unless to warn others?"

"Warn who?" Benton shrugged. "Who's left in the Coppola syndicate to warn? We've rounded up the major players, or rather, anyone who would do something like this."

Charlie glanced at the sky, and saw the crime scene wasn't about to be rained on anytime soon. He was tired, his eyes grainy from a night of no sleep, so he was grateful for the small blessing. No rain meant they could worry about preserving evidence, rather than protecting it from the weather.

Crouching next to the nearest body, he looked up to see Kevin Hilliard approach. About five-ten, one hundred and seventy pounds, his white hazmat suit and face shield were soiled with dirt and blood, and obscured everything about him except for his height. Kevin tipped his face shield up, revealing pale skin, blond stubble, and bloodshot brown eyes. The father of five kids, the youngest four months old, Kevin was chronically tired, and doing his best to kick a cigarette habit. He handed Charlie a set of latex gloves, stifling a yawn, smelling of Nicorette gum.

"Thanks, Kevin," Charlie said.

The tech nodded. "Wound stippling consistent with contact discharge. Me and Teresa removed the hoods to ID the vics. It's like this with all of them. Handgun, probably .22."

Charlie snapped on the gloves, aware of the hovering agents. They were impatient, because nothing was official until Charlie, the forensic pathologist on the case, said it was so. He lifted the white cloth enough to see the head and the top of the vic's torso. He lifted the head and saw the bullet had, indeed, been a through and through.

"No rigor mortis." Which occurs between four and thirteen hours after death, and it was ten in the morning now, so that made sense if these vics were shot at ten o'clock last night. He glanced at Kevin. "Who ordered you to take off the hoods?"

"Me," Benton said.

Kevin exchanged glances with Benton before turning back to Charlie. "Hoods are bagged and logged. I stopped photographing the scene when I saw you'd arrived. I'm halfway done."

"Anything standing out, Charlie?" Cynthia was biting her lip so hard, he feared she'd cut skin.

"Stop biting your lip." He frowned at her mouth, didn't turn away until she'd licked it, and glared at her fellow agents, who seemed interested in their byplay. He shut that distraction out and turned back to the body. Yes, he saw the "tattooing," or "stippling," of gunpowder residue around the wound. Also, he could see pieces of material embedded just under the skin. "Direct contact, muzzle pressed to forehead at time of discharge, consistent with a suicide or, in this case, with hands tied behind their backs," he said. "Execution."

"Ya think?" Modena snorted. "What gave it away?"

"Leave him alone." Cynthia scowled at Modena.

Charlie dropped the cloth over the victim, dismissing Modena's snarkiness. They were all on edge, and for good reason. He recognized this guy. He was a Coppola syndicate contract killer, which suggested the other bodies were also. Their executions should scare all of them. Special Agent Benton sacrificed a year undercover with the syndicate, and Modena almost died, and nearly lost the love of his life to these monsters. No one was happy to hear the words "Coppola syndicate" ever. His parents still hadn't forgiven him for torpedoing their lives when they had to enter protective custody for three months. Everyone that Charlie held dear became a potential target when he'd agreed to testify against Dante Coppola. His parents had understood the precaution, but hated the experience nonetheless.

"This will take time. Be patient, and I'll have a report to you as soon as I'm done," Charlie said, catching Cynthia's gaze. She nodded, and then stepped back, giving him the space to do his job.

Benton nodded, then he and his team moved to the next body, not touching, just conferring as they partially lifted the cloth his team had draped over the body to protect the evidence and hide it from unauthorized photography. There were six bodies, as Cynthia had described earlier, and the vics were lined up against the brick façade of the alleyway's wall. To Charlie, they represented ten hours with his assistants' help, of methodical evidence collection, which required exacting and exhausting focus. He felt an adrenaline rush thinking about it. Somewhere here was evidence that would clear Cynthia. And he was going to find it.

His second-in-command, tech Teresa Johnson, caught his attention as he headed to the forensic department's van. Though they met at the curb, well within the crime scene tape, the van's bulk protected them from news crews' cameras. Teresa stripped off her face shield, self-consciously tugged off the hazmat suit's hood to reveal mussed blond hair. She looked younger than her years, pale, and twitchy, which he attributed to the hot sun and, not incidentally, the fact that the crime scene smelled like a slaughterhouse.

"Everything's ready for you," Teresa said. "We did the perimeter, the walkthrough, and, as you can see, put down numbered placards. Kevin's still working on the close-up photography, but everything is pretty much documented but the bodies."

"Good job." His team was well trained, and this morning especially, Charlie appreciated their competence.

"I mapped the scene," she said, "made notes about each item collected. The chain of custody forms are here." Teresa lifted a clipboard, handing it to Charlie with a pen. "Property receipts are under that. Oh, and Kevin still needs to video before we move the bodies."

Kevin approached, holding the team's telescopic camera and hefting a video camera over his shoulder. Yawning, he was chewing more of his Nicorette gum.

Teresa peered beyond Charlie's shoulder. "I guess congratulations are in order." Charlie followed her gaze, saw Cynthia, then quickly donned a disposable hazmat suit over his clothes and slipped on a face shield.

"Thank you." He led them to the first body, crouching next to the vic. He lifted the cloth, saw a slight figure of a male, Caucasian, late twenties, blond man-bun atop his head. Charlie knew him, and knew he had a kill list longer than Charlie's weekly grocery list. Specialized in knives.

"You're certainly taking a big step, Charlie." Kevin smiled, pulling down his hood, revealing his unruly head of hair. The hazmat hood had electrified it, so some blond strands stood on end. "Next there'll be pitter-pattering of little feet."

Teresa flinched, making Charlie visualize slapping Kevin upside his electrified head. No, Charlie didn't want Teresa crushing on him, but he didn't want her feelings hurt, either. Kevin wasn't usually this insensitive. It was Kevin who mentioned Teresa's infatuation in the first place. He'd pointed out her lingering after hours at the lab, asking questions beyond the necessary, and her repeated hints that she'd welcome an invitation to Charlie's house after work. Once Kevin had put those instances through the prism of unrequited infatuation, it was hard for even Charlie to miss them. No, it wasn't Charlie's first social cue blunder and wouldn't be his last, but usually it didn't matter. This time, it mattered. He liked Teresa. She was a good tech. And neither had been happy after their meeting to clarify his *no fraternizing* policy. They left embarrassed, but Teresa stopped flirting, and…time would heal.

"You really proposed?" Teresa said. "At *this* crime scene?" She directed his attention to the blood spatter, the federal agents, and the general chaos.

Kevin snorted. "Are we pretending a different crime scene would have been better?"

Charlie suppressed a groan. The proposal really did make him look like a lunatic, but he'd been desperate. "In hindsight, yeah, a mistake. I'm not good with things like…" He paused, wondering how to categorize what was happening with him and Cynthia.

"People?" Kevin said.

"Women?" Teresa said.

"Cynthia," Charlie said, glancing at his newly minted fiancée. With a sigh, he shed all thoughts but the job and flipped through the clipboard paperwork, making sure all the appropriate forms were attached. Then he held it out to Teresa to make notations on while he worked the body. "Moving on. Anything I need to know before we start?"

Teresa nodded. "Vics' hands and shoes are bagged already. With the sheer volume of police presence, I was afraid of contamination if I waited until you'd arrived. I didn't know when you'd get here." She shrugged. Yeah, valid point, and not so subtle criticism.

"I photographed anything Teresa placarded," Kevin said. "Crowd shots, and far away shots, and body shots before we touched them. So I've got a few things left to shoot, but then all that's left are the detail shots of the bodies prior to bagging."

"Good," Charlie said.

"We still need to sample and log the spatter," Teresa said. "Slugs and casings were easy to find." Charlie forced himself not to tense up, or even respond. He needed to see those casings before anyone else, in case Cynthia was right and her prints were on them.

"Slugs were embedded in the brick," Kevin said. "Teresa dug them out after I took pictures. We were wondering." He exchanged glances with Teresa. "Usually, professionals police their brass. Dig out their slugs so we don't have access to them." Teresa averted her gaze, but he could see she was waiting for a response, too. Well, Charlie didn't have one. Obviously, the killer wanted these casings and slugs found. It was the "why" that gave him more than a little unease.

"We don't deal in *whys*," Charlie said. "We deal in *whats*. We gather the evidence, and allow the task force to investigate."

Speaking of *whats*... He studied the evidence list, looking for anything out of the ordinary. Blood samples, location noted and numbered by placards. He scanned the scene, picked out the placard location that was most probably where Cynthia had been pistol-whipped if she'd stumbled upon the crime scene in progress. Placard 126. Her DNA sample would be logged there. CODIS, the index of known perp DNA samples, would be searched, and come up short, because her DNA wasn't housed there. Charlie wasn't worried she'd be ID'd by CODIS.

Her prints on the shell casings would nail her.

Protocol would require Cynthia to surrender DNA to compare to samples found at the scene. She'd be forced to refuse, or risk being ID'd. Her refusal would trigger an investigation, maybe charges. Unfortunately, any attempt to subvert that process on his part would be illegal. They'd have to play it by ear.

Teresa pointed to the evidence list. "The duct tape is still attached to all the hoods, and bagged into evidence. The zip ties are white, non-releasable, seem generic, and they're still binding the vics' wrists. Hoods seem custom-made, so we might get lucky and find pertinent DNA there. Someone had to sew the brown cloth. I told Benton, and suggested they might have been ordered, so maybe they could find a name or credit card associated with a receipt at a local seamstress shop or tailor."

Charlie nodded. "Good job, Teresa. The vics were transported here from six separate WITSEC locations across the country, so even though they were killed here," he said, "we don't know how many other crime scenes this case might be looking at. Prepare for the long haul. As with anything Coppola syndicate related, it will be a pain in our asses." He flipped the page, glanced up, and saw Teresa pressing her lips together, looking a bit green around the gills. "Pray for some fingerprints," he said.

Kevin handed Charlie a manila folder. "Lab request forms." Charlie signed in the appropriate spots.

"Um, Charlie? I hate to bring this up, but—" Teresa exchanged glances with Kevin. "Last forensic tech crew that worked a Coppola syndicate crime scene had to enter protective custody. Do Kevin and I have to worry?"

Charlie shook his head. "The syndicate is dead." When Kevin and Teresa didn't seem consoled, he said, "Listen, I'll speak to Benton. See what he says." They nodded. "Good. Now let's get to work and bag these bodies. They've been on hot pavement too long."

With Teresa and Kevin assisting, they were done bagging and tagging within an hour. It gave Charlie a head start on paperwork, as his techs did a final sweep of the scene. After Charlie stripped off his hazmat suit, face shield, booties, and gloves, then tossed them in a medical waste container in the back of the van, he felt a hand nudge his shoulder.

"You almost done?" Cynthia had dark circles under her eyes. He found himself reaching for her, but then Teresa stepped to his side, pointedly ignoring Cynthia.

"Hey, Charlie?" she said. "Kevin and I came in the van. We're finished, so we should follow the ambulance back to the morgue." Teresa's gaze skittered to Cynthia, and then quickly away. Shifting foot to foot, he sympathized with her obvious embarrassment, but it was making things painfully awkward. "Meet you there?" she said.

"Charlie!" Kevin shouted from down the alleyway, just beyond the scope of the crime scene tape. He was waist-deep in a dumpster, next to a grimacing uniformed officer. Kevin's hand was raised above his head, and he was holding something. Charlie's heart sped up as it became clear what the tech held. "I think I found the murder weapon!"

"You always did have the luck of the Irish." Charlie exchanged an excited smile with Cynthia.

If this *was* the murder weapon, Cynthia didn't need to worry anymore. No matter what happened last night during her blackout, she wasn't implicated in these deaths. It meant they could spill everything to Benton and the team, and it even simplified his and Cynthia's relationship. Their marriage wasn't necessary.

He waved Kevin toward the van, forcing himself to patiently wait for the tech to deliver the evidence. Kevin carefully held it between his latex-protected fingertips, and was taking his damn time walking to Charlie. By the time he'd arrived, the task force had gathered, too.

"Good job, Kevin," Charlie said. Gilroy, Modena, and Benton leaned close, staring at the gun as Kevin held it aloft. "Teresa," Charlie said, "get an evidence bag, please."

The tech reached into the back of the van and pulled out a large, clear plastic ziplock evidence bag. She opened its top and held it out to Kevin, who dropped the handgun inside. Charlie took the bag, peering at it through the clear plastic. He sniffed.

"It's been discharged recently," he said. Cynthia's eyes were closed, and he suspected she was saying a little prayer of thanks.

Teresa hurried over to the van, and came back with the camera. Her hands trembled as she handed it to Kevin. Charlie didn't blame her. This multiple murder case, this *massacre*, was about to be busted wide open. The murder weapon would be traced through the ATF and would potentially tell them who'd bought it, and from whom. The serial number, plus any potential prints, could pinpoint exactly who'd wielded it.

After photographs were taken, and the camera was stored back in the van, Kevin and Teresa followed the ambulances back to the morgue. Now that the bodies were gone, so were the crowds and chaos of earlier. Uniformed officers guarded the scene, standing alone, looking bored as they stood at the crime scene tape perimeter.

"Let's hope the ATF can match the gun to its owner," Benton said. "Serial number was clear enough." He waved Modena closer. "Have them put a rush on tracking the buyer's ID. Six dead should bump us to the front of the line."

Cynthia seemed happy enough, but Charlie saw her hesitancy. "A Coppola contract killer wouldn't use a traceable gun for a hit unless they wanted you to know who owned it. And a Glock? No way. They pride themselves on using HKs. Serial number or not, it's unlikely that gun tells us anything they don't want us to know."

"Or they weren't killed by a Coppola contract killer," Gilroy said. "We don't even know if the gun is related to these kills. It could have been in the dumpster before, or even after, these vics were shot."

Modena vibrated with checked tension. "Even if we catch the killer today, it doesn't change that these witnesses were promised protection. They're dead. It will have lasting effects on our ability to recruit other snitches."

Cynthia nodded. "Newly enrolled WITSEC witnesses, snatched and grabbed, and then executed and left for maximum media coverage. We have the message. But who's the message for?"

"And who's the messenger?" Benton said. "I think we need a list of witnesses the FBI are grooming. See if they're somehow connected with these kills. Charlie, those crowd photos would be very helpful right about now. As soon as you can get them to us, please." Charlie nodded.

"You know Dante Coppola is probably involved," Modena said.

"He's in federal prison in Pensacola, Florida," Gilroy said. "He doesn't even have phone rights."

"And hard to see Coppola's motive, here," Cynthia said. "These vics snitched just like he did."

"I've heard rumors he's married," Modena said. "Living the good life in Club Fed." Rumors only, because Modena wasn't officially privy to

Coppola case files anymore. Not after he'd become romantically involved with Coppola's ex-wife.

"Yeah. Angelina Modelli," Benton said. "Records suggest they're hot and heavy. We're building a case against her, too, and she's not covered by Coppola's immunity deal." Charlie knew who they were talking about only because he'd been brought into the case at the very end when asked to replace their forensic expert at trial.

"I'd feel sorry for them if they weren't mass murderers," Cynthia said. "She's loved Coppola forever, had to live through his marriage to someone else, and now that she's got him hook, line, and sinker, the bureau is about to swoop in and separate them again."

"I don't feel sorry for them." Modena looked as if he'd bit into something bitter.

"Separate them?" Charlie said. "Coppola is in jail, right?"

"Conjugal rights," Cynthia said, avoiding his gaze. "Modelli is a *frequent* visitor of Coppola's at Club Fed in Florida."

"Charlie," Benton said. "I have to brief the acting lieutenant, and the special agent in charge. If you want me, call me. I'll be around. We need those crowd shots."

"I'll text Kevin when I get in the car," Charlie said. "Do you mind if I grab Cynthia for a quick lunch? We haven't eaten today." Benton nodded, and then left with Gilroy and Modena. The agents fell into deep conversation, discussing the case, leaving him and Cynthia alone to duck under the crime scene tape and head toward Charlie's car.

"It's a miracle," she whispered, glancing behind them. "The murder weapon. You said to wait until we see what the crime scene turns up, and you were right, but I didn't even dare to hope we'd find the murder weapon." Charlie didn't want to ruin her mood, and he didn't quite know how to explain himself, so he waited, hoping the right words would come to him.

"Let's grab some lunch." He was starving.

"Lunch?" Cynthia pressed her palm to her belly. "How can you think of food at a time like this?" Charlie led her past the news people packing their equipment and loading it into their vans. He had to get Cynthia out of there so he could think, and explain. Things were happening fast.

"Listen," he said, "I can't do anything until the bodies are at the morgue, and I have about a half an hour before they'll be expecting me at the hospital for a ten-hour shift. I need the food." He took out his car's automatic key and unlocked the door. He opened the passenger side door for her and waited until she'd settled inside before leaning toward her, his forearm on the roof. "How do you want to walk back this whole marriage thing? We should say you can't marry a man willing to propose at a crime scene."

She laughed, took off his MIT ring, and slapped it on his outstretched palm. If she'd kept her eyes on that ring a beat or two longer than necessary, or didn't retract her hand immediately, he blamed it on her exhaustion. He suppressed his urge to mourn, because the ring never belonged on her finger. It was too big and ungainly. Cynthia wore delicate jewelry, if at all. She deserved his grandmother's emerald—not that he'd be slipping a ring back on her finger any time soon. He had news. Not good news, and he wasn't sure how to break it to her, though he was positive withholding this particular bombshell was wrong, maybe even impossible. She had to know, if only to be safe.

When he slid behind the wheel, he reached for his phone in the console and texted Kevin, requesting the crowd photos to immediately be forwarded to the task force, and then put the phone back down. He scanned the street, saw no one watching them, and then turned toward Cynthia. Sun streamed in from her side window and transformed her normally straight blond hair into burnished curls of gold: a halo effect. It was stunning. She was stunning.

"You're spectacular, Cynthia." The words just popped out of his mouth, and he wasn't sure who was more surprised—him or her.

She frowned. "I look like shit. I'm exhausted, bloated, and I think my breath smells." She cupped her hand and breathed in it. He knew what she was smelling. Peppermint. Because that's what she'd tasted like when he'd kissed her after his proposal.

"Cynthia..." Damn, he just had to come out and say it. "The gun found at the crime scene is mine."

Cynthia's eyes widened. She blanched, but otherwise took it well.

"Combined with the evidence in my trunk," he said, "I believe someone is framing me for these murders. You need to be as far away from me as possible. Physically, and on paper. I know you won't agree to protective custody, but maybe we should bring Benton in on this, if only to add another level of security around you. I can't help thinking you're being used. They assaulted you and left you with six dead bodies. Somehow, you're playing a role in the killer's scheme."

The resulting silence in the car was complete, and seemed to have a weight to it, pressing down on him. He feared talking simply to fill it, so he remained silent, too, and focused on the sounds he made as he shifted in his seat, then tapped his thumb against the leather-bound steering wheel. Cynthia swallowed hard, and her chest rose and fell repeatedly, as if she were having a hard time breathing. Her previously pale cheeks flushed red, and she reached out, grabbed his hand on the steering wheel, and squeezed it tightly.

In the blink of an eye, she'd pulled his MIT ring from his finger and slipped it onto her left ring finger. Cynthia faced forward, staring out the front windshield.

"After long and deliberative consideration, Charlie Foulkes, I've decided to accept your proposal of marriage." She buckled in, looking as if she was in a daze, then lifted his iPhone out of the console between the two seats, typed in his passcode—her birthday—and opened the Google Maps app.

The animatronic voice resonated from his iPhone's speaker. "Starting route…"

He assumed she'd typed in a restaurant's address, that she'd decided where she wanted to eat for lunch, but Charlie wasn't hungry anymore. For the first time in ten years, he had no idea what he could do to save himself, and it sickened him.

But if Cynthia was hungry, he'd feed her.

"Where're we going?" he said, his voice sounding strained even to his ears.

Cynthia took a steadying breath. "The nearest justice of the peace."

Chapter Five

"And before you argue," Cynthia said, "I know as well as you do that once the West Virginia warehouse receives Modena's request to trace your gun, he'll hear back—"

"He won't." Charlie shifted into gear and pulled into traffic.

"—within a day. This is the ATF. Not the DMV."

"Even if they found the paperwork on my Glock—which they won't—"

"Of course they will!" She felt a panic attack coming on. Her heart was racing, and she was breaking out into a sweat. It was even becoming hard to form words. "I'm either having a stroke or a heart attack." She rubbed her chest. The only common denominator between the crime scene and Charlie was her. Maybe she hadn't been at the gym when that "blonde" appeared in his driveway. They'd yet to follow up on that, and she had been videotaped blocks from the scene with *her* recently discharged gun in hand. "By the time your gun is traced—"

"I bought it ten years ago." He took a sharp right, forcing her to steady herself with a palm on the dashboard. "At a Walmart that has since closed. It can't be traced back to me." His confidence seemed unreasonable, since the ATF agents were rock stars and finding records was their jam.

"*By law*, Charlie, these records must be kept, so they'll find them." Then Charlie would be called in by Benton for questioning, maybe arrested. "If you bought the gun, especially from a store, there'll be a record of the purchase—forms, maybe even a logged background check."

Charlie shrugged, slowing the car as they approached a red light. "You'd think, right?"

When the light turned green, he sped up and went through the intersection. All calm and collected. Whereas Cynthia's stomach felt like it was bursting with butterflies, Charlie was…shrugging off the ATF. She envied him his delusion. The man had always been an apple to her orange, and today was a prime example. As a student of behavior and interpreting the vagaries of the human mind, Cynthia's tools were statistics and, more often than not, gut instinct and opinion. Charlie's was data. So, what was she missing?

"This is me crying uncle," she said. "Tell me." He'd said he bought it at Walmart, so the gun wasn't purchased through private sale or a gun show. It was illegal to have a computerized national weapons register, or any register that could be used to create a national registry, but forms were mandatory. They just had to be on paper. "What don't I know?"

"We don't have that kind of time." His cheek kicked up, and his eyes crinkled with a smile.

She felt incapable of humor. "Charlie, even with its antiquated search process, the ATF can trace a weapon within twenty-four hours."

"The Walmart closed," he said, "and the stored records were destroyed in a fire."

Cynthia sighed with relief. "Way to bury the lead, but it sounds sketchy, and any prosecutor will say so in court."

Google Maps told Charlie to turn onto the freeway. "Stop looking so unhappy," he said. "The news could have been worse." He chucked her under the chin, making her feel like the naïve middle schooler she'd been when they first met. Back then, her biggest worries were math grades, and that she'd be flat-chested for life. "*Relax*," he whispered, though she wasn't sure if it was for her benefit or his, because Charlie seemed less than relaxed. "Whoever is framing me didn't do their due diligence. That's good."

"Are you positive it's your gun?" Hope tickled the edges of her despair.

"It my gun." He grimaced. "The serial number is mine, and Cynthia?" He arched a brow, his derision on display. "Really? You think I don't know my own gun?"

"But… How many people have your gun safe code?" It was her birthdate, just like his phone code.

"You and me, and it wasn't broken into. Whoever took the gun had the code." He kept his eyes on the road and his expression blank, but he had to be thinking it. He had to be thinking what she was thinking.

"Why would I steal your gun?" she said, in a small voice. "Or put that stuff in your trunk?" None of it made any sense.

"Stop it," he said. "We've been through this."

"We're both thinking it. We need to contact the gym."

"Of course, but you didn't do this." He squeezed the steering wheel until his forearms bulged.

She felt like a triggered jack-in-the-box. *"How do you know?"*

"Because you'd never hurt me." He said it quietly, clearly, and she heard the truth of his words. She'd never hurt him. "Your memory will return," he said, "and then you'll see. Until then, just…trust me, Cynthia. Okay?"

"I do trust you." But could she trust herself?

"You didn't break into my house and steal from me. You didn't plant anything. But someone did, and we need to find them." He glanced at her. "We'll call the gym. Between their records and your recollection of eating a falafel outside the precinct, you couldn't have been the one in my driveway."

"I'll call them now," she said, pulling her phone from her suit jacket.

"And Cynthia?" He kept his eyes on the road. "I can fight the whole of the BPD, the FBI, and all the alphabet agencies, but I can't fight you, too. So, work with me here." He looked exhausted as he turned the car, following Google Map's prodding down unfamiliar roads.

"It looks sketchy. That's all I'm saying." She sank deeper into her seat.

"It's not all bad news. My gun might give us a fingerprint, or maybe whoever stole it contaminated it with their DNA," he said. "Look on the bright side."

"I'm afraid for you, Charlie." He grabbed her hand and squeezed. She held on, squeezing back.

"We'll stay at my house, or your house, or we can just take turns, because of the cat. The killer is still out there." Fear tugged at his features. "I'm not giving him another shot at you."

"I'm still alive." That was a chilling clue. "Why'd the killer allow me to live? To walk away? Maybe you're right, Charlie. Maybe the killer is using me."

Google Maps directed them to take a right at the next block. He stopped for a red light and met her gaze as they waited for it to change. When the car's silence stretched out, and his expression gave nothing away, she wondered if she should just tell him. Everything. How she felt about him, what she wanted from him, what she feared, and all the crazy things that were suddenly on the table if it meant keeping Charlie safe. The only thing stopping her from confessing was the fear Charlie wouldn't welcome it. This was Charlie, after all. Uncomfortable with big emotions. Didn't like scenes. Didn't understand women. Staying silent seemed safer.

"Terrance would be horrified." He tucked a lock of unruly hair behind her ear.

She nodded. "He never really grew out of the whole 'girl germs' phase."

"Oh, yes he did." Charlie chuckled, glancing at the streetlight, seeing that it was still red. "We were college kids. We *liked* 'girl germs.' Terrance treated you like you were spun glass, and didn't act around you like he'd acted around…just about everyone else. Cynthia, your brother thought you walked on water. We both did." The light changed, he put the turn signal on, and soon they were down the street, parking at the curb outside a small white Cape Cod-style house sporting a shingle on the lawn advertising the JP's services.

"Joleen Champion, Justice of the Peace," she said. "I feel as if I'm in an alternate universe." Things like this didn't happen to people in Cynthia's family. They happened to other people.

Moments later, walking up the cobblestone path to the front door, Charlie pressed his hand to her lower back. Then they stood at the door, ringing the bell. A united front. Cynthia couldn't shake the feeling that they were there to question a witness. The neighborhood, and the rundown quality of the house, shouted meth, not matrimony.

Charlie knocked, and a lace curtain moved aside, revealing a small woman, mid-sixties, brunette, with short, curly hair, peering back at them through the top glass panel of the door. It opened, hitting a high-pitch bell at the lintel and revealing a quaint, cabbage flower-upholstered waiting room that smelled of roses. And cats. Lots of cats. They rubbed against their legs, mewing for attention as Cynthia and Charlie walked inside. He'd had to duck to get through the door, and the room was small, and the JP was small, and Charlie was so big. It made everything seem like they were in a life-size dollhouse, and she and Charlie were the toys. Suddenly, Cynthia felt faint, and it was hard to breathe.

More cats greeted them. More mewing. Cynthia's eyes welled up. She sneezed.

Ten minutes later, Charlie was finishing up paperwork with quick strokes of the borrowed pen, and then all Cynthia had to do was sign. Cynthia Deming. Her married name. Rather than Cynthia Deming, her maiden name. She didn't know how she felt about the whole marriage thing—hadn't had time to process it—but she did know it was necessary. JP Champion put her seal of approval on the form, smiled brightly, and then Charlie and Cynthia were officially married. Boom.

Cynthia could have cried. Felt like she still might.

"Okay! The dry, legal part of the wedding is over. So congratulations! You're married," the JP said, her brown curls bouncing as she vibrated with excitement. "Now for the fun stuff. Have you prepared vows to exchange?"

Cynthia sneezed. By now, her nose was red and drippy, and so were her eyes. She looked at Charlie, who stood frozen, staring at the little woman as if she'd suggested a three-way. It took Cynthia a moment to understand what was happening.

Charlie was choking under pressure. Vows? What vows? He was living the nightmare of taking a test without having studied.

Six gory, bloody bodies? Being framed for murder? Compelled to marry? None pushed Charlie beyond his ability to cope. Yet the idea of reciting hackneyed vows historically repeated ad nauseam by multitudes of romantics over the course of millennia? That was a bridge too far. Charlie choked. He was panicking.

For some reason, Cynthia felt no sympathy.

"Oh, for heaven's sake," she snapped. "*No.* No vows. We're good."

Cynthia snatched the paperwork from the surprised woman's hand as she walked out of the office and left Charlie to pay the fee. When she reached the walkway, she tilted her face up to the sun and wiped her tears, needing a moment to compose herself. She didn't get one.

"Hey." Charlie carefully closed the door behind him, ringing the bell overhead again. He hurried to her side. "I didn't know you were allergic to cats." She wasn't. "You okay?"

No. She wasn't okay. She was married. She hurried toward the car, needing to escape before she had a meltdown in a JP's front yard. "Let's go." She was Mrs. Charlie Foulkes. "I'm keeping my name."

"Me, too." He winked, but it was more of a "keep your chin up" wink, rather than a teasing wink. They got in the car, each silent, neither exhibiting an iota of the happiness usually associated with a wedding. She found it depressing. "Hey, I've been thinking," he said, turning the engine over. "We could simply be a diversion for the killer. While Benton is looking at me and you, the real killer is getting away with murder. Think about it. If we'd confessed immediately, all eyes would rightfully be on us. How could the killer predict we'd stay quiet? It's not like either of us."

"Planted evidence shows intent," she said. "But we'd have to prove it was planted. Good luck with that. Confession or not, we'll be screwed either way. At least now we can participate in the investigation."

"You shot six rounds," he said. "We'll find your casings, the slugs, and hopefully we'll discover you hit someone. I mean, the killer. Not one of the vics. And the killer's blood will then be on a slug."

"Or in all six vics. Nice try, Charlie. I'm screwed. You're screwed," she said. "Our one defense is this wedding."

Charlie grimaced, nodding. "We are totally screwed."

"All because I went to the gym last night." If she'd gone home instead, she wouldn't be Mrs. Charlie Foulkes. *Be still, my heart.* She glanced at him, saw he was deep in thought, pulling out of the parking lot and onto the road. She told herself not to be hurt that there was no pomp or circumstance to their wedding, no flowers or relatives throwing rice. What had she thought would happen? Platitudes? This was Charlie; their marriage was a practicality. She needed to be practical, too.

She dropped her gaze, noticed her nail polish was worse for wear. "What if the print on your gun is of a blond woman, five-six," she said, "weapons ready, has a penchant for manicures, high heels, expensive Kate Spade pocketbooks, can't cook, and is recently married?" Her description started out as a joke, but ended by depressing her. It was a real concern. "Bet you never thought you'd marry a woman who couldn't cook."

Charlie didn't smile as he hit his turn signal and pulled into the right lane. "I've survived worse." Yes, he had. Ten minutes later, he was parking at the curb in front of his house.

"What the hell? Benton will be waiting, Charlie." She'd been so distracted by the shit storm that had become her life that she hadn't noticed where he'd been taking her. Some investigator she was.

"I have to feed Socks, and we still need to eat," he said. "Lucky for you, you married someone who *can* cook." He released his seat belt with a snap.

"I'm not hungry." She opened the door and stood, slamming it after her.

"You'll eat," he said, catching her gaze over the car's roof. "And we have things to discuss."

"Such as?" This morning, she'd have assumed it was about their kiss, and her ghosting him and his parents. Now, it could be anything. He glanced up and down the street, as if he feared they'd be overheard, making her think that whatever it was, it was confidential.

"We're married," he whispered. "There will be questions." He stepped off the sidewalk onto his cobblestone walkway, heading up the stairs to his restored white Victorian. "And I need to hear this unsub's profile. He's targeted us; I want to target him." He no longer whispered, so she had to assume the sensitive topic had been their marriage and potential questions. "I know you and the task force are full-throttle looking for this guy, but it couldn't hurt to keep me apprised of what information you have. Knowledge is power. I want to help."

She frowned, annoyed, hurrying up the stairs onto his porch. "Why'd you whisper 'we're married'?"

He inserted his key into the door, using his hip to keep the intricately carved wood screen door open. "Huh?"

"Do you think people won't notice we're married?" She lifted her left hand, scowling as she walked through his now open front door. "This ring is huge." His MIT school ring had to be clutched in her fist to keep it in place or it would slide from her finger. "People will notice."

He not-so-subtly avoided her gaze as he stepped inside, too, closing the door behind him. "It's temporary."

"Damn right it is." As soon as this case was closed, she was getting a quickie divorce. No way she was any man's ball and chain, and certainly not Charlie's. Just thinking about how he must feel trapped by their circumstances was enough to make her die of humiliation.

"Hey," he snapped. "I was talking about the ring, not the marriage, but duly noted. You don't want to be married to me. Message received loud and clear. But we're married." Charlie rarely raised his voice, but now it echoed in the foyer and hall beyond. She turned to face him, unhappy to see the sun backlighting him, giving him a glow and putting his face in shadow. It put her at a disadvantage, because he could see her face crystal clear. "We're *really* married, Cynthia. It's not pretend." Fists at his side, feet shoulder width apart, he seemed poised to fight. Then he stepped toward her and flipped on the light. His eyes were focused on her lips.

They'd kissed twice. Once because of tequila, and the second time *at a crime scene.* He'd given her notice, walked her through the steps. "Get ready" he'd said. "Don't punch me," he'd said. But without an audience to convince, and bereft of tequila, she didn't imagine his eyes focused on her lips meant more than she probably needed lip balm.

"The marriage isn't real," she said. "It's not consummated." Cynthia batted her eyelashes, daring him to keep talking about something that was clearly making him uncomfortable.

He stepped closer, and Cynthia had to squelch an urge to step back. He was so big, and his presence overwhelmed her. Suddenly, Cynthia got the feeling Charlie's laser focus on her lips wasn't about chapped lips.

"Are you suggesting an eventual annulment," he said, "or that we consummate the marriage to make it real?" All in a tone like a waiter offering decaf or full-caf. The man was not luring her into sin.

"I'm just saying—" The words popped out of her mouth, because she couldn't allow *his* words to hang there, unchallenged, but she had no idea how to end her sentence. What the hell did she want to say?

He stepped even closer, so close she had to tilt her chin up to meet his gaze. "I, Charlie Foulkes, take you, Cynthia Deming—" His expression was inscrutable. "To have and to hold, from this day forward." She searched his eyes, hoping they'd give her a hint as to his purpose. "For better or worse, richer or poorer, in sickness and health." He cheek kicked up, and she saw self-deprecation in his gaze, though he remained guarded. "Sound familiar?"

"To love and to cherish, from this day forward," she said, feeling confused. "Wedding vows." That she didn't get. "What's your point?"

"It's you and me."

She looked around the hallway, saw all his family photos lovingly hung and showcased with expensive frames. She was in a few of them. She saw the sun streaming in through the front door, still backlighting Charlie, putting his features in sharp contrast. And she heard the silence in the house, reminding her they were alone.

"We didn't exchange vows," she said.

"No. We never did." He compressed his lips. "But we've lived them for ten years now. We're best friends, Cynthia. Nothing will ruin that, not even marriage. I promise."

"Me, too." But she still wanted him to kiss her. "Is that your point?" Because he was looming over her, looking as if he was hungry and she was red meat. It seemed contradictory if all he wanted was to reaffirm they were BFFs.

He shrugged. "You deserve better than a JP ceremony at lunch."

"It's what I got." She shrugged back, and then noticed a growing sense of panic about him, as if whatever was bothering him, he was about to drop his bomb now.

She braced herself.

"You deserve vows, Cynthia." He stared deep into her eyes, gathering her hands into his, squeezing gently. "You deserve to be kissed at your wedding." He watched her as if he'd asked a question, but she had no idea what response he wanted. "What I'm trying to say is, you deserve *more*, Cynthia." He said it quickly, measured, like it was a punch line.

His implication, of course, was she deserved more than Charlie. He didn't want her, was trying to let her down easy. And it hurt.

She had to clear her throat to talk. "Don't worry, Charlie. We're on the same page."

"What page?" His face scrunched up.

She pulled her hands from his. "Didn't you say something about feeding your cat?"

"Oh, right." He shook his head, as if dazed. Then he stepped into the living room, walked by the worn leather couch, the heavy green tweed-draped windows, the coffee table with a year's subscription of *Sports*

Illustrated on it, and disappeared into the adjoining room. "Socks! Here kitty, kitty."

Cynthia followed him into the kitchen, having a hard time wrapping her brain around such a low, masculine voice saying the words "kitty, kitty." It sounded more like flirty sex talk than caretaking. "I'm so tired," he said, "it's hard to hold a thought."

She dropped onto a kitchen chair, exhausted, and couldn't agree more. Then she propped her elbows on the table and rested her head on her palms. "If we make it through this day, Charlie, I'm going to sleep until I can't sleep anymore, or I won't survive. Maybe sleep will prompt my memory to return. Maybe I'll remember the murders when I wake." She heard cabinets opening and closing, but kept her eyes shut, giving in to fatigue.

"I wouldn't wish those memories on anyone," he said. "You think you're sleep deprived now? Try lying in bed, thinking about six executions." That got her eyes open, and she saw Charlie's commiserating smile. "I guess I could read you *Lord of the Rings* until you slept," he said, "though from my experience, that is more likely to keep you awake."

She smiled back. "We never did finish the series."

"I've read it three times over since then. Ham and cheese?" he said. She nodded.

"Benton will be itching for my profile of the unsub," she said. "And when I give it to him, he'll distribute it to every active investigator on the case, every pertinent individual and organization with something resembling a database." They both knew once she'd handed in the profile, her culpability would be official. There would be no turning back. "Tell me we're doing the right thing."

He opened a bag of bread and laid out the slices on two white plates. Then he assembled two ham and cheese sandwiches. "The unsub knows what we know." Charlie shrugged. "At the very least, we're his get out of jail free card." He pulled a bag of chips from the cupboard and put it and the plates on the table, but didn't sit. He opened the refrigerator and retrieved a Mountain Dew can and a water bottle. Cynthia reached for the soda and popped the top, taking a swig.

"I needed that." She looked at the food and wasn't sure she had the energy to eat it all, but she knew she should try, if only for the energy it would give her.

"Socks," Charlie called out, turning his face toward the kitchen door. He waited, peered out the doorway. When the cat didn't appear, he sighed and picked up his sandwich. "Damn cat never comes when I call."

They didn't talk much as they ate. Cynthia was formulating her profile in her head, and Charlie was keeping his thoughts to himself, periodically calling to his cat. Twenty minutes later, he opened a can of cat food and Socks came ambling into the room.

"Figures," Charlie grumbled, smiling as the cat stuck his face in the dish, sniffed, and then began to eat. Cynthia could tell he'd grown attached to the stray. "I'll be right back," he said, leaving her to finish eating alone. Or rather, with Socks, who continued to gorge on salmon. When the cat's plate was licked clean, Socks scurried under the corner jelly cabinet just as Charlie returned. Though still unshaven, his hair was damp and slicked back, and he'd changed into fresh jeans and a shirt, so she assumed he'd had a quick shower.

"Socks!" Charlie went on all fours, peering under the jelly cabinet. "He's a hoarder. I'm missing one of my favorite socks, and I suspect—" He pulled a bunch of odds and ends from under the cabinet. "He's stolen it."

Cynthia wiped her hands on a napkin, then joined Charlie, squatting in front of the jelly cabinet. "Well, what do we have here?" She saw a chess piece, a purple heart charm with an attached broken link, a black magic marker, and… Cynthia yelped and fell back, landing on her butt as Socks ran into the other room with a meow. "Charlie! That's a dead mouse."

Pushing off from the white and black checkered tile, she retrieved a broom from its place next to the sink as Charlie had a good laugh. "Go wash your hands," she admonished, sweeping the dead rodent into a dust pan and dumping it into the trash. "If this is what marriage to you is going to be like, it will never last." He used his wrist to turn on the faucet, still laughing, though he was smart enough to scrub with soap. After drying his hands, he gathered the other items from the floor.

"This yours?" He held up the one-inch purple leather bracelet charm from its broken ring, and it dangled there. Cynthia shook her head. "I don't recognize it," he said. "Maybe it's my mother's."

She studied it closer. "A little purple heart with Socks's teeth marks gouged in it." Her lower lip pooched out, and her face melted into all sorts of sappy contortions. "If that's not a perfect cat-owner allegory, nothing is."

"Hey. No picking on cats." He laid the items on the counter. "We should go. I've got six bodies waiting to be autopsied."

She looked around, trying to picture the woman—rather, women— Charlie dated coming to his house. "You've *never* brought other women here? Not even girlfriends? Dates?"

"Just mom." He tilted his head to the side, suppressing a smile. "If you want to know about the women I've had sex with, just ask."

"No!" She scowled, hands on her hips, trying not to stare at his amazing arms and flat abs. Or notice how his jeans hung on his muscular legs like they loved their job. "Stop laughing at me."

"Fact is, I haven't—" He stopped, as if second-guessing his decision to share whatever he'd been about to say.

"Don't leave me hanging, Charlie." His blush told her it would be juicy. He shrugged. "Since you'd kissed me." No other women since they'd kissed? "There. I've said it. Make of it what you will." His attempt to seem cavalier fell flat. His cheeks reddened even more, clashing with his red hair. He averted his gaze, focusing on Socks. "Now I have a cat."

"I was drunk." He couldn't possibly have read anything into that kiss. It's not as if she'd made declarations or anything. He couldn't possibly know her feelings. A flare of panic had her widening her eyes, wondering if she'd been grossly underestimating Charlie's ability to read her feelings. Could he know how she felt?

"You were *roaring* drunk. Me, too." He leaned against the sink, crossing his legs at the ankle, folding his arms. If that wasn't a defensive posture, she didn't know body language. And she did. "Tequila has a way of doing that to us."

"So, why?" Why stop his love life after one drunken kiss from her? Not knowing made it impossible for her to drop the subject. "You don't owe me—"

"*Bullshit.*" He narrowed his eyes, signaling he was willing to plant his flag and die fighting for this issue. She'd been about to say, *you don't owe me an explanation*, but the conversation turned, and now she didn't know what to say. "I owe you everything," he said. Familiar words, and as usual, they felt like a wall between them.

"Are you saying my kiss was so bad it put you off women altogether?" She stepped close, straddling his legs until the insides of her knees brushed his. It was a leading question, because they both knew he'd ended that kiss with a massive hard-on. Would he lie? "Why?" She leaned her palms on the kitchen counter on either side of his hips, and found herself smiling. "Talk to me, Charlie." His eyes grew hooded, and his lips thinned.

"Be careful," he whispered. His eyes flashed, only she couldn't tell if it was with anger or panic, but she knew she wasn't leaving this kitchen until he told her why her kiss had the power to put him off other women. He must have seen the determination in her gaze, because he pushed back with a challenge of his own. "I don't think you could handle the truth."

A thrill worked its way down her body, because a part of her suspected he was right, but his warning told her a great deal. He'd thought about it.

Charlie thought about them having sex. They'd kissed, and he hadn't had another woman since! Bingo!

That had to mean something. But was it enough?

He was still her husband out of mutual obligation, and it was temporary. If Charlie didn't break her heart, there was a good chance she could break his. Taking what she wanted had become even more risky now that they were married.

Her cell phone rang. She slapped her pocket, never taking her eyes off Charlie. Then his cell phone rang in his back pocket, but he didn't move. Neither moved, though Cynthia wanted to. She wanted to lean against him and see what would happen. Would he kiss her, and take the decision from her control? Or would he find an excuse not to kiss her, because he didn't know how he felt?

Whatever was going on in Charlie's head, she liked it, because he wasn't pushing her away, and she could see the bulge in his pants even from the corner of her eye. Cynthia didn't want this moment to end. Its delicious possibilities aroused and excited her, because for the first time ever, Charlie was signaling that he was attracted to her...maybe. She stared into his eyes, but couldn't be sure. It was driving her crazy.

As their phones continued to ring, they remained still, gazes locked.

She licked her lips and smiled when he immediately dropped his gaze there. "I guess we should probably answer our phones." He arched a brow. "But Charlie, this conversation is *not* over."

She stepped back, glanced at her phone. Benton. When she swiped to accept, the ringing stopped. She'd waited too long and the call went to voice mail. Then the ringing began again. Benton, again. She frowned, catching Charlie's eye.

"Modena's calling me," he said, also frowning.

Whatever prompted these calls couldn't be good.

Chapter Six

Benton and Modena wanted them at the morgue *now*, which suited Charlie just fine, because it saved him the delay of dropping Cynthia off at the precinct house. But the calls had upset Cynthia, and she wasn't saying why. He'd asked, and she'd put him off with a shake of her head.

Now, minutes from the hospital, he found himself frequently turning his attention from the heavy traffic to glance at her. *His wife*. It was crazy. Last night, when he'd received her "hang up" call, he'd raced to her house, assuming it was about the kiss. Her blackout meant he might never know why she'd called him, but it got him to her front door. Now they were married, him and Terrance's little sister. And she'd almost died last night. Those two things alone reshuffled Charlie's deck of priorities. He didn't know why the killer pistol-whipped Cynthia instead of planting a bullet in her skull, but Charlie would be forever grateful, and he was determined to deny the killer another shot at her.

He was still having a hard time processing everything that had happened, and from the looks of Cynthia, so was she. A reformed nail biter, she used lacquer nails to prevent relapses. Now, eyes unfocused as she stared out the front windshield, she kept lifting her thumbnail to her mouth, only to drop her hand just as quickly. She was stressed. So was he.

"Benton didn't tell you why he wanted to talk to you?" he said.

"No. Modena say anything to you?" He shook his head. Nothing. Just a request to meet Benton at the morgue. "Maybe they *know*," she said. "I wouldn't put it past them to know everything we already know, but they're waiting for us to say something."

"You're being paranoid. Stick with the plan," he said. "We'll be okay."

"The longer we remain silent, Charlie," she said, "the more time the killer has to plant evidence against you."

True. "And divert the investigation."

She tucked her hand between her thigh and the seat. "The planted gun worries me the most. Even if it can't be traced from point of sale, your prints are more likely to be all over it than the killer's."

Also true, but if there was even a partial print of the killer's on the gun, it would be more than what they had now. "It has to be processed," he said. "Tampering with evidence that might implicate the killer could give cover to the killer." Charlie couldn't take that chance. "It's important that we do what's right, and trust in the system."

"If we trust the system, we should tell Benton," she said.

He forced himself not to snap at her, but to concentrate on driving safely into the hospital garage and taking the ticket from the automated machine. By the time he'd found a parking space, he'd also found his reasoned response. "Someone is framing me, Cynthia. I've got skin in this game, and I don't want to be sidelined from the investigation any more than you do. If you tell Benton, I'm out." He shifted the car into park and pulled the keys from the ignition.

She'd folded her arms over her chest. "He and the team will help us. I know them better than you do. They'll be on our side." He tried to think of what he could say to shut this line of reasoning down. "You're not an investigator," she said. "Benton and the team are. It's what they do. Charlie, trust *me* on this." He unbuckled and turned in his seat to face her, reminding himself *not* to yell. "I can't take a chance that these murders will be pinned on you," she continued. "I can't. Let me tell them what happened last night, and I'll leave you out of it. I can do that. And we'll go from there, but they'll only know that I was at the crime scene. That piece of the puzzle might make the difference. You and me, running a shadow investigation, waiting to be arrested for murder? I can't handle the stress."

"Let me tell you what will happen." Charlie sympathized with her dilemma, because Cynthia liked to be in control, and this case stripped her of it. "Sooner or later, the FBI will find evidence that points to me. I'll be taken in for questioning, and *then* I'll tell them everything."

She threw her hands up, gasping with frustration. "You've done nothing."

"The team will make their case against me."

"*There is no case*," she growled, and then punched his chest. He knew she wanted him to lose control, because she was out of control, but neither of them had that luxury.

"It's Benton's job to build a case, and it's up to a jury of my peers to decide if it holds up beyond a reasonable doubt." He knew Cynthia was scared. She had nothing to do with what was happening to them any more than he did, so it was easy to understand her lashing out. He just wasn't used to her lashing out against him. "My point is they'll be looking at the wrong man, directing all their energies toward the wrong man. We won't be helping anyone, least of all ourselves, if we bring the team into this. You know we're innocent, but they can't assume that. It's their job to rule us out, and that will—"

"Waste time."

"*Yes.*" She understood his position. Relief and gratitude suffused his body and had him sinking deeper into the car's seat. Charlie scanned the garage, not seeing a soul. "So far, the evidence against me is circumstantial, but sooner or later, there will be evidence that exonerates me."

"Because you're innocent." She put her thumbnail to her mouth and nibbled on its edge.

"Every time the killer plants evidence, he's leaving a breadcrumb to find him."

"Maybe. Or maybe everything you just said is wrong." She stepped out of the car. Charlie followed suit, and the sound of the door closing echoed in the dim, fluorescent-lit garage. She was already walking toward the elevator, her pocketbook swinging from her arm. "Don't tell Benton anything, Cynthia. At least give me time to do my job before you blow my world up."

She didn't slow her gait. "We need to cut our losses and tell Benton."

"No. You want to make this Benton's problem," he said. Cynthia responded by walking faster. "I know I can't control you—"

"Damn right," she grumbled.

"—but it's both our necks on the chopping block."

Cynthia poked the elevator button, and then poked it three more times, each poke harder than the last. "Fine. *Whatever!* Okay!" He put a hand on her shoulder, wanting to calm her down. She shook him off. "Don't think I'm doing it because I'm an obedient *wife*. I just happen to agree with some of your arguments, and as an investigator, I'm willing to bend. As an investigator. Not as your wife. We clear about that?"

No. He was baffled. What the hell was she talking about?

The elevator door opened. He stopped her from walking onto it by grabbing her elbow, needing to calm her if only to make himself feel better. He hated fighting, almost as much as he hated Cynthia upset. He tugged, and instead of shaking him off, Cynthia pivoted into his arms, wrapping her arms around his waist and pressing her cheek to his chest. Charlie didn't think about the whys, mostly because he had what he wanted. Her, in his arms. So he held her close, resting his chin on the top of her head, taking this moment to enjoy a respite from the chaos.

The elevator doors clanked closed again, unnoticed. Cynthia's pocketbook fell to the dirty garage floor with a plop. The silence dragged on until her tight grip around his waist loosened and her breathing calmed.

"I'm sorry being my wife is fucking with your head." He brushed his lips against her soft hair. He'd meant it as a joke, to tease some of the seriousness from their hug, but she tensed in his arms. Big surprise. His first instincts with Cynthia always seemed to go terribly wrong.

"*Wife.*" She squeezed him, as if trying to break him, and thumped her forehead against his chest before tilting her head back to look at him. "Do you listen to yourself, Charlie? Neither one of us ever wanted marriage. How many times have we talked about that?" She gave him a shake, and then pressed her cheek back onto his chest. "There's a reason it took a mass murder to get us to the altar."

Charlie laughed. He tried not to, but she was being so adorable, it snuck out. Cynthia looked up, giving him a scowl for his troubles. She was right, of course. About the marriage part, anyway, though now he suspected his aversion to matrimony was a symptom of his disease. The disease being: he hated that he lusted after his best friend's little sister, but Charlie didn't want anyone else marrying Cynthia, either.

"That's right," she said. "Yuck it up."

"What about that guy you dated in college?" he said. "Andy...ah, someone. I thought you two were hot and heavy. My parents were positive you'd marry." And it had pissed Charlie off to no end.

"Andy Arnold?" She leaned more heavily on him, conforming her body to his. "I can't believe you remember him. The bastard wanted to marry me after I caught him cheating."

He narrowed his eyes, thinking of his fist in Andy's face. "What red meat did he throw to convince you to turn a blind eye to his cheating?"

"Money. He told me he was rich," she said.

Charlie chuckled, suddenly not so mad. "He didn't know you. Not really." He could smell her shampoo, and her scent under that, and he could feel her trembling. He would have given anything to know *why* she trembled. He told himself to be cautious. His track record of reading Cynthia correctly was hit or miss.

"Things happened fast after that, and I never saw Andy again," she said. The accident. It never occurred to Cynthia that she didn't have to support

Charlie after the crash. Most wouldn't have. She did, and he owed her for that. "Not that I would have married him anyway." When she didn't say anything more, he pulled back to look at her face, needing more information to understand why she'd gone silent. She seemed to be thinking.

"Benton's waiting," he said. She nodded, still watching his face, looking for something. "We should probably go upstairs." She nodded again, but now her eyes were focused on his lips. She tilted her chin up, lifting herself onto her toes. Charlie found himself clenching her suit jacket in his fists, pulling her hips flush with his.

Charlie gave her ample opportunity to avoid the intimacy. She'd flirted with him in his kitchen, against his counter. Had she only been flirting to make a point? He wasn't sure, but he wanted to be certain: she either wanted him or not. Asking seemed like a mistake, especially since the look in her eyes seemed to be asking him something in return, only he had no idea what the question was.

"We're married," he said. She nodded slowly, hanging on his every word. "In public, we have to appear in love." Her brows lowered. "Can you do that? We need to sell this marriage, or it might be used against us. They can claim it's a calculated move to subvert the law."

"Isn't it?" She slid her hands behind his neck, her tone quiet, almost a whisper. "Everyone who knows me knows I'd never marry. It's why the team is having such a hard time believing it." She exerted tiny bits of pressure, drawing his head down toward hers.

"So, we convince them." His mouth felt dry as he slanted his head to the side, aligning their lips to put them on the same slow trajectory so they could meet in the middle.

Her eyes widened and she froze. He supposed she'd noticed his hard-on.

"Charlie," she said. "Is that for me?" He opened his mouth to explain, causing his lips to brush against hers, and then her fingers threaded into his hair and her breath came in shallow bursts. He didn't notice his hands had dropped to her ass until they were squeezing each cheek. He lifted her, and she was so light that when he leaned her back against the elevator doors, it was with more force than intended. Her breath left her body with an *oomph*. He would have apologized, but their lips mashed together and the elevator binged. Then the doors clanked open.

Charlie and Cynthia fell, limbs entangled, onto the dirty elevator floor. It wasn't empty.

Benton stared down at them, his brows arched, clearly stunned. Then the elevator doors clanked closed on their legs, opened again, then immediately

closed again, hitting their tangled limbs a second time. Cynthia hopped to
her feet first, brushing herself off, keeping her eyes averted.

"Well, isn't this awkward." She tucked in her shirt and adjusted her suit
jacket before impatiently waving Charlie to his feet. Then she leaned out
of the elevator to retrieve her pocketbook off the garage floor as Charlie
cracked his neck and stood.

"I was waiting," Benton said. "I pinged your phone, Deming." His
blue eyes hinted at a harried state. "I figured I'd meet you in the garage."
Neither Charlie nor Cynthia responded, so Benton compressed his lips
and hit the elevator button for level three. "I received the crowd photos.
Thanks. The team is running them through the software, but I'd like to see
the evidence log. I spoke with Teresa upstairs, and she says she's waiting
on you to sign off on them." He glanced at Cynthia, then glanced away
quickly. Charlie almost felt sorry for Benton, except he'd interrupted a
kiss that had all the earmarks of being life-altering, so he wasn't feeling
all that happy with the team leader right about now. "Deming, you still
need a ride to the precinct?"

"Yes, please." She licked her lips, blushing, looking like a kid who'd
got caught with her hand in the cookie jar. Then it occurred to Charlie that
Benton didn't know, and Cynthia didn't look as if she was going to tell him.

"We're married," Charlie said. "Just came back from the justice of the
peace." He glanced at Cynthia, hoping that explanation would lessen her
embarrassment with Benton. When her blush deepened and he saw her
cringe, Charlie thought back to what he'd said and couldn't see how he'd
messed up. Benton seemed happy enough.

"Damn! You're a fast worker, Charlie. Congratulations!" They shook
hands, and then Benton gave Cynthia a hug. "This is all happening so fast.
No wedding? No white dress and bridesmaids? Hannah and Charlotte are
going to read you the riot act, but... *Good for you.* It's a chaotic, stressful
experience to throw a wedding. I don't blame you in the least for avoiding
it. But, wow, Cynthia! Modena is going to blow a gasket!" Cynthia groaned,
closing her eyes.

"Why?" Charlie said.

"Cynthia owes Modena five hundred bucks," Benton said, chuckling
under his breath.

She glanced at Charlie. "I said I'd never marry."

"Yeah." Benton chuckled some more. The elevator binged. Charlie
waited until Benton stepped off, then reached for her hand. Cynthia
slapped it away. Benton noticed, and walked beside Charlie as Cynthia
hurried ahead of them.

"You're driving her nuts," Benton said. "I don't think I've ever seen her like this." Charlie glanced at the FBI special agent. His expression was kind, and Charlie saw great affection there for Cynthia. "It's a good thing, Charlie. Honestly, I was beginning to think she wasn't human."

Down the hallway, to the right, shoes slapping on the white tile, they walked toward the morgue's entrance. The entire floor was quiet, which was the norm. Hands stuffed in her jacket pockets, eyes downcast, she seemed lost in thought. She reached the morgue's door first. He stepped to her side, used his ID to get past the door's security lock, and waited for the mechanism to beep. When Cynthia sneaked a guilty peek at him before she stepped inside, Charlie froze.

What did that look mean?

It gave him the distinct impression that she was about to go rogue and confess to Benton, *despite* their plan, despite her assurances.

Damn. Charlie should have known better than to think he could control Cynthia.

Chapter Seven

The florescent-lit morgue was large, had multiple stainless-steel gurneys in the center, and body refrigerators covered the back wall. There was a double desk set up off to the right for the techs, and Charlie's locked office to the left. His office was half glass on the top, obstructed by closed white blinds, and drywall on the bottom. Cynthia stood with her back to it as Teresa greeted Charlie and Benton. The tech acted as if Cynthia was invisible, which was...okay. Wired, embarrassed, and sexually frustrated, the last thing she wanted was a shallow exchange with her husband's groupie, especially minutes after Benton interrupted what looked to be Charlie finally deciding to rock Cynthia's world. That kiss-that-barely-happened would have been huge, and would have clarified a few things. Maybe Charlie's feelings weren't as platonic as she'd feared, and maybe Charlie was okay with her knowing that. In fact, she was beginning to suspect that obligation had nothing to do with Charlie's decision to kiss her just now.

Then Benton had to track her down and ruin everything.

So, it was with great disgruntlement that she found herself among the dead. They smelled, and they forced her to deal with reality. Right now, her reality was her boss hovering over a naked, partially draped corpse on the closest stainless-steel slab ten feet from her nose. She knew she should feel empathy for the dead guy, but she knew him—he was a stone cold killer—so she had no pity. She wished Benton would leave. Wished everyone in this room would go but Charlie. She wanted her kiss, and to forget that her life was a shit storm.

Teresa produced a clipboard of paperwork. Charlie took it without meeting the eager tech's gaze, then frowned, flipping through the pages. Cynthia wandered to Kevin Hilliard's desk and dropped her pocketbook onto its cluttered surface. She knew it was Kevin's, because of the many pictures of his wife and kids, and she'd seen him sitting there many times. Teresa's desk, abutting Kevin's, had a sole picture of her sorority sisters at NYU. Lots of teeth, all of them blond, with plenty of pink lipstick.

Cynthia turned her back on it and stepped to Benton's side, next to the slab, and studied the naked vic, too. Livor mortis, the patches of settled blood on the skin, was at its zenith. It meant the body was approximately twelve hours post mortem, which explained the awful stink. Mid-thirties, large and muscular, the man was Caucasian, pale, blond, and if not for the bullet to the brain, probably would have enjoyed another thirty years of life. She and Benton had interviewed him during the long months after Dante Coppola's arrest. He was given a choice: life in jail, or snitch. Hindsight's a bitch. Anthony DiGiacomo chose poorly. Though there was currently no proof Coppola was behind this, it seemed likely. All six WITSEC witnesses were connected to the Coppola case.

"So." Benton stood next to Cynthia, his tone quiet, his hands jammed into his pants pockets. "Married, huh? If this is a hostage situation, blink twice."

Cynthia closed her eyes, allowed the humiliation to flood over her without fighting back. She deserved it. How many times had she declared herself a bachelorette for life? And the bet she'd made with Modena after his engagement? She deserved every blush and cringe, so decided to woman up and take it.

"I love him," she said. It was true, so it sold easily. She loved three people in this world, and they all had the last name of Foulkes.

Benton glanced at Charlie over his shoulder, then shrugged. "I didn't even realize you knew the guy. I mean, beyond the professional."

He continued to wear a baffled, if not concerned, expression, which bothered Cynthia. Benton might do some due diligence, and with his penchant for solving mysteries, his concern might trigger an informal investigation into her and Charlie's lives. If so, the irony would be colossal. She needed to nip this in the bud. Direct his attention elsewhere.

"I've known him since I was a kid," she said, keeping her eyes on the decomposing body. "He was best friends with Terrance." She glanced at Benton, carefully keeping her expression neutral.

"Ah." His mouth opened, and he nodded, glancing at Charlie. "Well, you've always been private, but damn. You've taken it to another level. I guess I should feel privileged that I know you had a brother."

She nodded. "You should. I don't talk to many people about him."

"You don't talk to many people about anything beyond work, Deming. Not since I've known you. I'm glad you're happy." He pinned her with a sober glance. "You are happy, right?"

She glanced at Charlie, nodding. "He's my world."

As soon as the words left her mouth, she realized how true they were, and the analyst inside her was flummoxed. He wasn't just her best friend, he was her everything. Why'd it take so long for her to realize that? And how would Charlie feel if he knew he'd become her world? Surprised, most likely. Charlie lived in the present, dealt with facts and figures, and treated emotions as if they were colds: something to avoid. She feared if she laid it all out, telling him exactly how she felt, she might embarrass him. Pride had stopped her, and frustration. She'd fallen in love with a man who couldn't read her mind, and that pissed her off.

Charlie had stepped to Teresa's desk, and he leaned over it, signing things. The tech hovered over Charlie, prompting jealousy to seep into Cynthia's funk. The blond tech was too close to him, mere inches from pressing her boob to his arm. It depressed the hell out of Cynthia to admit, but they made a lovely couple. Both obsessed with dead bodies.

Charlie looked up, caught her watching, and winked. Cynthia scowled back. He smiled, and she found herself smiling back, though he didn't deserve it. Teresa saw their exchange, and looked away quickly with something resembling guilt on her face. Resembling? No, it was guilt. Cynthia recognized guilt when she saw it. It had been her constant companion for ten years. It was guilt. Teresa had designs on Charlie...a newlywed!

Cynthia stood straighter. She was Mrs. Charlie Foulkes now, so Teresa needed to back off. Well...Cynthia *would* be Mrs. Charlie Foulkes, if she took Charlie's name, which she wouldn't, because that was an arcane practice, but *still*. Charlie was off the market. Teresa knew this. Right? Cynthia lifted her hand, showcasing the MIT ring. Teresa did her best not to look, so Cynthia took that as a sign that Teresa had heard the news of her and Charlie's recent marriage. *The bitch.*

"Charlie," Benton said, "would you mind if Cynthia and I used your office to look those forms over? If I have any questions, I'd rather just shout them out than have to interrupt you with phone calls while you're performing the autopsies."

"Sure, of course." Charlie nodded, his glance in their direction perfunctory, completely oblivious to two grown women fighting a turf war over his delectable ass. If Charlie had an inkling, he wouldn't be Charlie.

Teresa copied the paperwork, opened the office using a set of jangly keys, and then handed the paperwork to Benton before leaving them to rejoin Charlie and assist with the first autopsy. First thing Cynthia did was close the door and open the blinds. She wanted to keep an eye on Charlie and his tech. See how they interacted. Maybe she'd read too much into Teresa's guilty glance. Charlie had a strict policy about fraternization in his crew, and Cynthia liked to think she'd have known if Charlie was dating someone. She'd get a feeling...hell, his mother would have called.

Soon, Benton's questions, the evidence, the grisly photos, and her job distracted her enough to forget about the potential relationship between Charlie and his tech. She and Benton fashioned a preliminary profile for the unsub. Nothing big. Just a framework. And every once in a while, she'd glance out the blinds and find Charlie looking at her. It sent a thrill through her, and she'd force herself not to smile and wave like an asshole. He'd smile at her, looking goofy behind his face shield, elbow deep in a body, wearing a bloody apron. So gross. Though she had to admit he wore it well. He was huge, and geared up he was even bigger. She *really* liked that about him. How damn big he was.

Kevin caught them. And Cynthia caught him watching as if she and Charlie were a tennis match. It was embarrassing, so Cynthia closed the blinds. It was a mistake, because then she worried she was missing Teresa pressing against Charlie's side, and no, knowing Kevin and a dead body were chaperoning didn't make it less frustrating.

Benton sighed, raking his fingers through his black hair. "We have to be careful with this one, Deming. If these kills somehow give Coppola's lawyers an in to reopen his case, all our work over the last two years is in jeopardy."

"I know. We won't allow it to happen," she said.

"Charlie has five more autopsies after this," he said, "reports to fill out and distribute, and then the tests need to be sent out. We're not looking at any answers for at least twenty-four hours."

"And he's exhausted," she said. "I don't envy him the next ten hours." A glance at the blinds had her wondering how stupid she'd look if she opened them now, a mere five minutes after closing them.

"Let's go to the precinct and confer with the team," he said. "They'll want to see what we have."

Cynthia nodded, springing from her chair, pulling open the door. "We're out of here." She kept her gaze averted, afraid of what she'd see if she looked at the threesome working on the body. Chin lifted, she did her best to walk like a queen as she headed for her pocketbook on Kevin's desk, past the smelly body et al. Benton drove like a NASCAR veteran in his cherry red Chevy, so she didn't want to get in his car queasy.

"One down, five to go," Kevin said. Cynthia heard wheels moving and risked a glance as she slung her pocketbook over the crook of her elbow. Kevin was transporting body number one, aka thug DiGiacomo, toward refrigeration as Teresa wheeled body number two from its slot in refrigeration. No gore. All sanitized.

"Once again, congratulations on the wedding, Charlie," Benton said. Cynthia headed toward the morgue's exit.

"You mean engagement," Teresa said, and Cynthia detected a thread of resentment in her tone.

"Yeah, so when's the happy day?" Kevin closed the refrigerator door with a crack.

"Today," Charlie said. "We got married at lunch."

His words had Cynthia stopping, mid-morgue. She looked at Charlie and saw him snap off his gloves, never once looking at the two techs whose jaws just dropped. Then he tugged off his bloodied disposable apron and protective gown like a stripper wearing Velcro pants, and tossed it all into a nearby red medical waste bin. "Speaking of which, excuse me and my bride while I say goodbye to her in my office." He grinned at Cynthia, and the naughty gleam in his eye made her nervous. "In private."

"Make it quick," Benton said, and then he rolled his eyes. "What am I saying?" Cynthia clutched her pocketbook to her chest, feeling her face flame with embarrassment, but she did her best to play along, smiling, shrugging, and hurrying along as Charlie took her hand and led her toward his office. "You know what?" Benton said. "I'll meet you in the hall." He left the morgue, pulling his phone from his suit pocket.

Kevin chuckled. "Teresa and I will prepare body two." Teresa's face flamed red.

Charlie closed the door behind them. Cynthia tossed her pocketbook on his desk, scowling. "Totally unprofessional," she said.

"Calm down," he said, his tone flat. She immediately understood she was talking to Boston Police Department's forensic pathologist, rather than her husband. "I wanted to speak privately, and thought it better that they believe we're kissing and talking dirty—"

"Talking dirty?" She couldn't even imagine Charlie doing that.

"—than conspiring to commit a felony. Where are your notes?" Charlie took the pad of paper she slipped from her pocketbook's depths, and then scanned her notations. "*The unsub is male, single, separated or divorced. Probably white, late 20s to 40s. No particular ideology. Gun bought legally,*" *probably evidence of mental illness, if killings are random."* His shoulders sagged. "What the hell is this? We both know these killings aren't random, and most people with mental illness are not violent."

She narrowed her eyes. "Is that why you pulled me in here? To critique my notes?" She preferred the dirty talk and kissing scenario, but should have known better. This was Charlie.

His brows lifted, and his surprise had him studying her expression. "What did you think I was pulling you in here for?"

"Nothing." She glanced toward the door, knowing she should just leave. It was hard to be reasonable with Charlie so close and oblivious. She was always afraid she'd give herself away and she'd be confronted with his apathy, or, worse, his sympathy. Was there anything more terrifying than the object of your affection feeling bad for you because you loved them? Probably, but she didn't want to experience those things either. She wanted the man who'd thrown her up against the elevator door to kiss her because he couldn't help himself. "My notes are generic and incomplete. I'll plug in details when you give me evidence I can use. You're the forensic guy. Give me something."

He leaned against the desk, folding his arms over his chest. "Well, I can tell you our killer isn't some random mass murderer."

"Just because the vics are Coppola syndicate alums doesn't mean Coppola is behind it." She bit her lip, knowing if Coppola was behind it, they'd all rest a little easier, because it would be easy enough to prove. "The killer, whoever he is, statistically *is* a misfit, loner, socially isolated male, late 20s to late 40s. Give me something else."

"I'm just saying—" She detected a prelude to mansplaining.

"Listen, *buddy.*" She poked his chest. "You leave the profiling to the professionals, huh? Or do you want me hip-chucking you aside to do your autopsies?"

Charlie grinned, glancing at her index finger still pressed to his chest. "Buddy?"

She dropped her hand. "There's a process, Charlie. Much like you with your bodies. Just because it's a GSW to the head doesn't mean the vic didn't die of something else before the bullet entered the brain. You still do an autopsy, right? Well, I need to do a complete profile so we don't miss anything."

He sighed. "Okay. Fine. I'm feeling impatient."

Cynthia stepped away from him, mostly because she didn't want to. Then she stuffed her hands into her suit jacket pockets and took a step toward the door. Benton was waiting, and she'd taken too long in here already.

"Let me test some guidelines, accumulate the information we have, and my team will do its thing, play out scenarios, see where we're at."

"It's a hitman, either in the Coppola syndicate or a rival syndicate," Charlie said.

She nodded. "Probably, but probably doesn't hold up in court. We need to support that assumption with compiled evidence. We haven't even received results from all the criminal databases yet. The vics are barely cold. It takes time." She put her hand on the doorknob, squeezing it, not wanting to leave but knowing she should. "I'm thinking this is a personal grudge." She leaned against the door, glancing back at him. "Who else would bother? These men already did their damage when they testified."

Charlie opened the window blinds and glanced toward his team preparing the body. Then he approached Cynthia, and she assumed he, too, was about to leave the office. She twisted the doorknob, but Charlie leaned his palm on the door, effectively preventing her from opening it. He was so close she could feel the heat of his body, and his face was lowered, his lips near her temple. "Do you sometimes feel," he whispered, his breath teasing her skin, "as if you're spinning your wheels? Accomplishing nothing? Different day, no closer to answers?"

Cynthia found it hard to breathe normally. "Are we still talking about the murders?" She tilted her head back, searching his gaze.

Then he kissed her.

Chapter Eight

Charlie kissed Cynthia for a reason. He had his excuse locked and loaded so that when she retaliated, he could explain without having to think. She'd said it herself. No one believed she'd want to marry, so the onus of convincing everyone was on them. Their greatest threat, unfortunately, was Teresa. She'd been working with him for months, crushing on him, always in his business. She'd have known if he and Cynthia were seeing each other, and she *knew* they weren't. What if she started rumors, and those rumors caught the ear of a particular special agent in charge?

The kiss was simple preventative defense. They'd get "caught" kissing and put his tech off the scent.

Just as his lips touched Cynthia's, it occurred to him that maybe he should have tuned her into his plan, but then her arms were around his neck, kissing him like a drowning woman in need of the air from his lungs. It surprised him. Then she pressed against him, on tiptoes, wiggling, fitting herself into his nooks and crannies. That surprised him more.

Suddenly, his chaste kiss for witnesses had been co-opted.

Charlie knew he should pull back, set her body from his, inform her that this level of intimacy in a workplace was—hell, he didn't want to. Charlie cupped her jaw, tilted her head to the side, and deepened the kiss to act out a few of his go-to fantasies connected with her mouth. Soon, he had her moaning deep in her throat. It triggered him. His stomach clenched and his hips arched toward hers, making her stumble back. Charlie caught her, guided her by the waist, and secured her back against the door with a thump. The door's blinds rattled, reminding him they had an audience. Without breaking their kiss, he swatted at the open blinds to his left until they closed, thinking Teresa had to be convinced by now.

Hell, Charlie certainly was. Cynthia wanted him as much as he wanted her.

At last.

He gripped her butt as she tugged his shirt from his waistband, dragging her lacquer nails along his skin, digging into the corded muscles along his spine. His eyes closed and his breath caught as tingles rode up his back and had his ass clenching, his hips thrusting. She clutched at him, widening her stance, inviting him closer. Charlie sunk his fingers into her waist and lifted, rattling the blinds as he dragged her up the door until their mouths were level, allowing him to deepen their kiss, lick into her mouth. She locked her legs around his hips, sending a shudder of desire through him. It had him pausing to absorb the pleasure of her soft heat against the straining fabric of his jeans' button fly.

Pinned to the door by his hips, she held on, and her mouth... He couldn't get enough of her taste, the feel of her tongue against his, licking into his mouth as their hips arched toward each other. He feasted as she held on, keeping their bodies flush, ignoring the noises, her elbows, his knees knocking the door, slapping the blinds. Locked in a mutual feeding frenzy, his hunger was too great to allow thoughts...*reasons* for caution. His feelings of triumph and desire battled it out, heightening his arousal, taunting him that all his fantasies were within reach now. But not here. Not in his office, techs ten feet away, Benton in the hall. When he made love to Cynthia, she deserved more, for him to linger and take his time.

But this kiss... It would stake his claim.

No walking it back. No ghosting. He was determined that when she left this office, she'd leave with damp panties, and the knowledge that they were consummating their marriage.

But not against his office door.

Charlie gripped her ass, then carried her three long steps to his desk and sat her there, never breaking their kiss, knowing he should. Paper scattered as she settled her weight holding his head in place, devouring his mouth. Pens bounced to the floor, files slid and fluttered away.

He had to stop. Time to talk, or he risked taking her here, now, on his desk.

Cynthia resisted his attempts to step away. Her legs squeezed his hips, her hands unbuttoned his shirt. He kept telling himself to stop her, to stop the kiss before it was too late. Then she'd moan and he was lost, thinking just one more kiss. He leaned, laying her down, resting his weight on his elbows. Her hand separated his shirt, now completely undone, and raked his skin from his pecs to his waistband's edge. It had his body shuddering with need.

When she broke their kiss he was almost relieved, but then she arched toward him, pressing her hot lips to his chest, tasting him. Charlie inhaled sharply, grinding his teeth against emitting a long, loud visceral moan. He'd dreamt of moments like this, and more. It felt right. Cynthia felt right. It had always been Cynthia.

And now he had her and wouldn't let her go.

A flicker of movement caught Charlie's eye. He titled his chin up and saw the blinds behind his desk were open. He'd missed that window, and for that sin, Teresa and Kevin were staring back at him.

Only Kevin looked amused.

Cynthia's tongue wrapped around his nipple. Charlie lashed out, swatting the blinds, hitting too hard, and they detached from the window's casement to land at a diagonal. Cynthia shrieked, curled her body to avoid the blind, and knocked into Charlie, who stepped back onto a displaced manila folder. Down they went, in a tangle of flailing arms. They hit the floor with a *thump*.

Face to face, still entwined, chests working like bellows, Charlie was afraid to speak. No, he was afraid Cynthia would speak and say this was a mistake, that she was humiliated, and never wanted to see Charlie again.

"Charlie," she gasped, whispering, "think we convinced them?"

Loud knocking.

His hands gripped her hard as his eyes tracked to the door. Instinct told him not to let her go, but damn…. This was not the time for the conversation they needed, so he kissed her, wanting to lock her commitment down but knowing that rushing it might ruin this opportunity. She was his now, whether she knew it or not. He'd be patient. Her kiss was hungry and had him rolling on top of her.

More knocking.

He blinked, rolled to the side, trying to remember what he was supposed to do. It was hard to think with Cynthia so near. She recovered quicker and hopped to her feet, slipping on paperwork, but Charlie caught her in time to steady her without crippling himself. His jeans' fly bit into his thwarted erection.

The room was trashed. "Help me clean this up," he said. On his knees, he picked up files, put the phone's receiver back in its cradle, and then back on his desk. Cynthia gathered up her pocketbook, hanging it over her elbow. Her smile couldn't have been wider as she waved at Kevin, who

Charlie could now see through the partition window. And that meant it was Teresa on the other side of his door. Or Benton, coming to gather Cynthia.

"Sorry, Cynthia." He hadn't intended to embarrass her.

Knocking again. More insistent this time.

"Don't be silly," she said. "The whole point was getting caught, right?"

Charlie stopped cleaning, and studied her. "You knew." She'd made that clear. It didn't mean she didn't enjoy it. She couldn't have been acting. Her composure and amusement had him second-guessing himself, and then suddenly he wasn't sure what to think. He opened his mouth to ask if she'd known that last blind was open, but by then she'd grabbed the doorknob.

Cynthia walked out, ignoring Teresa, who'd been mid-knock. It forced Charlie to turn his back as he climbed to his feet, or risk losing his last ounce of modesty. Teresa rushed in, gathering the paperwork off the floor as he donned a fresh disposable surgical robe and apron. After grabbing a pair of gloves, he rushed out of the office to catch up with Cynthia. She'd reached the morgue's exit, eyes on her phone's screen.

"The body is ready." Teresa had followed him. Charlie ignored her and the body, and stopped Cynthia from opening the morgue's door with a gentle hand on hers. She paused and tilted her face up, revealing mild curiosity.

Was this the woman who had been wild in his arms no more than a minute ago?

"Stay with Benton," Charlie said.

It hadn't been an act, he told himself. It couldn't have been.

Cynthia nodded, glancing at her phone's screen again. "I'll come back when you're done with the autopsies," she said. "I'll bring supper, so you'll be happy to see me." She aimed a distracted smile at Kevin, winked at Teresa, and then was gone.

Charlie wasn't happy now. He was disgruntled. What the hell just happened?

Kevin coughed quietly, then coughed again, louder this time. Charlie turned, slapping his gloves against the palm of his other hand. His tech was laughing without making a sound, and his eyes were tearing with amusement.

"You animal," Kevin said, and then laughter bubbled out of his mouth.

Charlie refused to blush. Refused even as he felt his face heat. He snapped on his gloves and compartmentalized the last ten minutes into a mental to-do box. He and his team had work to accomplish. Someone was killing people connected to the Coppola syndicate case, and Cynthia was in the middle of it. She wasn't safe until they found the killer, so that problem needed to be where he put his mental energies.

He approached the body on the slab, donned his face shield, and then pulled down the ceiling-affixed microphone to record his vocal autopsy notes. One glance told him that Kevin and Teresa were staring at him, rather than the body. Understandable, he supposed. They'd never seen him do anything so remotely human as kiss a wife.

"Love looks good on you, Charlie." Kevin adjusted his face shield in place, and then fluttered his eyelashes as he handed Charlie the bone saw. Teresa shifted on her feet, blushing behind her face shield. Charlie saw that his tech was upset, and hated that he was the cause, but it had been unavoidable. He was in love with his best friend.

"Let's get to work." Charlie smiled despite his uncertainty, because he'd kissed Cynthia, would kiss her again, and, yeah, he enjoyed his work. "One down, five to go." He hit the bone saw's on button, and its whirling sounded like an old friend.

Hopefully by day's end he'd have some answers.

* * * *

Sitting at his tech's desk, next to the newly sanitized slabs, he put his final notes on the paperwork. Day two of not sleeping had him dragging, beyond exhausted. It was eleven at night, his eyelids felt like sandpaper every time he blinked, Kevin and Teresa had just finished cleaning and locking everything, and he'd just nixed the seductive option of crashing on his office floor rather than driving home, because of Cynthia.

He was married. The thought prompted a smile, despite his clawing fatigue. He'd texted her a few times between autopsies to assure himself she was safe, though his excuse had been to give updates. Last he'd heard, she was at the precinct.

The morgue's door beeped. Kevin was close, so he was the one who opened the locked door. In walked Cynthia carrying her pocketbook, a six-pack, and a large Subway paper bag. As promised, she'd brought dinner.

"Anyone hungry?" she said. "Thirsty? I bought enough for everyone."

"Thanks, but no." Teresa's smile was taut, and didn't reach her eyes. She was notably exhausted—it had been a long day—so Charlie didn't blame her for retrieving her key chain from her pocketbook and heading for the door. "I need to crash." She glanced at Charlie, gave him a tight smile, and then ducked her head as he waved. She was gone moments later.

"Kevin?" Cynthia lifted the six-pack, offering him one.

"No beer for me. I have to pick up the wife, then drive the babysitter home." His wife, Charity, an internal medicine resident, had hours as bad as Kevin's. "Next time, definitely." He used a finger to indicate Charlie and Cynthia. "There's a story here, and I have a feeling it will take more than a few beers to get it out of you two, but one day, I'll get it." He laughed. Then he was gone, too.

Cynthia sat in Kevin's chair, her bags and beer on her lap, eyeballing the tech's cluttered desk. Even this tired, Cynthia was still the most beautiful woman he'd ever seen. Sitting across from her in Teresa's chair, he was thankful the last form of the night had been signed.

"How'd you get here?" He had an image of her falling asleep behind the wheel, wrapping her car around a tree, and had to shake it off. No one had to tell either of them how that scenario could ruin a life.

"Modena dropped me off," she said, sounding exhausted. "Get that worried look off your face. I was safer than POTUS." She set the bag and beer on the piece of desktop not devoted to Kevin's paperwork. "Find anything new?"

Charlie shrugged. "Maybe. Lots of DNA evidence. Our killer didn't work alone."

She set her pocketbook at her feet. "Yeah? Do tell."

"Multiple hair samples that didn't match any of the vics. Also, no puncture wounds on the body's skin, so it's unlikely they were sedated, though toxicology tests will give definitive answers on that."

"No sedation? That would be...impressive," she said. "How did the killer get six contract killers in their prime to a kill site? All neat and compliant?"

Charlie nodded. "They were big men."

"The federal marshals are all over the 'how.' WITSEC-protected, six witnesses, from six locations? They're baffled. Benton is pissed."

"Inside job?" he said.

"Don't go there." Cynthia closed her eyes for a moment, and shook her head. "I don't even want to think like that until I absolutely have to. We just went through that with our last case."

The smell of food coming from the bag made it hard to think beyond his stomach. Charlie gathered up his paperwork and locked it in Teresa's top drawer. Then he grabbed the nearest bag, looking inside.

"Six victims," he said, dumping the four hoagies and chips from the bag. "No defensive wounds. Zip. Nothing. Unless their stomach contents show sedation, they were stone cold sober when they kneeled, bound and hooded, and were shot in the head." He shrugged. "Let's hope the unsub prepped them for the kills. The more contact he had with the vics, the more likely we'll find his DNA."

"The hoagies are marked," she said. "I got different types because I didn't know what Kevin and Teresa would like." Cynthia grabbed a bag of chips and pulled it open. "Maybe the vics were compelled to hood themselves. Duct tape it in place. It's how I'd do it."

Charlie unraveled the paper around his roast beef with pickles. His favorite. He took a large bite, moaning with pleasure. When he could talk again, he caught her attention with a lift of his chin. "That's because you know what forensic experts are looking for, but this unsub is a low-educated contract killer. Am I right?" She shrugged, unconvinced. "If he's an evil genius, Cynthia, we're fucked. We'll never find him, despite our expensive tests. Tests," he grimaced, "that I just spent an hour signing off on."

She picked up a hoagie and unrolled the paper wrapper. "He's found a way to commit six murders, point the evidence toward us, and we haven't a clue about his identity. That doesn't sound like the normal class of clowns we usually find."

"The evidence will save us," he said.

"If it doesn't convict us first."

"Each hood had the same hair sample on it," he said. "Cross your fingers it's the unsub's."

Cynthia opened her hoagie, peeking inside. She always ordered a ham, cheese, lettuce, and pickles with oil and vinegar sub without tomatoes. Emphasis on *without*. When she grimaced, he knew the server had messed up, and probably layered sliced tomatoes on her sub. Mostly because they always did.

"If you tell them no tomatoes," Charlie said, "all they hear is tomatoes. Just don't say tomatoes when you order the sub, and you won't put tomatoes in their head. I keep telling you this, but you never listen." He took a big bite of his perfectly prepared roast beef and pickles hoagie.

"Not true. Tell them or not, they always give me tomatoes," she said, methodically picking them off. "Might as well order it the way I want it." Then, like clockwork, she ritualistically blotted the tomato juices off her cheese. Same channel, same show. "So," she said, "the geographical profile has no surprises, and is useless as written. Two words: east coast."

"How many years of college to make that assessment?" When she narrowed her eyes, flashing him some attitude, Charlie couldn't help but chuckle. "What? You want congratulations on *not* narrowing down the unsub's location? You didn't think it would be easy, did you?"

He was already halfway through his hoagie, and Cynthia hadn't taken her first bite. Her slow eating always baffled him, though he'd memorized her explanation. She chewed her food. Implying Charlie didn't. Charlie chewed; he just chewed faster.

"No, I didn't expect easy." Licking her fingers clean of chip and salt, she picked up her sub, holding it near her mouth as if about to bite, only she didn't. "The syndicate's reach has migrated to Florida now that Coppola is incarcerated there, and now we have to consider every damn state along the east coast. Data index searches will be barely useful. We need more personnel, but I don't see that happening since the bureau considers the Coppola case closed, and its budget is nonexistent. The vics were killers, so there's little sympathy, or political willpower to hunt down an unsub that many see as doing the taxpayer a favor." She took a bite of hoagie, as if punctuating her explanation, and then frowned, because her bite was too big. She was having a hard time keeping her mouth closed while she chewed. Charlie almost laughed, but didn't want to embarrass her, so he popped a chip in his mouth and did his best not to notice her difficulties.

"Boston wasn't part of Coppola's turf either until the trial venue was moved here," he said. It's how Charlie was tapped to be the bureau's forensic expert for the Coppola syndicate case.

She dipped her fingers into her chip bag, pulling out a chip, still struggling to chew politely. "We're thinking our killer knew the vics were witnesses for the prosecution. Anyone with a laptop or a library card had access to that information, so we can't say definitively it's a Coppola syndicate hit."

"But it probably is." He popped the last of his hoagie into his mouth and chased it down with more chips.

"Yeah." She took a smaller bite of hoagie this time, and when she finished chewing, she said, "The syndicate is dead, but someone connected to the case could have hired an outsider. A victim of a vic, maybe. We're thinking motive is revenge. Benton's got Vivian O'Grady chained to the databases, looking for hits of suspects, but the list is long, and getting longer. That means lots of pressure on the crime scene evidence, Charlie. We need your DNA samples to pan out with a name."

"Doing my best. Let's see what the tests show." Charlie popped some chips in his mouth, and then licked his fingers.

She took a bite, talking around her food. "I was so hungry, I almost ate at the restaurant, but felt too guilty knowing you were here, and you'd probably not eaten since we saw each other last."

He rubbed his face, leaning back in his chair. "I'm so tired I can barely think."

She nodded, licking her lips. "So, is this a bad time to talk, then? 'Cause what I have to say requires you to think. To really think, Charlie. About us."

Yeah, it was a bad time to talk about "us." Them. On a good day, Cynthia could talk him in circles. Now, he was punch-drunk tired. She'd want to talk about what happened in the office, their latest kiss, and he wasn't feeling particularly flexible about what it meant. If she didn't see things the way he did, he didn't think he had it in him to be polite about it.

"If you want to talk," he said, mostly because he suspected that was the right answer, "we'll talk."

"*If I want to.*" She took another bite, lifting her brows. That, more than anything, told him maybe he'd miscalculated the "right" answer. Shit. Sometimes he thought he would have a more successful social life if he threw darts at a board of prewritten responses and just said whatever the dart landed on. No dartboard on hand, he was forced to dig deep and hope he could keep up.

"Do you want me to apologize for kissing you?" He'd do it, but he wasn't sorry. He'd kiss her again. And soon.

She snorted and finished chewing. "I'm not looking for apologies, Charlie." She grabbed a beer and used her keys to take the bottle top off. Handing it to him, she then grabbed one for herself. "I'm looking to understand." She chugged until it was half gone.

"I think it's pretty clear why I kissed you." He took a pull off his beer. He'd kissed her because she was damn sexy, and he wanted her. Wanted her bad. And he'd wanted to kiss her, and more, for years. Did she want to hear that? He wanted to tell her.

She lifted her brows, not looking convinced. "Are you looking for sex as sport?"

He recoiled from the idea. Not that he hadn't had his fair share of sport. He just had no intention of doing that with Cynthia. Damn. Was their latest kiss a result of her being horny, and Charlie making himself available?

"No." He hadn't meant to sound so…sanctimonious. But he was kind of offended.

She tilted her head to the side, avoiding his gaze, and then opened her hoagie again, picking at the cheese and meat. It told him she wasn't hungry anymore. "We're married, Charlie, but I've got ambitions and a career I'm focused on. I'm no one's 'little woman.'"

He felt his stomach twist with irritation. Did she just accuse him of attempting to turn her into a housefrau? It was a kiss. And it had been hot. "What do you want me to say?"

"Nothing. Just so we're clear." She sipped her beer, avoiding his gaze.

"We're not. Why don't you spell it out for me?" Like always.

She sighed, putting her beer down. "My life is my career on purpose. I've fought hard to be taken seriously in the FBI, and in this precinct in particular. Everyone thinks profiling is woo-woo soft science, so add that on top of my gender, and I'm always walking a fine line here between acceptance and…well, and not."

He nodded. He'd heard her fears and complaints from day one, right out of Quantico. "You have a well-earned chip on your shoulder. So what? I think it lends you charm." He winked, hoping to lighten the mood. She grimaced, picking at her sandwich again, eating the innards, then licking her fingers. "Cynthia, nothing's changed between us, except we're married. And it's a piece of paper, right?"

He ate some chips, watching her closely. Would she take his bait and rail against him? Would she declare their marriage wasn't just a piece of paper, and their kiss meant their marriage was more than a get-out-of-jail card? Her eyes lost focus, and he thought she wouldn't respond…until she did.

"You're the only one I can be completely myself with, Charlie." She caught his gaze, and he saw her fear. "I don't want to lose that. I don't want to lose you."

His bait had caught unexpected booty, and he didn't know what to do with it.

"Listen, I know I'm clueless, but humor me. Why would you ever lose me?"

"You're not clueless." She shook her head, grimacing. "You're…blunt, reason-driven. A methodical thinker." She sipped her beer, smiling. "It's one of my favorite things about you."

"One, huh?" His cheek kicked up.

She was being kind. When emotions fell into the equation, he *was* clueless, and she knew it. Well, he didn't want to be clueless with Cynthia. He wanted to understand. Was she telling him to back off? That it was better to keep some of what they had than lose it all? He tried that idea on, then instantly dismissed it. He wasn't sure he *could* back off. He loved her. He wanted her. And he knew she wanted him back. There was no faking her responses to him. At least, that's what he was telling himself.

Sipping their beers, neither said another word, nor even met the other's gaze until they were done with their hoagies and chips. Then Cynthia slung her bag over her elbow and gathered up the trash, putting the empty bottles back in the six-pack holder.

"We need to sleep," she said. "We're dragging."

"Your place or mine?" As exhausted as he was, he feared tonight would be another night of no sleep. Wanting her the way he did, he'd be thinking of her under the same roof, wanting to touch her, but with Cynthia's little pep talk, he wasn't sure that was in the cards for them.

"Socks," she said. "Shouldn't we stay at your house?"

"He's fine. I keep kibble out, and we'll stop by in the morning to feed him canned food. I think you'd be more comfortable at your place, especially after the day you've had. You'll want your things around you."

She nodded, her lower lip jutting out. "You make me sound pathetic. What about you? Don't you want your things around you?"

He shook his head. "I have you, and my go-bag in my trunk. That's all I need." Cynthia studied his face. "What?" he said, but she shook her head, and then walked toward the door.

"Is that go-bag the same one in your trunk that has the hoods, duct tape, and zip ties?"

"No," he said. "I logged all that into evidence." He opened the morgue's door for her.

She stepped into the hall. "Charlie, what am I going to do with you?" She waited for him to lock up behind him, then they walked toward the elevator. Her gait was markedly slower than his. "The evidence is mounting, and you being a stickler is helping the unsub."

"Maybe. But I won't break the law." He slid his hand into his pocket, reassuring himself that he had his car keys. "I didn't do anything wrong, so evidence will bring us the lead we're waiting for. Until I'm pulled from this case, I'll work it."

"Feels like a mistake," she said. Feels. Feelings. Since when did feelings close a case?

"Emotion has no place in evidence collection," he said. "We follow protocol and hope for the best. I'll leave feelings for the jury."

The lights had been dimmed in the hall because it was after hours. The other offices were dark also, and everyone was gone but for a skeleton crew. Charlie saw a pretty, blond housekeeper pushing her cart around the hall corner as Cynthia dropped the trash into a bin. She tucked the two extra hoagies into her cavernous pocketbook, tossed the empty beers, and then caught up with him at the elevator door. It binged, and then opened. Charlie held it open as she stepped inside.

The moment felt so *normal*. As if this could be his life from now on. Meeting up after work, going home together. He wanted to get used to it, maybe even take it for granted, and he liked to think Terrance would have approved. Of everything. His position as a forensic pathologist. Cynthia as an FBI profiler. He'd have been happy for them. Maybe was, looking down on them from heaven.

She arched a brow, silently asking him a question as the elevator doors closed them inside. "You're smiling," she said, and then punched the garage floor button.

"Terrance. I think he'd be proud of you." His smile widened when she predictably grimaced.

She clutched her bag to her chest and kept her back to the elevator wall. "Terrance thought I was his irritating little sister. 'Clinging,' I believe was the term he was fond of using. Your memory is faulty."

Wrong, but this was an old argument. "I remember just fine. I remember always liking you."

Her jaw dropped. "You didn't know I existed."

"I just hid it well." She was just so damn cute. "Lusting after my best friend's little sister would have earned me a pummeling. A well-deserved pummeling. You weren't even eighteen," he said.

"Lusting?" She seemed no less stunned.

He didn't see the big deal. "I wasn't blind. The better question is: who *didn't* lust after you? All your curves and swinging blond hair, swaying hips, and pale blue eyes." He perused her curves until he noticed her blush. "I was a sophomore in college. You were in high school and too young. I had no business thinking about you."

Her eyes lost focus, and he suspected she was reviewing that era of their relationship through a new lens. *About time*, he thought. "I didn't think you knew I was alive," she said.

His cheek kicked up. "You were too busy reading." When he took the remaining beer cans Cynthia held dangling from their plastic loops, she lifted her fingers to the back of her head. "Does it hurt?" he asked.

"I'm fine." But she winced a little before dropping her hand. "Got to admit, though, I'm a bit stunned. Where were all those lusting boys you talk about when it came time for prom? If you'll recall, I never went. Was never asked."

"*Senior* prom?" She'd been at the hospital, reading to him in a loud enough voice to be heard over his respirator.

Her spine straightened, and then a familiar expression of guilt and anxiety contorted her face. "Sorry," she said.

"What for?" He knew. They both knew, but he was so damn tired of it that he called her on it.

She held her bag to her chest a little more tightly. "For reminding you."

Not what he'd expected her to say. He'd expected mea culpas for her brother's part in landing Charlie in the hospital. He hadn't heard one for years, thankfully, but that was usually her go-to response.

"I don't mind reminders." His scars were daily reminders that he'd *survived.* He glanced at the light on the wall indicating the elevator had arrived at the garage floor. "I'm the man I am today because of that accident."

"Not the accident." She peered at him. "Your reaction to it." She slung her bag over her elbow. "You know you're wonderful. Right?" She thought he was wonderful. His cheek kicked up, but he didn't trust his voice to speak without embarrassing himself. "And—" She glanced at the lights indicating the door was about to open. "And I like kissing you, Charlie, but I don't want you to think I expect anything from you because of it."

"You're saying my virtue is safe?" He smiled, because she made no sense.

"Exactly." She nodded, as if they were on the same page. They weren't.

The elevator door clanked open. His stomach tightened. "And what happens if I don't want to be safe?"

Charlie hit the door-close button, then pulled Cynthia into his arms. Her pocketbook fell to the floor as their lips came together and he cupped the back of her neck. The kiss was rough, hot, and wet, with lots of tongue.

The door binged and opened again with a clatter. He heard a gasp, and knew it wasn't Cynthia's, because her tongue was in his mouth. He forced his eyes open and saw Teresa, framed by the darkened garage. Her hand held the elevator door open. He and Cynthia broke apart.

"I left my identification card in my desk," Teresa said. "I thought you two would be gone by now."

Cynthia took a shaky breath, grabbed her pocketbook off the floor, and then hurried off the elevator into the garage.

Charlie nodded. "I left the signed forms in your desk, Teresa. Ah, see you tomorrow." He caught up with Cynthia, draping an arm over her shoulders as they walked to his car.

The elevator door binged and closed with a clank, triggering Cynthia to look left and right. They were alone. She shrugged off his arm, looking irritated, and continued to brood on the drive to her house.

Charlie didn't mind. He figured she was processing what he'd already come to accept. It was just taking Cynthia longer. Like eating. She took longer, but sooner or later, she'd come to terms with their new reality.

They were forever.

Chapter Nine

The first and only time Cynthia ever cold-cocked someone was in college, freshman year. It was a defining moment in her life, directing her to seek a career in law enforcement, with a focus in criminal psychology. And she owed it all to Charlie.

Six months after the accident, when he was still in the hospital, she'd convinced him and MIT that he should end his scholastic medical leave and attend classes again, despite still being wheelchair-bound. He'd graduate late, but he'd graduate. It took some finagling, but by scheduling her classes Mondays, Wednesdays, and Fridays, she could bring Charlie to his classes on Tuesdays and Thursdays.

The "cold-cocking incident" happened early that first semester, when no one knew yet if Charlie could meet this challenge. She'd parked his wheelchair in class, and then left the hundred-seat auditorium to use the restroom before class started. At the door, Cynthia passed two perfectly coiffed students, smelling of Chanel and wearing designer clothes. The young women noticed Charlie, his wheelchair, and his medical devices, and were visibly and vocally recoiling. Cynthia ignored it, until one—phone in one hand, spiced latte in the other—curled her lip, and said, "I'd rather die than be disabled."

Cynthia remembered stopping, as if she'd run into a wall. She remembered her fingers clutching the door's handle and her vision blurring as fresh memories of Terrance's wake and funeral resurfaced. She was told later—in her MIT-mandated anger management counseling session—that she'd snapped. Many reasons were suggested, but even now, the last thing she remembered of the incident was their tittering and giggles. Then, nothing. But there were plenty of witnesses.

Cynthia cold-cocked the student. Tackled her.

Her father happily wrote a large alumni donation, smoothed things over with the student's family, and Cynthia found her major, which eventually landed her at The National Center for Analysis of Violent Crime (NCAVC), a major branch of the FBI's Crisis Incident Response Group.

All because of Charlie. No one screwed with him, not while Cynthia was around.

But she'd yet to find a way to protect Charlie…from Charlie.

She worked that problem well into the night, too stimulated to sleep, and it was the only reason she heard the suspicious noises in the apartment. Rolling out of bed, she quickly and *quietly* shrugged into an oversized T-shirt and a pair of panties. If there was an intruder, she wasn't getting caught naked. Then she slipped her gun from its holster, also quietly, and carefully turned the knob on her door to prevent any telltale sounds from giving her away. Then, on nimble feet, she hurried down the hall to investigate, gun at the ready, fearing an intruder had broken in while she and Charlie slept.

But it was just Charlie. Not snoring on the couch, per se, so much as making noises in his sleep. She allowed the gun to hang at her side, feeling a bit ashamed at her disappointment. She could have used the workout an intruder would have provided.

Cynthia approached the pullout couch, her path lit by moonlight peeking in from between the drapes. First thing she noticed was his quilt had slipped off the mattress. Second thing she noticed was he was nearly naked, and his boxer briefs left little to the imagination. She gawked with zero shame, admiring his body splayed on the queen-sized mattress too small for his length. She loved how big he was, and all his nakedness was making her feel aflutter.

In college, during his hospital days, she'd seen his body waste to skin and bones as he healed from injuries that miraculously didn't kill him. He never looked like this back then. This version of Charlie had easily fifty pounds more muscle mass, sculpted calves, heavy thighs, wide hips, flat belly, deep chest, and massive shoulders. He was perfection.

Even with the scars. They'd faded pale, but she could see every one of them, and knew their stories. One ran from his belly button to beneath the waistband of his underwear, where dashboard shrapnel had ripped into his body. No longer raw and puckered, every scar bore tribute to the violence that almost killed him. His stomach was peppered with them, as was his right shoulder, left arm, and his leg.

His leg muscle flexed, pivoting her gaze to his face. Had she woken him? A study of his features told her no. He still slept, so she peered at his leg scars again, frowning. Not because the scars were unattractive. They were Charlie's scars, so they were beautiful scars. The most beautiful scars ever. But the muscles beneath twisted and spasmed before her eyes. She'd found the origins of his pain, and marveled that he could sleep through it.

Cynthia leaned close—so close she could smell him—and peered at his eyes. Was he faking sleep? Wishing she'd leave? His eyes remained closed, and he seemed asleep, so she thought no. The guy was just so used to his chronic pain that he'd trained himself to sleep through it.

He'd been on his feet all day, irritating the lesions that had formed since the accident, that pulled on muscles, and caused cramping. He'd stood for ten hours in the morgue, hovering over the vics, and hadn't slept for forty-eight hours straight. Charlie should have anticipated these cramps.

She glanced at his go-bag, wondering if he had a bottle of muscle relaxers in there. Just as she thought to rummage inside, she second-guessed herself. It seemed counterintuitive to wake him if the pain was partially induced by exhaustion.

She should turn around and walk away. Go back to bed.

In the morning, he'd act as if he were fine, and it would be as if this never happened, as if she'd never stumbled upon his half naked body, witnessed his gorgeousness, and walked away. But she'd worry tonight, and didn't have the stomach for more worry, especially since she was having a hard time sleeping.

But what to do? Massage, probably. Sitting next to him on the thin mattress, she put her gun on the side table and gathered up the quilt, wondering how best to massage without waking him. And where to start? There was so much of him.

He threw his forearm over his furrowed brow, casting his eyes into shadow. Cynthia froze, saw he still slept despite his clenched fist. Then she tossed the quilt over his body, thinking to keep him warm as she massaged him limb by limb.

Charlie's right hand shot out and painfully grabbed her wrist before the quilt had even settled on his frame. His eyes opened, and their gazes locked. Cynthia watched as his sleep faded, and with it, his inner warrior. Then his grip loosened, but instead of releasing her, he tugged her across his chest until she was draped over him, the quilt separating their bodies.

"Charlie. You're in pain," she said.

He flipped them onto their sides, spooning her, resting his chin on the top of her head as he held her close. "Go to sleep." His voice sounded gravelly, and she knew he was exhausted, but sleep wasn't making his pain go away.

"You need a muscle relaxer," she said.

"You're my heating pad. Go to sleep." He yawned, and then smacked his lips, settling more comfortably behind her, until his body conformed completely with hers, his hand pressing to her belly, her T-shirt riding up, her bum nestled deep in the crux created by his groin and thighs.

"You're in pain," she said. "I want to help." She feared the weight of her head on his bicep would exacerbate his cramping, so she struggled to rise. His arm clamped down, pinning her in place.

"Shh," he sighed. "Sleep, baby." Then his arm grew heavy, and soon, his breathing pattern suggested he slept.

Suggested, because Charlie was sporting an impressive hard-on, and it ran the length of her ass crack. He *was* quietly snoring, and his breathing had mellowed to slow and rhythmic, so she thought maybe he was sleeping. His leg muscles weren't spasming anymore—she'd have felt the cramping against her legs through the thin quilt. She certainly felt everything else going on with his body through the quilt. So Cynthia relaxed, her worries dismissed, because Charlie had relaxed.

And she felt coddled, so she drifted off to sleep.

* * * *

The sun was bright, the birds were chirping, and Cynthia was draped on a bed with a heartbeat. *Tha-thump. Tha-thump.* Its rhythm increased. Not by much, but enough to notice, and if she wasn't mistaken, it still had a hard-on, only this time it was nestled along the notch of her thighs.

Charlie.

Cynthia lifted her brows to encourage her lids to open. First thing her sleepy eyes saw was his nipple, and her fingertip on it. Then she noted the pressure of his hand splayed on her ass, his middle finger tucked in its cleft. His other was under her T-shirt, palm flattened between her shoulder blades.

"Run while you can," Charlie whispered.

His grip contradicted his directive and tightened. Cynthia felt stupid. She should have anticipated this come daylight, and maybe made a decision or two last night.

At least shaved her legs.

Instead, she found herself tempted by morning sex, with morning breath, and glaringly bright morning light to illuminate all her flaws. Butt dimples and puffy face notwithstanding, sex with raccoon eyes was best done in the dark. Now, splayed on his chest, his hands pinning her in place, she didn't want to run. Didn't even want to delay. She just wanted forgiving lighting, a sexy negligee, and brushed teeth.

Awkward.

Charlie wasn't waiting for a response, unless Cynthia *not running* was all the answer he'd needed. His hands caressed her butt in slow, circular motions, and, strangely enough, his palms and fingertips were packing a wallop, dredging deep, arousing feelings in the clenching bits between her legs. Pleasure had her flexing her thighs, and wiggling on him. Could he tell?

Charlie moaned, inhaling sharply. He'd noticed.

Inconveniently, a yawn worked its way through her body, and though she struggled to mitigate its effect, she arched nonetheless, dragging her swollen lady parts against his rock-hard erection. Tingles fanned out across her body, and then it was her inhaling sharply and releasing it on a dragged-out moan.

It stilled Charlie's hand, making her wonder if her response had shocked him. Embarrassment forced her lazy eyes open to see his unsmiling face, his mental gears working, weighing repercussions of what they might do, what they *would* do, if she had anything to say about it. Her cheeks warmed, and she couldn't help wishing Charlie would think less, and direct that focus to…other pursuits.

"I know," she whispered. "Sex would be a complication." She gave him a suitable excuse to bail, because Charlie wasn't wired for anything but blunt honesty, and she wasn't sure her ego could handle blunt at the moment. If he changed his mind, no harm, no foul. She'd probably molested him in his sleep anyway, and his dick had done all the thinking up until now. "But it doesn't have to be. It can be—"

His finger nudged aside her panties and slid inside her wet heat. Her mouth opened, and she lost focus. Charlie cupped the back of her neck and pulled her lips to his, sweeping his tongue inside her mouth, drugging her with expert kisses. Did his mouth muffle her long, hungry moan? Most certainly, because his fingers knew what they were doing. It was his fault that she couldn't control her response.

Cynthia ran her fingers over him, relishing the feel of his crisp chest hair as she widened her knees, straddling his hips, giving him all the access he could possibly need to keep doing what he was doing. She licked into his mouth, cupping his cheeks, rocking on his hand. His fingers had her tipping toward climax, but she rebelled. She wanted Charlie with her. This time. Their first time together, she wanted Charlie inside her, orgasming while she orgasmed. She'd been fantasizing about that too long to give up that dream.

Cynthia stilled his hand, broke their kiss, and pushed off his chest, sitting on his thighs. Then she watched his face as she slowly lifted her T-shirt, revealing her breasts to his hungry gaze. His response had her trembling in anticipation. She tossed the shirt aside and gathered her hair on top of her head, because it made her breasts look perky and Charlie seemed to like it. When he cupped her breasts, his thumbs teasing their tips, the look in his eyes told her she'd been right. Charlie was a breast man.

"I want your briefs off, Charlie."

His cheek kicked up as his gaze lifted to hers. "I want your panties off, Cynthia." He was too much in control for Cynthia's tastes, especially since he'd gotten her a hiccup away from coming already. She wanted him weak with passion. Needed it, or how would she know they were on equal footing?

Cynthia stood, planting her feet on the mattress on both sides of his hips. Then she inhaled deeply to remind him, yeah, she had great breasts and he liked them. One look told Cynthia he didn't need reminding. He was staring at them. "Then take my panties off, Charlie."

He smiled, propping himself up with his fists. It put his lips on level with the very panties she'd told him to remove. One glance told her Charlie wasn't feeling so cavalier anymore, but now that his hot breath and lips were touching her through the lace, she wasn't feeling in control in the least. His tongue snaked out, pressing against the lace, the wet pressure licking at her until she didn't notice the lace between them, and all she could focus on was Charlie's tongue and how he was making her feel.

Her knees gave out.

Charlie caught her before she landed on the mattress and guided her onto her back. When she opened her eyes, his fingers were drawing her panties down her hips and then her thighs, bending her knees as his gaze locked on her exposed, swollen, clenching lady parts. His obvious hungry anticipation almost had her coming then and there, but he distracted her by tossing her panties aside and catching her gaze. He smiled, grabbed her knees, and then spread them wide.

She propped herself up on her elbows, helpless to do anything but watch in wonder as his chest rose and fell, like he was exerting great effort to control himself. Yet all he was doing was staring at the apex of her thighs, licking his lower lip, looking as if he'd found Nirvana.

Then his mouth covered her, his hands gripped both ass cheeks, and Charlie gorged on her, using his shoulders to support her trembling thighs. He was reverent, at first, and as she watched, she wasn't sure she'd survive his teasing. Then he wasn't, and she was positive she wouldn't survive. Her elbows gave out, and she was flat on her back, eyes open, blind to all but how his mouth was making her feel. Waves of arousing jolts ratcheted her toward a helplessness that bordered on agony, because it would bring her to an ecstasy that would end this feeling. She wanted both. She wanted Charlie. She was coming and didn't want to.

"Inside me," she gasped, turning on her side, pulling away from him.

He kissed the back of her thighs, her ass, and by the time he was done, he'd tasted every inch of her. Every. Inch. Of. Her. No more secrets. Butt dimples? He'd had the time to count them. And when she couldn't tolerate for one more moment his keeping her poised at the cusp of orgasm, she begged him, "Please, Charlie. Now, Charlie." He pulled her toward him by her knees, positioned himself above her.

"Put me inside you." The words seemed ripped from his throat. "Cynthia, now."

She cupped him and guided him forward. Then he had her wrists in his hands, and trapped them over her head as he moved into her body, his weight bearing down as he buried himself to the hilt while kissing her. His hips thrust so powerfully she was moved inches up the mattress as he filled her completely, stretching her. She saw stars.

And loved him. She loved him.

As the thought blossomed in her heart, she allowed herself to crest and surf the pleasurable waves of a powerful orgasm as Charlie's kisses muffled her cries of passion. He was wild above her, fierce as he dominated her body, then he took his release with a shudder, an arch of his back. Arms taut, tremor preceding a great stillness, he was glorious to see as she floated there, in heaven on earth.

Soon his body began to relax, and his elbows dropped, digging into the mattress on either side of her shoulders, and though he continued to move inside her, drawing out her pleasurable aftershocks, she wondered if he was thinking what she was thinking: that she didn't want it to end. That it was wonderful.

She didn't even care about the sweatiness, and the fact that her breasts were mashed flat against Charlie's chest. She didn't care. Didn't care that her hair was tousled and not aligned. Didn't care. Every whimper, gasp, and word of pleading, every touch they'd shared… She remembered. And wasn't embarrassed. She felt no shame, and would do it again.

"I forgot to ask," he said, still deep inside her, brushing his lips against hers. "You on birth control?" She nodded.

"Hm." She'd planned on weaning off. Such was her sex life.

He smiled, and his eyes crinkled, but said no more. Then he rolled off her and lay on his back, pulling her to his side. She missed him inside her already. She was swollen, still clenching with aftershocks.

He kissed her, long and lingering. "I can't believe I denied myself that for ten years."

She propped herself up by the elbow, looking down at him. Ten years ago? Why would he bring that up? It was obviously a reference to the accident. To Terrance. And all references to Terrance were somehow connected to his sense of obligation.

"We weren't the same people ten years ago." She studied his expression, doing her best not to panic. Sex had been amazing. She'd thought it meant he… She thought it meant he was in love with her and wanted to spend the rest of their lives together as man and wife.

He smiled. "You were jailbait."

She narrowed her eyes. Was she overthinking things? "I was nineteen. My mom was married and pregnant with Terrance when she was nineteen." He kept his focus on the ceiling, looking relaxed, as if he had no idea he was playing with fire. She kind of envied him that oblivion.

"Ten years ago, you'd assigned yourself my nurse. My babysitter. You went from off limits to out of my league."

She sat on the mattress's edge, hating the memories he'd dredged up. "I wasn't on bedpan duty. I visited. Read some books." He leaned on his elbow, caressing her back. It was comforting, which made her suspicious. Why did he think she needed to be comforted?

"I know what you did," he said, "and I know why you did it." She glanced over her shoulder to tell him to drop the subject, and then saw his chest. It shut her up. The daylight was unforgiving. There was no shadow, no dim lighting to soften the scar's impact. And they broke her heart.

"You're my hero, Charlie." When their gazes met, he wasn't relaxed. He seemed pissed, and she couldn't blame him. He'd caught her feeling sorry for him.

"You deserve a better hero," he snapped.

"You let me worry about that." She draped herself on his chest, kissing him until he stopped frowning and grew playful, rolling her onto her back. Then his caresses had her forgetting about everything but how Charlie made her feel. He took his time, was methodical in his seduction, exploring, teasing responses from her, showing her what she liked even as she discovered what made him moan with pleasure. An hour later, they found themselves lying on their backs on the floor next to the pullout couch, naked, and a bit stunned.

"Four orgasms," she huffed and puffed, "is definitely a record."

He gasped for air, smiling. "It's all about setting goals."

"Feed me. Need coffee." She flopped her left arm on his chest, pressing her palm over his heart, and then noticed the MIT ring was gone. "Shit. The ring. Charlie, I lost your ring."

Charlie's heart was racing. She could feel its beat under her hand. "I put it on the side table." He reached up, slapped the top of the side table a few times, and when his hand covered hers on his chest, he'd retrieved the ring and slipped it back on her finger. "My parents need to be told," he said.

Cynthia shook her head, feeling the hard floor press against her bruised laceration. She didn't want to tell them until things were settled. Yeah, she and Charlie got married. Yeah, they'd had *phenomenal* sex, but… This marriage thing. It might not last.

"Let's not deal with that now, okay?" Telling Delia and Paul Foulkes would set in motion things she wasn't sure either she or Charlie were ready to commit to. Meaning they'd have to make decisions. 'Til-death-do-us-part decisions. And she didn't want to challenge what they had now. It was still too new, and, yeah, they still had a killer out there trying to pin a mass murder on Charlie. "Too much is going on. I feel good. Let me enjoy this."

Charlie hauled himself to his feet, then pulled on his boxer briefs. "Just saying."

"First you bring up your parents, then you put clothes on. What did I ever do to you? Look at me." She indicated her nakedness with a wave of her hand. "I can barely stand. My dignity is in tatters. Help me up." She held up a hand. Charlie took it and tugged her to her feet.

"They have to be told, Cynthia. It will hurt their feelings to hear it from someone else."

"It could drag them into our troubles," she said. It was a worry.

Charlie shrugged. "We're married. Married people have troubles."

"Chicken and the egg, Charlie. We married *because* of trouble. This is a whole different thing, and you know it." Cynthia arched a brow, patting his chest. "You must consider how your parents will feel when this case is closed, we're not in jail, and I drop you like a stone." When and if she married, it would be to a man who declared his endless love, and white-chargered her ass off into the sunset. That crime scene proposal could not stand.

"Already planning on breaking my heart?" he said, smiling.

If Charlie took her threat seriously, he gave no indication of it as he grabbed his go-bag and left her weakly swaying on her feet, so well-loved and satiated, all she was good for was watching him walk out of the living room in his boxer briefs.

Damn, he was sexy as hell.

When she heard the bathroom door close and the shower turn on, she still didn't know what to make of his response. What she was absolutely positive of, however, was she didn't have the guts to call him on it, either. Didn't want to rock the boat.

She loved him and couldn't tell him.

He had to say it first, because otherwise, Charlie would *never* divorce her. Her declaration would effectively trap him in their marriage. He had to pull that particular rip cord first, or no matter how their relationship progressed, Cynthia would never be sure what was in his heart. Such was the insidious nature of his obligation. It even made her question the motive behind orgasms.

Her phone rang. The screen said Benton. Cynthia hurried into the kitchen, all her naked bits bouncing and ignored as she found Charlie making coffee. "It's Benton," she said. "I don't want to answer. What is wrong with me?" She couldn't think. "I'm having a panic attack. I don't have panic attacks, but I think that's what this is." She huffed and puffed, then stopped breathing altogether when she became dizzy. The phone continued to ring.

He compressed his lips, nodding. "Nothing's changed. He's your friend as well as your boss." She nodded, still not breathing, and hit "accept."

"Deming here." She sucked in more air and held it, squeezing her eyes shut.

"We need you here," Benton said. "Now. There's been movement on the case. Are you with Charlie?"

Her heart skipped a beat as she stared at Charlie. His hand stopped scooping coffee into the filter as she slowly inhaled, doing her best to sound normal. "Yeah. I'm with Charlie."

"Don't tell him anything, just… Bring him here, Deming. Bring him to the incident room." Benton hung up. Cynthia's hand trembled so much, it was hard to turn her phone off.

"What did he say?" Charlie gripped her upper arms, studying her features.

"He said *don't tell Charlie*." She dropped her forehead to his chest. "I'm scared. What are we going to do?"

Chapter Ten

Charlie had a hard time stopping Cynthia from throwing on clothes and rushing to the precinct, but he calmed her enough to convince her to shower and eat first. It gave him time to think, clear his head. What evidence could prompt such a request from Benton? Was he asking a newlywed agent, a *friend*, to deliver her husband to an interrogation? Not necessarily, unless the evidence was so clear they were convinced of his guilt. But then, wouldn't they fear for Cynthia's life and break down the door to save her? It seemed more likely they wanted to see what Charlie would do. Run? He didn't know. Interpreting this sort of machination wasn't his strong suit, but he didn't want to ask Cynthia, either, because…well, she was upset.

He told himself not to worry. He wasn't guilty of anything, and as BPD's chief forensic pathologist, he knew, sooner or later, evidence would clear him. Truth didn't have a timeline, and it could be unkind, but the evidence was out there, waiting to be found. He thought it might be a good time to remind Special Agent Benton of that.

A half hour later, they'd eaten, showered, dressed, and were ready to leave. Charlie stopped Cynthia before she could open the front door, wanting one last moment before they allowed the world to intrude into what had been his version of heaven. He took her hand, earning a worried smile from her. She was doing a good job of pretending she wasn't upset, fidgeting with her pocketbook strap, but he knew the signs. Her hands trembled, and she was having a hard time holding his gaze.

"We'll get through this," he said, "and it won't even be the hardest thing we've ever done." She nodded, only stopping when he dropped a kiss on her lips. She was being so brave. "When this is over, you and me, we're going to have a long conversation about you and me." He lifted his brows, waiting for pushback, or agreement. She gave him neither, refusing the bait to think beyond the coming meeting.

She scowled. "You don't get to take the fall for this. I won't allow it, Charlie. You understand me? Be careful about what you say to Benton. I don't know what they think they have, but it's incriminating, or he wouldn't have tipped me off." She dropped her bag and grabbed his shirt with both fists. "Promise me you won't do anything stupid, or I swear I'll do something stupid, too, and we'll both regret it. I'll make sure of it."

He covered her hands until she loosened her grip, then he brought them to his mouth, kissing them, lingering on the knuckle above his MIT ring, her "wedding" ring. It reminded him to do something about replacing it. "We're investigators," he said. "Experts in all the many ways a crime is committed, and I promise you, these killers are fucking with the wrong people. We're going to nail them for these murders and make them pay for what they've done."

"I hope you're right." She slipped from his grasp and bent, retrieving her pink pocketbook, to sling it over her elbow. "But until then, worry is going to eat me alive. I have no idea how you're so calm." He opened the front door, waiting for her to step through first.

"We both know if I'd planned this crime, I wouldn't have gotten caught. Benton has to know that, too." She nodded, frowning, hurrying off the porch to the sidewalk.

"Good point," she said. He clicked the key fob, unlocking the car, and then opened the passenger side door and waited for her to sit. She tucked her bag at her feet as he leaned, one hand on the roof, the other on the open door.

"And don't think your decision to ignore my comment about talking later went unnoticed. I noticed," he said.

"Sounds like a threat." She buckled in, avoiding his gaze. He grimaced, closing the door, not knowing if he should drop the subject, or push his advantage. After all, they'd just had a morning of mind-bendingly amazing sex. Surely, if ever she'd be inclined to commit to a lifetime as his wife, this morning would be the best time to ask. Before he was arrested.

He walked around the car, worrying the problem. Being arrested certainly wasn't a good selling point. It could explain Cynthia's hesitancy. What had she said? *Sounds like a threat.* Hard to argue, so he didn't, but rather slid behind the wheel, disgruntled. Now was one of those all too frequent times when he wished he knew what was going on in her head.

"We both know you run rings around me when it comes to things like this." He buckled in and started the car.

"This?" He caught her smiling, and then caught her suppressing it when he'd caught her.

"Yeah." He used his hand to wave between the two of them. "This." He grimaced, even as he realized a grimace probably wasn't his optimal expression if his objective was to butter up his wife. "And don't think I'll forget your merciless exploitation of that strength when the dust clears. Next time we have sex, maybe I'll only give you three orgasms, rather than four."

"You mean five, if you count the one you slept through last night."

Her words hit him like a pie to the face. But in a good way. He found himself smiling. "I stand corrected." Hands on the wheel.

She pressed her lips together, as if forcing herself not to say more, and then looked out the window. "I'm sick to my stomach."

He froze. "Because we had sex?"

She physically startled, her expression one of surprise. "Huh?" So, *no.* Not because they'd had sex. He gave up. If she wanted him to know what was on her mind, she'd tell him, just like always. He'd have to be patient, *as always*, and hope for the best. "Because of the meeting, the questions they'll ask, what evidence they've dug up. I feel as if I'm leading a sheep to slaughter."

He stopped himself from rolling his eyes by concentrating on driving, pulling into street traffic. "I'm no sheep."

"No. You're right. What if they use that against you? Maybe you should act less fierce. You can't be less muscular overnight, or less smart. They'd never believe it, but—"

Her words were a balm to his soul. "You forgot to mention sexy."

"No, I didn't." She folded her arms over her chest. "It was a deliberate oversight. If you were any more conceited, your head would explode."

Conceited? "Have you met me?" When all she did was narrow her eyes and then turn her head away, Charlie laughed and focused on his driving. "Maybe I should head for the airport, grab a flight to Costa Rica, and sit on the beach drinking frosty beverages while Benton finds the real unsubs. Would that make you happy?"

"Not Costa Rica." She sighed, running her manicured fingers through her hair. "Thirty-two countries don't have extradition treaties with the United States. Pick one of those."

He glanced at her. "Costa Rica isn't one of them?"

"No. We'd have to go farther afield. Choose a country, preferably, where I won't be penalized for being a woman."

We. She'd said *we.* His chest tightened with emotion, and it took a moment to hide it, because Cynthia couldn't have been clearer. She'd run with Charlie. No questions. Wasn't that the answer he was looking for? "We're staying. We'll fight this and win." He had plans for them, and they didn't include prison, or being a fugitive.

She nodded. "Like always."

Fifteen minutes later, parked at the precinct house, they stepped out of the car. Cynthia appeared somber. They both shouldered their fears silently as they made their way inside. It was morning, so the place was hopping as they checked in at security, hustled to the elevators, and then stepped off on the homicide department floor. A multitude of desks were manned by distracted detectives clicking on keyboards, interviewing people. No one paid them the least attention, and that was a good thing, because Cynthia's hands were shaking. She looked guilty. As they hustled down the hall, Charlie couldn't help worrying she might make a scene if things went south in his meeting with Benton. It would do neither of them good if she was fired, or even suspended. Cynthia represented a wild card layered on top of his other concerns.

By the time they reached the incident room at the far end of the department, Charlie had come to terms with the uncertainty. Nothing he could do about it. Cynthia was her own woman.

He opened the door for her, saw her take a bracing breath before she entered, and then followed her inside the large room. Desks were to the left of the door, and Special Agent Jack Benton stood in front of them by a six-foot-tall murder board. Six vic pictures were taped on the white surface, above erasable-marker handwritten notes. To the left of the board was a table with a coffee machine, paper cups, stirrers, sugar, and a doughnut box. It was the doughnuts that caught Charlie's attention. He headed straight for the box and chose glazed from the selection.

Special Agent Vincent Modena was hunkered down at his assigned desk off to Charlie's left, near the door. One look noted Modena only had eyes for Cynthia. It stilled his hand, freezing the doughnut inches from his lips. Then Charlie saw that Modena seemed sympathetic, and relief had Charlie eating that doughnut in three bites. It was delicious.

Cynthia pegged it right. Fingers were decidedly pointed at Charlie. He wondered what planted evidence was found.

Special Agent Gilroy stood to Charlie's left, in the back, rubbing his big hand over his shorn blond hair. He didn't look happy. BPD's IT tech, Vivian O'Grady, stood at Gilroy's side. Mid-thirties, brown hair, tweed suit, she was flushed and clutching her pearls. Rumor had it O'Grady and Gilroy were dating, and Charlie had noticed they'd seemed happy lately.

Vivian didn't seem happy now. Her gaze shifted to settle on Charlie, and she glared at him. It told him two things: the evidence was damning, and whatever personal currency he'd accrued by working with the team had been spent. Benton turned his attention away from the murder board, his eyes zeroing in on Charlie leaning against the coffee table.

"You want to do it here?" Charlie said, licking the sugar off his fingers. "Or in an interrogation room?" Benton's eyes narrowed. Cynthia tossed her bag onto the nearest desk, scowling.

"Shut up, Charlie," she said, just as Benton said, "Interrogation room 1."

Cynthia gasped. "Benton!" Charlie shook his head once, willing her to be silent. "Fine!" she said. Then she turned toward Benton. "I trust you, Benton, but I trust my husband, too. Remember that when you question him."

Benton exchanged glances with his team, then gathered folders from his desk. "Deming, you know you can no longer have anything to do with this case."

"No," Cynthia said, visibly shaking, eyes narrowing. "I don't know that. Why don't you tell me why?"

Benton glanced at Modena. "Keep her out of the room."

Then he tilted his head toward the door and Charlie followed. To interrogation room 1. Benton flipped on a switch, and a red light in the ceiling camera turned on. It told Charlie this interview wasn't casual, it was official, would be recorded, monitored, and logged into evidence. Charlie sat in the perp chair, the one facing the camera, and told himself to be calm, because… Well, fuck, he was innocent.

Benton sat, eyes on an open manila file filled with the pictures Kevin took of the crime scene yesterday. "Doesn't look good, Charlie."

"Can we dispel with the games?" Charlie said. Not knowing what they had was making it difficult to digest the doughnut.

Benton tapped the photos with his index finger. "You think six executions of WITSEC witnesses is a game? I thought the killing would stop when we put Dante Coppola behind bars. The syndicate is dead, its operations halted, but now this. Believe me, Charlie. I'm not playing."

"Yes, you are," Charlie said. "It's textbook for an interrogator to use photos of gory vics for shock value. I autopsied them, so unless you have pics of the Loch Ness Monster in that folder, you're not shocking me. Why am I here?"

Benton nudged a copy of a bank statement from the file. Its letterhead was unfamiliar to Charlie. "Where were you the night before last?" he said. "I'm going to need a detailed accounting for every hour, into the morning."

Charlie glanced up from the paper, curious. "The vics were shot around ten PM. You know I was leaving to drive to Cynthia's house around 10:15 PM, because I called you as I was leaving. Hell, I called everyone I could think of to find Cynthia when her phone went dead. Use the GPS card on my phone to track where I was that night."

"Where your phone was, you mean. You're a forensic expert, Charlie. If anyone knows how to finesse the system, you do, and it's not an alibi if you were alone."

"So why would I be that sloppy?" Charlie saw the flaw in Benton's logic immediately. "You're suggesting I advertised that I was alone and drove through Boston with a phone that could track my whereabouts because I'm attempting to avert suspicion? Is that also why I called the people most likely to investigate the mass murder?" He shook his head. "You're describing someone who wants to be caught."

Benton's lids lowered as he studied Charlie's features, and his body language. "Most serial killers want to be caught."

Charlie decided not to take offense, since Benton's words sounded like rote. The team leader was only doing his job. "I drove straight to Cynthia's apartment, where I stayed until morning, and then I drove her to the ER, and then to the crime scene."

"Where you proposed," Benton prompted, "in a spectacular fashion." When Charlie simply lifted his brows and didn't add to his comments, Benton grimaced. "My assumption is Cynthia can corroborate your alibi."

What alibi? Then Charlie realized that Benton assumed Cynthia had been at her apartment when Charlie arrived that night. She hadn't been. She'd been gone all night and Charlie had been alone, waiting and worrying at her apartment. Not that he'd tell Benton that. Compromising Cynthia helped no one.

Charlie was careful to keep his thoughts hidden, because Benton was staring, the camera was recording, and whoever was watching through the monitor was taking notes. Lying to a FBI agent was a felony, so Charlie had to answer carefully.

"Isn't that a question for Cynthia?" he said.

"I'm asking you."

"You're playing games," Charlie said, "and you're fishing for information. Tell me why I'm here."

"When was the last time you saw these vics?" Benton indicated the photos.

They were autopsy photographs. Benton knew exactly when he'd last seen those men. "You mean alive?"

"Yes, Charlie. When they were alive." Benton's lips tightened.

"Never." Charlie watched Benton lean back in his chair, his blue eyes fixed on Charlie's face, as if weighing his answer for veracity. "I've seen pictures of them, because I had to study the case for the trial, but until I arrived at the scene, I'd never been in their presence." Charlie picked up the copy of the bank statement and read the letterhead. Stone Industries, LLC. "What is this?"

Benton lifted his brows. "That's exactly what I said when I found it slipped under my apartment door this morning. Whoever delivered it knows where I live, and what case I'm on, and had access to confidential information on a foreign bank account."

"Foreign?" Charlie was completely lost, and it must have shown on his face, because Benton seemed uncertain for the first time since Charlie sat his ass in the hot seat.

"The company is based in the Cayman Islands," Benton said. "I had our forensic accountants do their magic, and it didn't take long to discover Stone Industries is a Coppola syndicate money-laundering shell company."

Now, isn't that interesting, Charlie thought, scanning the document. His attention was immediately subverted by the interrogation room door slamming open and hitting the wall. Cynthia barged in, face flaming red, her eyes flashing with anger.

"This is the Coppola case then. What the hell is going on?" She glared at Benton. "If you don't tell me right now, I'll lawyer Charlie up so fast your head will spin!"

Benton's shoulder's sagged, and he sighed, glaring at the camera affixed to the ceiling. "Modena. You had one job."

"Don't try to put me off," Cynthia said. "I'm serious, Benton." Her fists rested on her hips. Charlie thought her magnificent, and couldn't stop smiling. "This isn't funny, Charlie! Benton! Talk to me!"

"Look at this." Benton handed her the bank statement. Charlie stood, looking over her shoulder. Halfway down the page, there was a withdrawal transaction highlighted with yellow. "An even million," the team leader said. "Look at the date." Two days ago, the day before the murders. Charlie shook his head, still flummoxed. He exchanged looks with Cynthia and discovered she didn't seem to have a clue either.

"What are we looking at, Benton?" Charlie said. Benton handed him another piece of paper. Same bank, but this time, it was a printout of the destination of the million-dollar transaction, also highlighted in yellow. No names, just account numbers.

"We've subpoenaed the bank," Benton said. "The one in the Caymans shrugged us off when we called, but the destination bank in the United

States must comply, so we'll discover what account this transaction landed in soon enough. We believe our source is revealing the killer's identity, as well as the one who ordered the hit."

"But why show us these statements?" Cynthia had grown more incensed the longer Benton spoke, making Charlie think her question was rhetorical. Cynthia handed the bank statement back to Benton.

"I thought it would be wise to give Charlie the opportunity to refute our source's claim," Benton said.

"Your source is claiming I kill people?" Charlie said. "For a million dollars? My net worth is twice that size, and the IRS can attest it was earned the old-fashioned way, not by moonlighting as a contract killer. If this transaction landed in my bank account, it's because someone is framing me. Your forensic accountants need to work faster to uncover this manufactured motive."

Benton expression was neutral. "You willing to allow us access to your bank accounts?"

"Hell no," Cynthia said.

"Someone is framing me for murder, using my banking system," Charlie said. "Seems counterintuitive to help them by helping you."

Benton nodded. "Fair enough, but I have to do my job." He sent a sidelong glance to Cynthia. "You know that, right?"

"She knows," Charlie said, because Cynthia was too busy scowling at her boss.

"The subpoena is written and submitted," Benton said, "in anticipation of your"—he shrugged—"sensible response, but it's only a matter of time before we gain access to the account."

"Who is your snitch?" Cynthia said. Benton made a big show of ignoring her, futzing with the paperwork. "We deserve to know who is accusing Charlie."

Benton's jaw muscles flexed. "That's what a trial and discovery is for."

Alrighty then. Benton had a reputation for hardball. There were no surprises here.

Benton focused on Charlie. "You should be upset. Surprised, maybe. Why aren't you?" He glanced between him and Cynthia, who from Charlie's perspective seemed upset enough for them both. "Six dead. Payoff from a Coppola syndicate shell company transferred to your account. If you're being framed, you are mighty calm about it."

Benton's goading failed to move Charlie. "'No man knows the value of innocence and integrity but he who has lost them.' William Godwin."

Benton narrowed his blue eyes. "You confessing?"

"No!" Cynthia snapped.

"To what?" Charlie said. Now was the moment of truth. Would Benton come right out and accuse Charlie, instead of simply insinuating?

"Murder one. Six counts," Benton said. Not a flicker of skepticism. It hurt.

"Screw you," Charlie said. "The real killer is out there, the case's lead investigator is chasing ghosts, and the case's forensic expert is conveniently sidelined by defending himself from murder charges. Someone knew what they were doing when they chose me to pin these murders on. You get that, right?"

Cynthia pulled out her phone. "I'm calling my lawyer. Stop talking, Charlie. We're done here."

Charlie wondered if Benton would be surprised to discover his head had been nodding as Charlie had been defending himself. It made him think maybe Benton and he were on the same page after all.

"And yet." Benton pulled a piece of paper from the folder and nudged it across the table toward Charlie. "Where's your gun?"

The paper was a copy of a Walmart receipt. For a Glock. He leaned, reading without touching, and saw that it seemed to be a good facsimile of the receipt he received from the now-defunct Walmart. Except it couldn't be authentic. Those gun sale records had been destroyed in a fire, and that wasn't his Visa number. Yet his "signature" was clearly written on it, as well as on the accompanying Visa receipt. Charlie's eyes hit on the discrepancy immediately.

"I didn't buy my Glock from that Walmart, that's not my Visa, and my gun was stolen." All three statements were true, so they fell from his lips easily, despite Cynthia's frown. She wanted him to shut up, and he probably should have, but he wanted this case solved, too. "Whoever falsified this information is connected to the killings. I'm not."

"Stolen, huh?" Benton said.

"Charlie, not another word." She curled her fingers into the muscles of his neck as she leaned close. "You hear me?"

"The receipt is falsified." Charlie pulled out his wallet and showed Benton his Visa card. "Sloppy work by my accuser."

"Means nothing. It's easy enough to open secondary accounts." Benton pressed his lips together, frowning at the card as Charlie allowed him to take a photo using his phone. "I'll need a credit report to verify your claim. I'm assuming you'll want to sign off on that to avoid a subpoena."

"Subpoena all you want, Benton. He's not giving you anything," Cynthia said.

Her cheeks were flushed, and she had the flavor of panic about her. Charlie felt bad that she was this upset, and a little confused. Why hadn't she anticipated these questions? *And* a few surprises?

"So far, we seem to be doing fine without his help, Cynthia. We called Walmart," Benton said, "gave them the receipt number, make, and model, and obtained the serial number of Charlie's gun. It matches our murder weapon."

"Let me guess," Cynthia said. "Your anonymous source who fed you the bank statements and pointed to Charlie's bank account. Unless you can prove that Visa account was opened by Charlie, and that the receipt *isn't* falsified, and that the serial number proves it is his gun, and that Charlie was in possession of that gun *during* the killings, none of this proves anything. So, no, you don't get Charlie's anything. Got it? What else do you have?"

"Deming." Benton compressed his lips, looking fit to be tied. "There is a reason why you shouldn't be in this interview. *This.* This is why. You know I have to ask these questions. If it's not me, it will be someone else. Someone who doesn't know Charlie—"

"I don't care who's asking. Charlie isn't talking without his lawyer in the room." She waved her phone in the air. "And once I get a call back, then…" She nodded her head, looking hesitant for the first time since she stormed in the room. "Then you'll be sorry."

Benton rolled his eyes. "Is the murder weapon yours, Charlie?"

"You can't ask him any questions now," Cynthia said. "He lawyered up. Stop trying to use our friendship to pin a murder on my husband!"

Charlie wanted to answer. Yes. The gun was his. He'd known that from the moment he saw it at the crime scene. "Are you saying the gun matches the slugs and casings that killed the vics?"

"Yes," Benton said. Charlie felt relief expand his chest, and it was hard not to show it. Cynthia's gun wasn't the murder weapon. "So?" Benton said. "Is it your gun, or not? Your silence doesn't help your case. Either someone is going to a lot of trouble to paint you as the unsub, or you really are the unsub. Which is it?"

Cynthia threw her hands in the air and looked ready to blow a gasket. Charlie moved to her side and embraced her, pressing his lips to her ear. "Stop," he whispered. "Benton is doing his job. We *need* him to do his job." When she nodded, Charlie loosened his grip and turned toward the team leader. "I'm innocent."

"Yes, dammit! He's innocent." Cynthia, still clutching Charlie, was now struggling to hide a quivering chin. Her eyes were round with hurt, and she looked helpless. Charlie knew that was when she was most dangerous.

Kris Rafferty

Cynthia didn't like helpless. She lashed out. He feared she'd do something rash, like confess.

"Cynthia," Charlie whispered. "Let's be calm."

"How can you think he's guilty, Benton!" She scrunched up her face, scowling. "I mean"—she gave Charlie a squeeze—"look at him! Does he look like a killer?"

Benton lifted his brows and scoffed. "You're biased. And you're ignoring the evidence. If you weren't married to the man—"

"But I am! *He's being framed.* All of this can be explained away, or disproved."

"I know," Benton said, leaning back in his chair, folding his arms over his chest.

"Because of the bank account?" Charlie could feel her relax in his arms. She'd switched easily from outraged spouse to investigator in the space of a heartbeat, and then stepped from Charlie's arms. He almost smiled. Then she paced the small interrogation room. "Anyone with access to the internet can find a bank's routing number."

"I know," Benton said.

"And we both know it's not hard to find someone's bank account if they're motivated," she said. "I bet I could find *yours* if I wanted, and Charlie said the gun was stolen."

"I said *I know*, Deming." The weight of Benton's stare seemed to finally get through to her. "And you're his alibi that night. Right?" He shrugged. "So, the question is, who is trying to frame Charlie? That's probably our killer."

Cynthia's mouth dropped, and her hands clenched. Meanwhile, Charlie's stomach had grown queasy. This was the test. Did he trust the justice system or not? Cynthia seemed poised to lie for him, and if he'd allowed her to do that, to commit a felony, they'd have to live with that lie for the rest of their lives, or face the consequences. Careers over. Maybe jail time. It would stain them both, and maybe help the real killer.

"No," Charlie said. "She wasn't with me that night." Cynthia gasped and turned toward Charlie, her heart on her sleeve.

He'd been right. She'd been moments away from lying to her boss, a federal officer.

Cynthia turned her back to the camera and leaned her shoulder against the wall, hiding her face from Benton and Charlie. He wanted to go to her, to explain why he did what he did, but he knew now wasn't the time. Benton was staring at the table, and didn't seem surprised, which made Charlie wonder if he'd been baiting them to lie, waiting to see if they'd give a false alibi.

"Why the sudden marriage, Charlie?" Benton kept his tone low, almost gentle, either because he knew the atmosphere in the room was combustible and he didn't want to trigger another outburst by Cynthia, or because the topic was marriage. Feelings. And those were always combustible. "Did you hope your association with Cynthia would buy you leniency? If so, you've miscalculated. I care for Cynthia. She's like family. As her husband, that puts you under more scrutiny, not less, if only to keep her safe."

"I'm innocent," Charlie said.

"You can't even answer why you married her," Benton said. "Don't think that goes unnoticed."

"Charlie," she shook her head, her back still to the room. "He's not the enemy."

"No," Benton said. "In fact, I might be the only thing standing between you and jail." Benton stood, leaned his palms on the table, and leveled a no-bullshit glare on Charlie. "I'd like an answer, please. Why did you marry Deming yesterday?"

It was complicated, especially since the question implied Charlie was using Cynthia as a shield. Just posing the question wounded his pride, but it was a grievance best left to resolve after the real unsub was found. Then Benton could eat crow, when, ironically, he and Cynthia no longer needed to be married.

Charlie shrugged. "I love her." Cynthia's shoulders shook, as if she were silently sobbing.

"Oh, *Charlie.*" She glanced at him over her shoulder. He stood, held out his arms, and felt his heart swell when she raced into his embrace. "I love you, *too.*" Then she was squeezing him as if to give him strength, or maybe because she was that afraid. Hiding her face against his chest, she sobbed. Charlie felt sucker punched. She loved him, too. She could mean many types of love, but at that moment, he needed to believe she meant it the way he'd meant it. He was in love with her. If she meant something else... Well, he'd fix that later, when he wasn't trying to keep them both out of jail.

Chapter Eleven

Cynthia felt the tension in Charlie's body the moment she embraced him. He was taut, and upset in a way he hadn't been even when Benton was accusing him of being a murderer. She'd seen his face, knew her words of love had shocked him, and now, mortified beyond all belief, she had to find a way to move past this humiliating moment. But she couldn't stop crying!

For an unforgivably obtuse moment, Cynthia forgot that Charlie was playing a role!

His "love" went along with their "marriage." She knew Charlie had to be desperate, if not horrified, that she'd put him in this untenable position. He was covering for her, hiding that she was at the crime scene.

Charlie would *never* hurt her on purpose. Never.

She'd confessed her love for him, and he'd seized up, stiff as a board. If that didn't answer her question about his feelings, nothing would. She cringed to think of what he'd do to smooth things over with her later. It's not as if Charlie was fully armed when it came to navigating social situations. Would he melt, act lovey-dovey, thinking that's what she'd want? Ugh.

Time to put her big girl pants on. None of this mattered.

She loved Charlie. This case was going to kill her career. She might as well save her relationship with Charlie. It might be all she had left afterward. Sniffing, brutally shutting down her tears, Cynthia pulled from Charlie's embrace, grabbed his hand, and squeezed to signal she was on his side.

"Benton," she said, "all you have is a snitch's accusation." Charlie squeezed her hand back, but it felt as if he were cautioning her. "If your snitch was credible, we wouldn't be standing here. Charlie would be in handcuffs, being led to holding. In fact, I'll go out on a limb here"—she used the back of her hand to wipe a tear that spilled past her lashes—"and say you don't trust your snitch." Benton's gaze flickered, telling Cynthia her instincts had been spot on, and her relief was incalculable. "We're leaving." Cynthia tugged on Charlie's hand. He didn't move at first, but instead looked between her and Benton, calculating if leaving was a good idea. Finally, after a long pause, he nodded and led the way to the door.

"Cynthia!" Benton barked out her name. When she paused and turned, Charlie did also. Benton looked at the camera affixed to the ceiling and used his fingers to make a slashing motion to his neck. He continued to stare at the camera until the red light flickered out. "Just so we're clear," he said, his tone low, at almost a whisper, "I am not releasing Charlie because I don't have probable cause to hold him. I'm protecting the Coppola case. Charlie was the bureau's expert witness. If it gets out the forensic pathologist we used to prosecute the Coppola case is now the prime suspect for the deaths of these witnesses, Dante Coppola's conviction can be overturned. The bastard can file a petition for mistrial, and will, in a heartbeat. He'll receive *at least* a retrial, as will any defendant from any case that Charlie touched. This is bigger than Charlie, Deming. You have to see that."

Cynthia shook her head. "No. I don't. All I have to see is Charlie. Something else you never knew about me."

"Deming—" Benton snapped her name out, as if he wasn't done.

"The prosecutor has to assume his culpability. I don't." She almost mentioned spousal privilege, and that it meant she didn't even have to *talk* to Benton about Charlie, but she feared solidifying his suspicions that she and Charlie had married because of the murders.

"Benton," Charlie said. "Does it occur to you that I wouldn't want all the cases of my career to be challenged? It's not just the bureau and the FBI that will be affected. My life's work will be ruined. Keep that in mind when you're looking for a motive."

"Hmm." Benton didn't seem convinced, and that panicked Cynthia even more. "I'm thinking a man willing to kill six people for a million dollars might not value the legacy of his day job." Benton might not want Charlie to be guilty, but he was telling them he wasn't ruling it out.

"Consider this my official request to take time off for a honeymoon." It stopped Benton from putting her on administrative leave. "You need me, call me, but if it's about Charlie, call his lawyer. I'll email you his contact information." *When she found a lawyer.*

Cynthia and Charlie left the interrogation room. She quickly grabbed her pocketbook from the incident room, avoiding her fellow agents' gazes, hoping to just leave. Gilroy, Modena, and Benton hovered, a gauntlet of detectives that she and Charlie had to walk by.

"Deming?" Modena said. "You want to wait to settle that bet?"

The marriage bet. He was asking her if she had any hesitation about whether Charlie was guilty. "Nope," she said. "Expect the money on your desk when I get back." Modena nodded, his brow furrowed, his green eyes bright with concern.

Vivian O'Grady stepped to Gilroy's side. "Call me if you need me," she said. Cynthia nodded to the IT tech but couldn't hold her gaze, because Vivian's tears were threatening to make Cynthia cry again.

"When the subpoenas are issued," Benton said, "it won't take more than an hour to have our answers." He followed them out into the hall, hounding their steps.

Charlie stopped walking, and turned so abruptly that Cynthia stumbled against his side. "Do what you've got to do, and do it fast, because you're wasting time. The real unsub is out there, and it isn't me. Tell my techs—" He paused, as if he had no idea what to say.

Cynthia took pity on him. "Tell Kevin and Teresa that Charlie is on his honeymoon. We'll be at his house or mine, but call first. We'll be busy." Her smile was tight, and she didn't feel any pity for Benton, Modena, and Gilroy's embarrassment. Vivian, however, smiled.

"Enjoy!" Vivian said, her hand pressed to the silk bow at her throat.

When they reached the elevator and stepped onto it, Cynthia leaned heavily against the inside wall. "Honestly," she said, "I didn't think they'd let you leave, but then again, after almost two years of struggles to put Dante Coppola behind bars, Benton's not excited about allowing your conviction to ruin all that work. I suspect he'll be a good ally. It's in his best interest." She hoped she was right, because Benton would also follow the evidence and the letter of the law.

Charlie pressed the button for the ground floor. "We were right to get married."

She swallowed hard past the lump that suddenly appeared in her throat. It was hard to be reminded that their marriage served a purpose other than the best sex she'd ever had in her life, but Charlie's reminder was necessary. If it had come sooner, she might not have gushed with such enthusiasm in the interrogation room. Now she looked like a fool.

"Masterful strategizing." Desperate to salvage her pride, she masked her embarrassment best she could, hiding her sweaty palms in her suit jacket pockets. "That whole 'I love her' moment in the interrogation room? Even I bought it."

Charlie focused sharply on her face. Anger radiated from him, from his stance to his glare, and she didn't blame him. Her words were indelicate, especially after declaring her love in that nakedly emotional manner. He must be embarrassed. She wished she was a better steward of his feelings.

"Of course, they 'bought' it," Charlie snapped. His phone buzzed in his pocket, distracting him. "A text from my mother," he said. "Our engagement made the local news. She's going to be upset when she discovers we didn't invite her to our wedding."

Her heart stuttered. His remark seemed so…normal. It forced her to swallow the lump in her throat before speaking. "The engagement made the news, but not in relation to the murders, right?" He nodded, and then the elevator doors opened and they stepped into the precinct lobby. They were in his car before Charlie spoke again.

"We're kind of screwed from here and back again," he said.

She tucked her bag into the back. "Yup." Didn't need to ask what prompted that assessment. The list was long, but knowing Charlie, it probably had something to do with his parents not being invited to the wedding.

He still hadn't started the car. Sitting there, staring out at passersby on the sidewalk, the traffic paused at the streetlight ahead, Charlie gripped the wheel as if it had offended him, but made no move to put the car into gear and drive.

"Our access to the investigation is over," he said. "We're at the mercy of Benton, the team—"

"And the killer."

He looked at her, studied her eyes, and then nodded once. "Yeah." He started the car and merged into traffic.

"I trust Benton and the team. You do, too. We haven't lied. We haven't killed anyone. I say we're in a good place."

He widened his eyes, looking as if he wanted to argue, but didn't. "I have to feed Socks. My parents are meeting us at my place for lunch." She sank in the seat, groaning. "I know you said you didn't want my grandmother's emerald, but mom said she was bringing it, and the matching wedding ring. Will you wear it?" He glanced at her, and then turned his focus back onto the road. His expression remained devoid of emotion.

"Of course." She used her thumb to press the oversized MIT ring against her finger. "The rings are…they're beautiful. I'd be honored to wear them…for however long…." She felt emotion welling in her throat and couldn't finish her sentence. Damn. She just needed to shut up. Every time she opened her mouth something more and more stupid popped out.

Charlie nodded, frowning, and they spent the rest of the drive silent. When he pulled up to the curb outside his house, she caught him glancing at her, probably gauging her reaction to his parents' car parked out front. They were here already.

He shifted into park, took the key out of the ignition, but didn't move to leave the car. She figured he wanted to talk, get their stories straight. They were about to stand in front of his parents, after all, and tell a bald-faced lie, which they had to sell.

"Listen," Cynthia said. She squeezed his thigh. "I know our world is blowing up. I know we don't know what tomorrow will bring, but *please*—" She tilted her head, seeking his gaze. His parents had to believe they were madly in love or she'd be mortified. "Don't..." She didn't know how to say 'don't make your parents feel sorry for me.'

He frowned. "Don't worry, Cynthia. It's just my parents." Then he got out of the car.

Pasting a fake smile on her face, she slung her bag over her elbow and hurried to catch up with him. She didn't want to be so far behind Charlie that it caused further questions from his parents. They were supposed to be in love, dammit! He should be all over her.

This marriage had been Charlie's idea. If he left her hanging—

His front door was flung open, and Mrs. Delia Foulkes greeted them with open arms. A tiny woman, wearing jeans and a striped jersey shirt, she hugged her son the moment he stepped into the foyer. The difference in their sizes was notable. Charlie seemed the adult, and Delia the child. Her husband, Paul, so like his son, was burly and grizzled. His red and gray hair was neatly clipped, combed, and he was clean shaven, every inch the Norman Rockwell father of old. He was smiling, his eyes revealing familiar delight as Cynthia approached. He spread his arms wide and waited impatiently for her to enter his embrace. She did so with enthusiasm.

"You're engaged! I can't believe it," Paul Foulkes said.

"Married, Dad." Charlie smiled. And he *seemed* authentically happy, announcing to his parents that he'd withheld the experience of attending their only child's wedding...a once in a lifetime experience. His parents reacted predictably. At first, their smiles collapsed, and Cynthia saw their hurt, but then they rallied quickly and were all smiles again. Cynthia launched herself at Charlie's mom, hugging her, her cheeks cramped from forcing her smile.

"It happened quickly. Don't be mad," she whispered.

Delia held on tightly. "Sweetheart, don't be silly. We couldn't be happier. Tell her, Paul."

Paul hitched his jeans up and rolled his shoulders, making his floral print shirt sit more comfortably around his large frame. It was such a

Charlie mannerism that Cynthia couldn't help but smile. "What she said," Paul said, laughing.

The Foulkes weren't stupid. They knew how complicated her and Charlie's relationship was, and had to know this revelation was unexpected on many levels. Mostly because never once did either she or Charlie indicate they were anything more than friends.

"I have to feed Socks," Charlie said. "Come into the kitchen, will you?"

They all moved down the hall, through the living room, and into the eat-in kitchen. Charlie's father opened one of the windows and sat next to it at the table, batting the yellow checkered drapes away as the breeze pressed the material against his arm.

"I'd love a cup of tea. What about you, Paul?" Delia glanced at her husband before putting on the kettle. Charlie grabbed a can of cat food from a shelf, and as soon as the automatic can opener buzzed, Socks wandered into the kitchen. "A cat *and* a wife." Delia chuckled. "Charlie, those are two things I never thought you'd ever take the time to find." She pulled down her favorite blue mug from his cupboard as Charlie spooned cat food into Sock's dish. "Which came first?" She winked at Cynthia before choosing a teabag from a glass jar on the counter.

Cynthia sat across the table from Paul Foulkes, fighting a case of the nerves. This moment seemed surreal, an alternative universe, because in her world, she and Charlie were in trouble with the law, their marriage under scrutiny by Benton, and here they were, having tea with his parents, feeding the cat, when what they really should have been doing was studying countries with no extradition treaties with the U.S.

"Socks came first," Charlie said. "Because it took an inordinate amount of time to convince Cynthia I was husband material." Charlie rinsed out the can before tossing it into the recycle bin. "Do you have the rings?"

His father nodded and reached into his pants pocket. "You betcha I do. This is very exciting."

Charlie dried his hands on a dishtowel as he approached her. She saw Paul place the old ring box on the table, and suddenly it was hard to breathe and her vision grew blurry. The ring box was worn green velvet, looked old as dirt and well loved. The antique emerald ring and matching wedding ring with tiny diamond clusters inside that box had been in the Foulkes family for ages. It was the most valuable thing the family owned, and now, Charlie was giving it to Cynthia. For a "kind of" marriage. She feared fainting was a possibility, until she thought, *This was Charlie's idea.* As soon as the thought hit her brain synapses, it spilled from her lips.

"This was Charlie's idea." She forced a smile to soften the stridency of her tone.

Charlie picked up the ring box, gave it a little toss, and caught it. Then he narrowed his eyes as he hovered over Cynthia, watching her. "I take full credit," he said, then dropped to one knee.

Face to face, Cynthia studied his features, and to her horror didn't have a clue about what was going on in his head. Charlie was usually so... predictable. He had simple tastes, simple needs: no drama, good food, and challenging work. Charlie, on his knee, three people staring at him, had never been more unpredictable. Intensity radiated off his body; his gaze danced between anger and recklessness. As he stared at her, he kept squeezing that damn ring box, like he wanted to throw it.

And his parents were noticing.

Cynthia brightened her smile and did her best to give Charlie cover. "He gave me his MIT ring as an engagement ring, and as much as I'll miss it, I confess I'm a bit relieved to replace it. It kept slipping off."

Delia nodded. "That ring is too big for you. The emerald is more appropriate. I had it sized this morning, so it should fit. Charlie, honey, what are you waiting for? The floor can't be all that comfortable. Do you want us to leave the room?"

"We missed your wedding," Paul said. "The least you can do is allow us to see you put the ring on her finger."

Charlie opened the ring box with a snap and showed the rings to Cynthia. His eyes were still intense, but watchful now. Delia clasped her hands and stepped to her husband's side, resting her hand on the back of his chair. Paul's arm slid around his wife's waist as he watched his son present the rings to his bride. Tears welled in her eyes, despite her attempts to be stone cold. When she blinked past them, she saw Charlie was smiling as he took the rings from the box.

"'Til death do us part, Cynthia Deming Foulkes," he whispered, sliding the rings on her finger.

Cynthia took his MIT ring and slid it onto his left ring finger. "'Til death do us part, Charlie Foulkes." For her part, she thought Charlie deserved an Academy Award. He sold it.

Delia clapped, bouncing on the balls of her feet. Then she grabbed her husband's cheeks and pressed a quick kiss to his lips. Then Paul stood, his arm around his wife, and nodded a few times, watching Charlie and Cynthia.

The kettle screamed.

Charlie stood, pulled Cynthia to her feet, and embraced her. His kiss was quick, and then he was pressing his lips to her ear. "Hold it together," he whispered. "Confessing all will only implicate my parents in this mess."

She nodded quickly, sniffing, forcing her smile to relax and be more natural. Charlie was right. She and he were radioactive, and all they could do now was quarantine themselves and hope for the best. This show for his parents was necessary, and if it scourged her soul a bit, it was worth the price.

The Foulkes left after lunch, and without a word Charlie hurried into his study. Curious, Cynthia followed, hoping he wasn't avoiding her. The room's walls were lined with bookcases filled with textbooks, reference material, and Stephen King novels. They surrounded his large wooden desk, big enough to accommodate Charlie's size. The desk sat in front of the lone window in the room, whose blinds were closed. He sat, moving the wireless mouse until his laptop lit up. It had been in sleep mode.

"Subpoenas take time, and I don't want to be taken by surprise," Charlie said.

"You want to see if that million-dollar deposit is really in your account," she said.

"If it is, Benton will arrest me."

"He'll have no choice," she said, peering over his shoulder. Charlie clicked on his bank's app, and his obscured password immediately showed under the log-in information. Charlie clicked "log in" and gained immediate access to his accounts. "Well, shit, Charlie. That's stupid. Never put your bank password on autofill." The screen showed his accounts, and even without clicking on his checking account, Cynthia saw the balance. There was over a million dollars in that account. "I'm going to assume you don't usually keep well over a million dollars in your checking account."

"And your assumption would be correct." He clicked on the account, and the list of transactions filled the screen.

"Whoever broke in and stole your gun had instant access to your bank account through your laptop. You leave it on sleep, and you have your log-in information autofilled. You need a keeper."

"I already have a wife." He winked, then turned back to the screen. "How was I supposed to anticipate that someone would break into my house and transfer a million dollars *into* my account?" He dropped his hand, leaning back into his office chair.

"Up. Get up. I want to look at something," Cynthia said.

He stood and stepped away from the desk, giving her access to the monitor and keyboard. "And I certainly couldn't predict someone would frame me for murder."

Cynthia sat, grabbing the wireless mouse and clicking on the deposit information. "Shit. Will you look at that? Just like Benton said. It was deposited the day before the murders." The screen froze, and a banner flashed. Cynthia pushed away from the computer, throwing her hands up. "I didn't do anything! Don't blame me!"

Charlie leaned over the desk. "This isn't you. They've frozen my accounts. One guess who's behind that."

She leaned back in the chair, covering her mouth. "What the hell can we do?" Her words were muffled, but she could tell he heard her.

He shook his head, leaning against his desk. "I don't know. It's as if whoever is behind this knew exactly how to tie our hands. We have no access to the evidence, the databases, the files." He leaned his head back, staring at the ceiling, then closed his eyes. "Now, my money. I'm beginning to second-guess our marriage. I should have predicted this."

Cynthia held her left hand out, admiring the engagement and wedding ring. "I should have stepped up and told Benton what I remembered, how I was there." She licked her lower lip. "I should do it now."

He pinned her with his stare. "He'll arrest us both immediately. We've bought time, and right now only I'm at risk." Then he folded his arms over his chest. "I'm sorry, Cynthia. I never should have married you. You'd still be working the case if we hadn't married. I was trying to keep you safe, and I'm so sorry it's backfiring this way."

A million things popped into Cynthia's head, and she didn't have the courage to say any of them. She settled on something that wouldn't make any waves. "You're not getting rid of me that easily. I've got the rings, I've got the paper, and the marriage is already consummated."

He chuckled, then tugged her onto her feet, into his arms. "Yeah? You remember that? It seems like forever ago." She stood on tiptoes and wrapped her arms around his neck, melting against him. He pressed his face into her hair, close to her laceration, and the pain made her flinch.

Just like that…she remembered.

"Cynthia?" Charlie had noticed her reaction, and tilted her chin up to study her face. "What?"

"Oh, Charlie." Her chin quivered. "It's worse than we thought."

Chapter Twelve

"Worse?" he said. It was near impossible for the truth to be worse than what he'd feared. "Talk to me." Cynthia was hyperventilating.

"I was leaving the gym." Breathless, she swallowed hard. "I'd stayed longer than expected."

"You sparred with Sergeant O'Neil. Did he hit you on the head?"

"No." She shook her head dismissively, shaking off his hands. "No. I parked a few blocks down, next to the safe house, because there was no parking near the gym."

"Which explains why your car was there." She didn't seem to hear him as she clutched his waist.

"I remember putting my gear bag in the car, and I called you for some reason. I can't remember why." She bit her lip, and then pushed away from him, pacing the small office. "Yeah. I did. I did call you, but then—" She stopped, covering her eyes. "I heard screams. Male screams from down the street." She shook her head, dropping her hands. "It was horrible." Sniffing, she grimaced. "I… I dropped the phone in my bag, grabbed my gun, and—" She wiped a stray tear, talking fast. "I slammed the car door and ran toward the screams."

"To the crime scene."

"Yes." Her frown deepened. "They were kneeling in front of the brick wall, right where we found them. The streets were empty. The area was in shadow, just outside of the streetlight's reach. I was running, down the street. It was too quiet, except—" She covered her mouth, so all he saw were her eyes, revealing fear.

"What the hell were you doing running toward an active crime scene without backup?"

"My phone died. I thought I'd catch someone's attention along the way. Have them call it in. What was I supposed to do? Ignore it? But there was no one on the streets. No one."

He pulled her into his arms, feeling helpless. "Tell me what happened."

"I saw them. They were alive. I don't remember seeing anyone else."

"Doesn't mean the killer wasn't there," Charlie said.

She tilted her head to look at him. "I didn't see anyone. I don't know who killed them. I never saw anyone." He wiped a tear, and then gave her a squeeze. "Then I tripped." She touched the back of her head, glancing at him. "No. I remember being hit from behind." She sighed, draping herself against his chest.

"Do you remember hearing gunshots?" he said. She shook her head. "Then the kills happened when you were unconscious."

"When I woke at the crime scene, they were dead, and I still had my gun. It had been used; I could smell it." She grimaced. "My pocketbook and my phone were in the car, so I still couldn't call it in. The vics were dead, so I left, more afraid of contaminating the crime scene than anything else. I was walking back to the car, and felt faint. I knew I couldn't drive. I remember heading toward the safe house, climbing the stairs, and then it gets fuzzy. I don't know how I managed to find a bed to pass out on, but I did. I don't know why I didn't call anyone."

"We might never know. It's a miracle you survived," he said. "Your DNA is at the crime scene and will be processed with the rest of the samples. If your gun casings are there, too, with your prints, they'll request a DNA sample." Her lips tightened, and she nodded. "The connection will be made, and you'll be implicated."

"If I'd only managed to stay conscious just a little longer, I might have called Benton, and we wouldn't be in this situation."

"I don't know about that," he said. "Your gun was discharged. The killer allowed you to live for a reason. Those seem to be two bombs that haven't gone off yet. Odds are the next call Benton receives from an anonymous source will cause him to call you in for questioning."

She rubbed her face, clearly shaken up. "Who shot my gun?"

"A better question is, when will the safe house techs discover you were the culprit that deleted video?"

Her forehead thumped onto his chest, and her fingers bit into his waist. "Charlie, I look guilty as sin." He nodded, but she couldn't see him agreeing, so he didn't feel bad about being brutally honest.

"Our unsub knew you were there," he said. "He knew you. Didn't kill you." She nodded. "We have to assume they thought better of killing an FBI special agent."

Cynthia grimaced, shaking her head. "They thought of a way to use me."

"What's the odds the killer is our anonymous source?" Charlie said.

"You're the math guy. You tell me." She lifted her brows, sniffing. "Got a plan?"

"My last plan isn't working out so well," he said.

Cynthia's gaze softened, and the look in her eyes made his heart swell. "It was a fine plan," she said. He kissed her, and didn't stop kissing her until she was wiggling in his arms, arching toward him.

"I want to make love to you, Cynthia." His heart was pounding, and his fingers were inching to strip her bare as she wrapped her arms around his neck, pulling him close.

"I want you to make love to me, Charlie."

This is it, he thought. His chance to have it out with her finally about how their relationship was about more than simply loyalty and friendship. She *loved* him. Really loved him. It was time for her to admit it.

"Cynthia?" He'd just blurt it out and hope for the best. If his declaration of love made her run for the hills, well… He'd do what it took to change her mind.

"Yes?" Her eyes were round, barely focused as she stared at his lips, nipping at them, luring him into kissing her again. "Charlie?" The phone rang. "Crap." She pulled the phone from her suit jacket pocket, and then exchanged glances with Charlie. "Benton."

He nodded and loosened his grip, stepping back. "Answer it."

Inhaling sharply, she visibly steeled herself before accepting the call. "So, found the unsub yet?" She listened, her stricken expression at odds with her cavalier tone of voice. "Well, what's taking you so long?" Cynthia turned her back on Charlie but leaned against him, pulling his arms around her waist as she adjusted the phone so he could hear what Benton was saying.

"…warrant for Charlie's bank statements was denied due to lack of evidence," Benton said, "but we're still digging. With enough culpable evidence, the judge will relent. Try to convince Charlie to release his bank statements, please. He's being stubborn, and I'm positive the more cooperative he is, the quicker we can clear this up and direct the team's attention back toward the real killer. You should already know this, Deming. You're allowing your feelings for Charlie to cloud your judgment."

"Sue me," she snapped.

"Don't tempt me. The longer he waits to give his accounts up, the guiltier he looks. Tell him," Benton said. "He'll listen to you."

"I'll think about it," Cynthia said, but Charlie knew she was simply stalling. They both knew what was in his account ledger: an incriminating million dollars. "I'm on my honeymoon, however, so I can't promise anything."

There was silence on the line for so long Cynthia was soon biting her lower lip. She glanced over her shoulder at Charlie, but he had no idea what the silence meant, either. She's the one that knew Benton well.

"Understood." Benton hung up. Cynthia's shoulders sagged and she leaned against Charlie as if her legs were about to buckle.

"I can't take much more of this," she said.

Charlie thought about Benton's words, then smiled. "I think we just got good news."

Cynthia turned in his arms and embraced him. "Don't trust it."

"We have a reprieve," he said. "I'm not in jail, and you don't have to check in with the boss."

"Hmm." She smiled. "In a perfect world, I'd say take me to bed, lover."

He smiled, seriously considering her idea. "We could make the world perfect."

"Or," she said, tilting her head to the side, studying his expression. Then she left his arms and rushed out of the room. Charlie caught up with her in the living room, in front of the television. Remote in hand, she was watching the local news, and reports of the Chinatown Massacre were on every channel. "I think we need to see one of the scariest people I've ever met."

He folded his arms over his chest, watching her rather than the news. "If it's an either-or, I vote for stripping naked and having sex." When she ignored him and instead frowned at the television, he sighed and collapsed onto the upholstered chair next to his couch. It gave him a bird's eye view of another pile of Socks's plunder. Dropping on hands and knees, he peered into the corner, under the television. A black magic marker, a stuffed cat toy mouse, a tiny, shiny purple flower charm, and a pair of sunglasses. Another cache of Socks's stolen booty.

"Huh? What did you say?" She was now frowning, arms akimbo, the remote forgotten in her hand. "Why are you on your hands and knees? Aren't you even curious to know who I think we need to interview?"

"You want to interview Dante Coppola," he said, peering under the television stand. "The Coppola syndicate crime lord. Am I right?" He glanced at her to see her nod. "My idea is better."

"What idea?"

He swept his hand under the stand and pulled out more items from under it. "We make glorious, hot, sweaty love, as I..." Tell her how much he loved her. *Damn.* As if she'd be capable of focusing on anything but her desire to interview Coppola and save their careers, their freedom. Nope. Long, drowsy kisses, and multiple orgasms would have to wait.

"As you what?" Now he had her attention.

Charlie sat, the pile of Socks's booty at his side. "Let's put a pin in my idea. I'm thinking our anonymous source might be getting as antsy as we are, and might decide to drop a bomb before we're able to fly to Florida and back."

"That's what I'm thinking, too," she said.

"Might as well go down swinging." He hopped up from the floor. "Do me a favor? My arm isn't small enough to reach all the way under there. I've got most of it, but I can't get the last bit."

Her lip curled with distaste. "It better not be dead, whatever it is."

"Cats are supposed to kill mice. It's what they do, but whatever this is, it's not dead or alive." He sat on the floor, indicating under the television with a flick of his fingers.

She grimaced and bent, crawling on her hands and knees until she was close enough to lay flat and retrieve the pile. "This is getting old."

"I've had her for over a week now, and it's just getting worse." He was no better at understanding cats than he was understanding women. "I think I need a cat whisperer."

"Hmm," Cynthia said, handing over a sock, sunglasses, and a desiccated baby carrot. "Gross."

He shrugged, slipping the sunglasses into his pocket and gathering up the other items. He placed them on the side table. "Will the FPC warden allow us to see Coppola?"

"It's a minimum-security federal prison camp. I'm listed as one of the arresting agents, so I have jurisdiction."

Charlie arched a brow. "Club Fed. Should I bring a bathing suit?"

"Do you own a bathing suit?"

Now that he thought about it... "No."

She dusted her hands off and allowed Charlie to help her to her feet. "We lean on him, see what happens. Couldn't hurt."

"Sure it can. Florida is out of state." She averted her gaze, as if that changed the fact that what she'd proposed could land them in jail. "Benton will find out, and when he discovers we're interviewing Coppola, he'll label us flight risks. Best case scenario, he'll see our visit as obstruction of justice."

"Or conspiracy. I know," she said. "Hopefully by the time he hears anything he'll be thanking us, because we'll have a lead." Her expression told him even she knew that outcome was a long shot.

"Since when did you start believing in fairy tales?"

"You think too much," she said. She grabbed her purse and left the living room, leaving him to turn off the television.

He gathered up the marker and the purple charm, tossed the toy mouse back on the floor, and followed her out into the hall and into the kitchen. The other Socks plunder remained on the counter where he'd left it earlier. Charlie added this stuff to the pile, putting the purple flower charm next to the purple heart charm. Pieces of a set? He supposed they could be his mother's…. Charlie took a picture and texted it to Delia before turning his attention back to the growing pile. He was worried about Socks, who was weaving his way around Charlie's ankles. Every time Charlie attempted to pet the cat, Socks ran away, only to come back and rub against his legs again.

"Cynthia, did I ever tell you that Socks reminds me of you?" Cynthia didn't answer. When he looked up, he noticed she'd left the kitchen. "What do you think, Socks? Do you think she'll keep us?" The cat wandered away, not deigning to answer, or maybe Socks didn't know either.

Chapter Thirteen

Charlie was a rules guy, and as a Quantico-trained investigator, Cynthia admired that, but it meant he was less than comfortable going rogue. Charlie being Charlie, he supported her efforts anyway. Didn't mean he liked it, or liked crossing state lines and interviewing a man linked to a murder case that was implicating him. They were inviting a ton of blowback, so flying to Florida was a stupid move. That was a given. *Especially* since any investigation involving the Coppola syndicate put Dante Coppola on the top of a short list of suspects. So, in effect, two prime suspects speaking privately…collusion, anyone? Or worse, conspiracy. The optics were bad.

She knew it, but felt they didn't have much choice. Waiting around for the other shoe to drop wasn't her style, and if one more person impugned Charlie's integrity, Cynthia feared another cold-cocking incident. Benton's treatment of Charlie had been the final straw, flipping her between furious and afraid and back again whenever she replayed the interview in her head. *As if* Charlie could murder six WITSEC witnesses. For money he didn't need? Did Cynthia believe Benton was sold on Charlie's culpability? No. In fact, she believed Benton didn't *want* to believe it, but he had to follow the evidence, so that meant Cynthia had to fight back. With Florida. She needed to redirect Benton's attention to where the true evidence pointed… with a little help from Dante Coppola.

It took them just under five hours to fly from Boston's Logan Airport to Pensacola International. Soon she and Charlie were flashing their credentials at security personnel to gain admittance to Federal Prison Camp (FPC) Pensacola, Florida. It was a minimum-security facility, low staff-to-inmate ratio, with dormitory housing. More Sandals resort than *Orange Is the New Black*. The limited perimeter fencing screamed third-world luxury, not corrections department. Even so, it was a legitimate work- and program-oriented prison, with inmates who were allowed "approved" visitors. It was Friday, 7:00 PM, *within* visiting hours, so she and Charlie avoided an awkward petition to the warden that would have triggered Benton being notified otherwise. FBI credentials and a call to the appropriate correctional counselor (CC) was all it took to be included on the visitor's log. The visit was approved by the time Charlie drove the rented Camry onto the FPC's grounds.

Entering the main complex, parking, nodding to armed guards in khakis and polo shirts as they walked by, Cynthia found it hard to hide her roiling stress. Charlie kept close, the picture of an affable, if a bit bored, "partner." She knew it had to be an act, because if Charlie was framed and convicted, he wouldn't land in a Club Fed. He'd do hard time amidst a prison population that would know he'd spent his career putting people like them in jail. How could he not be stressed?

She ran her thumb along the edges of her wedding rings like they were worry stones and scanned the grounds, taking note of the multiple security look-out towers to their left and right. Yesterday, they'd joked about going on the lam, but this place was no joke. The evidence against Charlie had accumulated past the point where spousal privilege would tilt the balance for or against a conviction. Posh though this FPC was, it clarified a few things for Cynthia.

Nothing was off the table if it stopped Charlie going to jail.

And if that included knocking him over the head to get her way and hauling Charlie's ass to a non-extraditing country, so be it. Some asshole thought he could frame Charlie and use their lives as chess pieces in some fucked up machination? Unacceptable. Cynthia had…a future still nebulous in detail, but it was hers, and she wanted Charlie in it. She didn't share this red-line-that-could-not-be-crossed to Charlie, of course. They still had options to explore, but she'd made confidential calls on a burner phone to her investment manager and sent preliminary, non-traceable texts to contacts out of country. Cynthia had backup plans, and she was not playing.

They moved down the long walkway bisecting the two fenced-in outdoor grounds. Every guard seemed to be staring, curious or bored. A dark haired, buzzed cut young guard opened the entry door, and then she and Charlie stepped through into a fluorescent-lit foyer. It was bare, shining white tile, white walls, with a visiting room security booth ahead. She and Charlie exchanged glances, and he gave her a perfunctory grin and wink before they approached the booth and flashed their credentials. The guard was female, mid-thirties, with short, curly hair and an imp-like face. She wore a Kevlar vest over her tan uniform, was armed, and seemed deadly serious as she studied their credentials, matching the photos to their faces.

Experience had her leaving her pocketbook in the car to streamline vetting. Now she only needed to surrender weapons through the slot in the Plexiglas window, and her expensive Kate Spade would remain safe from rough searching hands. Last time, it cost her a bundle to repair their mistreatment of its delicate lining. Unsheathing her ankle and belt knife, she passed them and her gun in through the slot and watched as the guard logged them and moved them into a bin on the wall in the back.

"Special Agent Deming. Dr. Foulkes." The guard nodded.

"We're here to see Dante Coppola," Cynthia said. "You should have the paperwork and approvals already."

The guard consulted a computer monitor to her right, and then nodded, returning their credentials through the slot. "Before you enter, protocol requires a pat down, so if you have any other weapons on your person, please relinquish them." She looked at Charlie in particular, since he hadn't handed any weapons over.

Charlie shook his head. "Nothing."

Two burly corrections officers, men as tall as Charlie, wearing Kevlar vests and side arms, approached. If their sizes didn't intimidate, watching them snap on latex gloves and their surly attitudes would. The pat down was thorough, and ended with an even more thorough metal detector wand sweep. Afterward, forms were signed, log entries updated, and then they were led through metal doors to the left. The curly-headed guard who had originally processed them into the building met them on the other side of the doors. She seemed less intense now that they'd passed screening. She was even smiling.

"I'm Officer Bentley," she said. "Mr. Coppola already has a scheduled visitor. We weren't sure when you'd arrive, so we didn't cancel on her," she said. They walked down the gray-carpeted hall, passing multiple closed white metal doors.

"Her?" Cynthia said.

"His new wife." Bentley lifted her brows, and gave the impression she had lots to say on the subject, but wouldn't. "Today is her normally scheduled visit. Now that you're here, we'll cut it short."

"Angelina Modelli." Cynthia said.

"Angelina Modelli *Coppola* now." Bentley nodded.

Charlie frowned. "Isn't she the one that—" Whatever he saw on Cynthia's expression had him rethinking his words. "A known Coppola syndicate contract killer," Charlie said. "Since when did this FSC become married housing?"

"She isn't housed here, or in jail at all. She turned snitch," Bentley said. "Negotiated a hush-hush deal with the bureau recently. That's all I know about it." Charlie glanced at Cynthia, as if looking for clarification. Cynthia shook her head, not wanting to get into specifics with Bentley around.

Bentley pulled a ring of key cards off her utility belt as they continued down the hall.

"Technically," Cynthia said, "she's out on bail for assault." That was public record, and something Bentley, if not Charlie, would already know about.

They had Modelli pinned on those assault charges and were holding them over her head for leverage. That didn't mean they weren't pursuing murder one, though evidence was scarce for that more egregious charge. Witnesses against Coppola's new bride were either dead or not talking, so warrants, subpoenas, and surveillance requests were regularly denied by judges. But they still had the assault charges to keep her in the country, and her husband to keep her near Pensacola, Florida's FPC. Anyone who knew anything about the case knew Modelli had loved Coppola for nearly a decade. Obsessively. So she wasn't going anywhere, and though arguably just as much a monster as her husband, Modelli was busy, presumably kept out of trouble with her assault case, negotiating her deal with the FBI, and managing her husband's visitor schedule. No small beans. That meant Modelli was someone else's problem, which was a good thing, because Cynthia had bigger fish to fry...and her own husband to worry about.

Officer Bentley used a security card to gain access to the visiting room. The atmosphere felt relaxed inside, lots of chatter, very much Club Fed: white walls decorated with murals and paintings. There was even a vending machine against the back wall. At this moment, three kids were feeding it bills. Guards manned the room's corners, their expressions friendly, and fifteen round tables with plastic chairs sectioned off the visitors per inmate.

They were led to the farthest table in the room, where Dante Coppola, dressed in hunter green prison garb, leaned on his elbows, conferring with his wife. Cynthia had never seen Angelina's dark brown hair down. She now looked more like the "Lina" she was known as in syndicate circles rather than the "Modelli" that Cynthia saw when looking at the woman's mug shots. In those pictures, the ones stacked in her file, she always wore a black pantsuit, white open-collared shirt, and had her long, dark hair upswept into a serviceable bun. It was a uniform of sorts for the notorious Coppola contract killers, of which Modelli was "allegedly" a member, though no one on the FBI task force believed she deserved the presumption of innocence the "alleged" indicated. Too much anecdotal evidence to pretend otherwise.

Now, however, Lina seemed girly, wearing a tight black sheath dress, red stiletto heels, and lots of makeup. Large-boned, shapely, and muscular, Lina was taller than her husband, and outweighed him. From her expression, it was clear she loved him, worshipped the ground he walked on. From all appearances, however, Coppola seemed to take Lina's adoring glances for granted. Flagrantly arrogant, despite his fall from grace, the handsome ex-crime lord still wore his black hair slicked back as if he were holding court in his multimillion-dollar mansion's compound in Saddle River, New Jersey. Though he'd lost weight, and there were dark circles under his eyes, Coppola seemed much improved from when last Cynthia saw him: bleeding, whimpering in pain after his ex-wife, Avery Coppola, nearly killed him.

Bentley was right. The couple was real cozy. Lina's eyelashes were aflutter, and though Coppola's black eyes still had that dead fish quality about them, there was a hint of amusement in his smile. Apparently, this new marriage suited him. Psychopaths in love? Weirder things had happened, Cynthia supposed.

The three of them stepped up to the table. "We need to cut your visit short, Mrs. Coppola," Bentley said. "This is—"

Lina threw up her hand, palm facing Cynthia. "I know who she is." Other than a tightening of the skin around her eyes, Lina gave no indication that she was put out by the interruption. "I'll see you soon, my love," Lina said. Then she stood, rock steady in her super high heels, and bent at the waist, kissing Dante Coppola full on the mouth, lots of tongue and smacking noises. When she straightened again, Coppola was smiling at Officer Bentley as if he knew the corrections officer would be unsettled by the display. Cynthia watched the byplay and recognized it as pure Dante Coppola. The man lived to manipulate those around him.

Lina was making a big show of facing Cynthia, using her middle finger to fix her red lipstick line, but keeping her gaze averted. Then the woman grabbed her purse and walked to the exit, shimmying and rocking her hips with enough force to cripple a man if he happened to get in her way.

"She loves me," Coppola said, when the door closed behind his bride. "And she's afraid the bureau will stop us from seeing each other, so forgive her poor manners." He shrugged, as if to say, "What can you do?"

"And what about you?" Cynthia said. "Are you afraid the bureau will stand in the way of true love?"

Coppola chuckled, shaking his head. "She loves me, so she has something to lose. I didn't say I loved her. There is nothing I want that the FBI can give me." His eyes narrowed. "How is my lovely ex-wife?"

"Dead," Charlie said. Which wasn't true. Avery Toner Coppola was currently planning to wed Special Agent Vincent Modena, and she was ecstatically happy because she had been accepted into three engineering colleges in Boston. Cynthia knew for a fact that she was leaning toward MIT. "The obituary was in all the papers," Charlie said. Planted obits. She and her sister now lived under aliases with Modena.

"Dead, huh?" Coppola's cheek kicked up. "If my Avery was dead, I'd know it."

"Yeah?" Cynthia said. "How?"

He touched his green uniform shirt and clutched the material over his heart. "I'd feel it."

The man was obsessed with his ex-wife, and was lucky Avery didn't kill him when she'd had the chance. Didn't mean Cynthia didn't believe Coppola, because she had that kind of connection with Charlie. If he died first, Cynthia was positive she'd feel it, and knew it would probably feel as if a hole had been blasted through her heart. She felt the urge to mirror Coppola, and had to stop her hand from clutching her chest. She wanted to look at Charlie, but couldn't, because Coppola still held her gaze, searching, studying her response. Still clutching his uniform over his heart.

She wondered how he'd feel if she admitted Avery was happy, living her life, never thinking of him. Cynthia couldn't taunt him about it, as much as he deserved it. Not without compromising Avery, anyway, but she wanted to. Cynthia wanted to taunt Coppola something fierce, because he was proof that a connection that strong could easily be one-sided.

"Green is definitely your color." Cynthia sat at the table, across from him, well out of reach. Though she didn't think Coppola would attempt to harm her; it wasn't his style. Coppola hired people to do his dirty work. Cynthia's skin crawled when she got too near him. The man was a living, breathing monster.

"I want a cigarette, or this interview ends now." Coppola folded his hands on his lap.

Charlie sat next to Cynthia, looking his affable self. "I'll buy you a pack. No, I'll buy you a carton. You'll have it when we leave."

"What are you? Good cop?" Coppola chuckled, looking Charlie up and down. "I remember you." Cynthia supposed once someone met Charlie, it would be hard to forget him. His size, his coloring, his deep voice had a way of sticking with a person. When he sat in the witness box at Coppola's trial and put his considerable academic and professional weight behind the forensic evidence findings, and explained it to the jury in an understandable manner, everyone watching knew Charlie had put the final nail in Coppola's coffin.

Charlie nodded. "Charles Foulkes, BPD."

"The forensic expert." Coppola narrowed his eyes. "You were at my trial." He turned to Cynthia. "A special agent and a forensic expert walk into a prison in the sunny state of Florida. Sounds like the setup to a bad joke." He lifted his brows, not hiding his derision. "Miss me, did you?"

"Six of your men are dead," she said. Coppola didn't seem surprised, so Cynthia supposed Modelli had shared this syndicate-related gossip. All other avenues of inside information with syndicate associates had been cut off by the FBI to prevent Coppola from becoming puppet master while behind bars. Modelli's visits were okayed because Cynthia's own risk assessments suggested it was in Modelli's interest to keep her husband in jail. If he was free, the woman had to know there would be instant competition for her husband's affection, which was notoriously fickle.

"Only six?" Coppola projected boredom, but didn't attempt to sell it. Even though he was the one caught in a trap, he still acted like the cat playing with the snared mouse. Cynthia exchanged glances with Charlie, who seemed the image of patience. It reminded her to be cool, to not give anything away for free. To Coppola, information was currency, and she needed him to think he was bankrupt.

"You're in here," she said, "your syndicate gone, your power nonexistent. No one left to impress, really. Why bother with the hits? And who was stupid enough to take the contracts on spec? You don't have a dime."

"All true." Coppola nodded and caught Charlie's gaze, winking, his lips cracking a smile. "Special Agent Deming is practicing what is referred to in the biz as a 'leading question.'" He turned back to Cynthia, his smile fading. "I'm in jail. My deal with the feds requires me to cut all ties with past associates. I'm not the man you used to know, Special Agent. I'm humbled. They bus me to a nearby plant, where other inmates supervise my work and tell me what to do. Plebeians, the lot of them, and not one with a sense of humor."

"Working stiff, huh?" Cynthia studied Coppola, wondering why he'd bother to explain his day. He had a motive. Coppola wasn't a man who wasted his time, but then again, time was all he had left.

"It's pretty hairy work, actually. Hazardous materials at Pensacola NAS. Funny story." He chuckled. "My supervisor was a CEO for a major hedge fund before he was incarcerated. Very high maintenance, this man. Reminds me of myself. He runs his fiefdom like he's still on Wall Street and I'm his intern. He makes twelve cents an hour, just like the rest of us, so he's not doing it for the money." His eyes narrowed as he looked between her and Charlie. "He's doing it because it's his nature."

"Said the scorpion to the frog," Charlie said. Coppola laughed, nodding.

Cynthia frowned. "Your immunity covers past offenses. If we discover you're in any way involved in these six murders, you'll lose your deal. Withholding information could land you in Fairton Federal Prison, rubbing shoulders with New Jersey's finest."

"Which tells you all you need to know," Coppola said, the image of disgruntled.

Cynthia studied the man, his body language and expression, and couldn't see that he was lying. Didn't mean he wasn't. "I've been monitoring your visitor logs," she said, "and keep seeing familiar names."

"None are past syndicate associates." Coppola shrugged. "All vetted by my CC and signed off by the warden. Whom on the list do you have a problem with?"

She felt Charlie's sneaker nudge her foot. A glance told her Charlie didn't so much as flicker an eyelash, but she knew he was reminding her to be careful, that she was here for information, not to give it. Coppola's eyes narrowed, his speculation clearly on display.

"Six months of visits from New Jersey friends," she said, resting her elbows on the table. "If I were suspicious"—Coppola smiled—"I'd suspect you were arranging a reunion here in Florida. Are you? Maybe activating a pipeline to pull Coppola syndicate strings from behind bars?" It would explain six contract killers publicly murdered. It certainly reiterated the message that screwing with Coppola will get you dead. Were these murders a signal that Coppola was back in the game? It was a reasonable motive, and would be an easy sell for a jury.

Coppola's smile widened. "Catch me if you can."

"Look around," Charlie said, his tone flat and unemotional. "You're caught."

Cynthia saw a flash of anger slip past Coppola's projected nonchalance, and could have kissed Charlie. He'd succeeded in forcing the crime lord to reveal his first authentic emotion since they'd arrived.

"Once"—Coppola snapped his fingers, glaring at Charlie—"you wouldn't be so quick to speak to me that way. You'd be smarter. Know better." Coppola's inner monster was peeking out from behind his new worker bee persona. No one, least of all Cynthia, was surprised. This was the man she knew, who she'd devoted two years to putting behind bars.

"If you didn't arrange for the hits," Cynthia said, "who did?"

"I don't know. That's the truth." He seemed disgusted. "I'm in prison, minding my own damn business, so leave Lina and me alone."

Cynthia grimaced. "Maybe Lina will be more willing to talk than you, especially if we escalate her court date for assault. It's a slam dunk, Coppola. You know I can do that, right?" She lifted her brows, taunting him. "You think life sucks now? Try living it without conjugal visits."

"You're a bully, and you're wasting your time with us." Coppola's all-powerful crime lord persona diminished as his inner toddler took center stage. He still wore his crazy eyes, though. "I don't take a shit alone, so not incidentally, *I have an alibi*." He folded his arms over his chest. "*My* alibi is rock solid." Cynthia forced herself to not move, to not even flicker an eyelash. He was telling her something, and instinct told her it was important, and dangerous. Her heart was racing, and it was hard not to look at Charlie to see his reaction. To see if he'd picked up on it, too. *What was she thinking?* This was Charlie. He'd be no help. Was she imagining the triumphant look in Coppola's eyes? He didn't hide that he wanted to hurt her, and triumph would indicate he thought he had. "Cattle breeding cattle," Coppola said. "Is there any wonder why there's a 'one percent' in this world? It's because *we're* not cattle. We think, and we live accordingly."

"In prison." Charlie stood and glanced around the crowded room that seemed more church social than federal penitentiary. "Yeah. Cattle. Gotcha." He exchanged glances with Cynthia. "I think we've got what we need."

Coppola narrowed his eyes. "I want my promised cigarettes."

"You know they cause cancer, right?" Charlie arched a brow, paused, and stared at Coppola until the man was forced to acknowledge him with a nod. Charlie smiled, ever affable, and seemingly without guile. "I'll make sure you get them before we leave." Charlie glanced at the nearest corrections officer leaning against the wall. The guard nodded and spoke into a walkie-talkie affixed to the shoulder of his Kevlar vest. Moments later, Officer Bentley stepped into the room.

Cynthia stood, dejected. Their options had winnowed down to the unthinkable. Coppola most likely knew more about what was happening to them than they did, but there was no way to prove it...or beat it out of him.

Bentley caught the attention of the nearest corrections officer, and then indicated the exit with her hand. "If you would escort Mr. Coppola back to his room, I'll show Special Agent Deming and Dr. Foulkes out."

Twenty minutes later, after Charlie gave Bentley cash enough to buy Coppola his promised cigarettes, they were back in the parking lot, and Charlie was hustling her into the car rental. "Cheer up," he said. "It could be worse. It could have been me in there, and you visiting, torturing me with a tight dress and heels."

"Not funny." She slammed her door, cutting him off mid-chuckle.

Moments later, Charlie slid behind the wheel, keys jingling in his hand. "Let's spend the night at a posh hotel, do some beach time, and have a taste of that honeymoon you keep telling people we're on." His smile told her he was teasing, which meant he couldn't understand the severity of their situation.

"There's probably a BOLO out on us," she said.

Charlie shook his head. "Benton would have called first."

True, she thought, *but still...* Coppola throwing the word "alibi" around meant he knew something. She was sure of it. Did he know the extent of her and Charlie's alibi deficiencies? Or was there a snitch in the Boston Police Department, giving Modelli an earful about Charlie and his problems? It wouldn't be the first time there was a snitch. Wouldn't be the last, but it was damn frustrating and intimidating to think someone like Coppola, in Florida, was more informed than even Charlie's parents.

"I think Modelli shared intel about us to Coppola that could have been lifted straight from Benton's investigation notes," she said.

"That would make it a no on the beach?" He didn't bother waiting for a response. He just started the car. "Airport it is, then." Charlie threw his arm over the back of the seat, looking out the rear windshield as he backed out of the parking space. "What else did your voodoo pick up?"

"Voodoo?" Why did that sound familiar?

"That's what Modena calls it," he said, chuckling, carefully driving off the FPC, leaving the guard towers, the guns, the oppressive taint of lives on hold behind them. "That thing you do with suspects. Well, with everyone, actually." He meant body language and facial cues assessment. "When you asked Coppola if he knew about the murders, did you believe him?" Charlie was a lot of things: brilliant, learned, methodical, but Cynthia had been in love with him for years, and Charlie still hadn't a clue. Body language and facial cues assessment was not his strength.

"It's a dangerous thing to believe anything Coppola says," she said. "He lies as easily as he breathes, so I don't know. That crack about his alibi, though, is freaking me out."

"Crack?" He curled a lip as if confused. "I don't remember. He talked a lot and didn't say much."

"Take my word for it," she said. "It was a crack about him having an alibi, and the implication that we don't." She held onto the door handle as he took a tight turn, leaving the compound.

"Okay." Charlie nodded. "I can tell you this. Implications aren't evidence. They're subjective, and—"

"I know I'm being sensitive because we have shitty alibis, but didn't you hear the emphasis he put on that word? *Alibi.* He said it twice."

He shook his head. "I remember, but he was having a tantrum at the time, right?"

"Seems important."

"Seems a stretch." Charlie shrugged. "Maybe Modelli knows I'm under suspicion and my alibi is nonexistent. How hard would that be to find out?"

"Not hard, if they had insider information. Someone in the know is talking." She didn't want to believe it, especially since she *wanted* to believe Coppola was behind their troubles. It would be much easier if they could drop the full force of the FBI on a known felon's shoulders than some stupid cop trying to make a buck to put his kids in braces. "My *voodoo* is on the fritz, I guess."

Charlie turned onto a ramp and drove onto the interstate toward the airport. Once he settled on a lane, he reached out, eyes still on the road, and gave her hand a brief squeeze. She felt his thumb press on her wedding rings, something that she had found herself doing a lot. She knew why she rubbed them: it calmed her down. Why did he? To remind himself they were there, or that he'd get them back soon? Cynthia wished she knew, but she didn't have the guts to ask.

They drove the rest of the way to the airport in silence, and other than small talk, using each other as sounding boards for the case, they kept their personal thoughts and worries to themselves during the flight to Boston.

Charlie had to feed Socks, and neither were up to driving there and then to her place, so they crashed at his house. She was in bed, asleep soon after they stepped through the front door. She roused a bit when the mattress dipped, and her body rolled into its depression, stopped suddenly by Charlie's wide, naked chest. She curled around his warmth, struggling to open her eyes.

"Cynthia," he whispered, tucking a lock of her hair behind her ear. "I need to turn myself in."

"*No.*" She barely recognized her voice. It sounded rough, and weak from sleep.

He pressed a kiss to her forehead. "Our silence enables a killer."

Confessing increased the chance of kissing her career goodbye, abandoning the life she'd created, her friends, her country. She thought of the money she'd moved to offshore accounts, the fake passports that wouldn't be available until tomorrow. Charlie might be willing to sacrifice his future, but Cynthia would do what it took to stop him. She wished he'd be reasonable, though, and chill out, wait for Benton to do his job.

"I was at the crime scene," she said, struggling to find the right words to make him see reason without triggering him to double down on his stubbornness. "Should I turn myself in, too?"

"No." Predictably, Charlie shook his head. "Listen. Our investigation stalled with Coppola. We both knew it was a Hail Mary pass. It failed. More delay will expose me to obstruction of justice charges."

"Us, not just you."

"No, *me*. You have to allow me to take the fall for this, Cynthia. It will leave you on the outside, working to prove I'm innocent. It's the only way."

"No." She pressed her cheek to his chest, holding him tightly. "I can't allow you to do it." Panic flushed sleep from her mind, but the fear replacing it didn't make it easier to think. Tears spilled past her lashes.

"Why?" He searched her face. "Because we're friends? Because Terrance was driving?"

They'd shared so many heartaches, struggled to move beyond them, and both had the scars to prove it, but no. She couldn't let him sacrifice himself because she loved him. How could he not see that? "Charlie, I—"

"I shouldn't have asked." His thumb caressed her lower lip, stopping her words. "No, don't say anything, because I think you don't know, Cynthia. Not really. And if you say it, and then change your mind, I don't think I'd survive it." He closed his eyes for a moment, hiding his emotions, and when he opened them again, his determination had reasserted itself.

"Silencing me doesn't change a damn thing, you fool. I love—" His kiss cut her off, and she wanted to argue, to demand he know what was in her heart, but Charlie either didn't want to hear, or wasn't ready to believe. His kiss then became a consolation prize.

He licked into her mouth, rolling her onto her back, pressing his knee between her thighs as he moved on her, his arousal a stark reminder of the ways a woman could convince a man she loved him. Cynthia was eager to try.

His weight pressed her deep into the mattress, knees akimbo, her thighs clenching his hips. Overpowered by his size, his strength, Charlie made her feel safe in a world that was anything but. Did he understand her? Sometimes. *Enough* times. What mattered was he loved her. He hadn't said it the way she wanted him to say it, but he'd been saying it for ten years with every look, every gesture. She believed him now. And she loved him. That's what mattered. And now that she knew she had it, she wasn't giving it up.

Wrapping her arms around his neck, she opened her mouth wider, welcoming his thrusting tongue, their kiss breaking only when he moved down her body, kissing her everywhere. Teasing her breasts, caressing her thighs, her belly. He had her squirming under his hands, wiggling against his mouth, seeking to be closer, needing more of him. She sighed with anticipation as he kissed his way back up her body, and when his lips covered the tip of her breast, her breathing hitched, and a shot of electricity moved from her breast to her swollen, wet center. It curled her toes and had her arching her hips toward him. She'd never wanted a man like she wanted Charlie. He'd awakened something inside of her, a spark that felt like it was burning her from within.

"Charlie," she sighed, "please."

Lying between her legs, his arousal pressing against the apex of her thighs, Charlie rested his elbows on either side of her shoulders as he brushed his lips against hers. Cynthia searched his eyes for intent, drawing her fingertips along his scruff. She moved beneath him, and he saw her impatience. His lips cracked with a smile.

"I want you so much I ache." His tone surprised her. It reeked of humility, when he deserved to crow. "I knew it would be like this."

He covered her mouth with a searing kiss, and it felt as if she were drowning in it, holding him, feeding off his hunger. When they broke apart, out of breath, she felt a moment of panic. What if this was her shot to make him see reason, and she was so distracted by his touch that she was blowing it?

"Then don't leave me." Cynthia's words tripped over themselves as they rushed from her mouth. He averted his gaze, and her voodoo was going off the charts. It convinced her that Charlie had decided to martyr himself at the altar of Cynthia, and he might not be persuadable. His sense of obligation risked their future. "I won't allow you to take the fall. Don't you know me better than that?" She lifted her head as she pulled his head down to hers. She nipped his lower lip, and then soothed it with a swift kiss before she dropped her head back on the pillow. She'd convince him, or die trying.

"I know you," he whispered. Then Charlie moved his hips, dragging himself against her swollen lady parts. Her body clenched inside, longing to be filled by him.

"If you think I'll give you a divorce"—it was hard to talk, or keep her eyes open as he moved against her slickness and waves of pleasure promised heaven—"simply because you're incarcerated, you've got another think coming." With a trembling hand, she cupped his arousal and guided him to her entrance, and cupped the back of his neck with her other hand. "I'm keeping you, Charlie Foulkes." Charlie smiled.

"My wife," he said. Two words, but they landed hard.

Then Charlie moved inside her, filling her completely, forcing a gasp from her mouth.

"Mrs. Charles Foulkes," she said.

Blinking fast to chase away stupid tears, Cynthia did her best to balance her fear and love as both hammered at her for attention. He arched his hips rhythmically, kissing her face as his eyelids became hooded. "I thought you were keeping your name?" he whispered.

"You're threatening to leave me," she said, wrapping her arms around his neck. "To give up and let them ruin our lives." He kissed her, and his tongue had her moaning low in her throat. Her arousal was weakening her certainty. Was he right, and she wrong? Should he turn himself in, or should they run and take that flight she had on standby? "If your name is the only thing I get to keep of you, I'm keeping it."

"*Oh, Cynthia.*" Charlie buried his face against her neck, then he cupped her bottom with both hands, gripping it, and then his thrusts were no longer slow and seductive, they were demanding and rough. It became impossible to keep up, or think, and she was racing toward release…it was happening too fast. She wanted more…and pushed against his chest. Charlie stopped, out of breath, his eyes wild.

"You okay?"

"On your back," she demanded. He laughed, as if relieved, and then flipped onto his back

Now he was smiling up at her, his hands behind his neck, giving her a front row seat to his amazingly fit abdomen, broad chest, massive shoulders, and biceps that made her lick her lips. She inhaled deeply, needing to clear her head. Then she raked her fingertips down his body, loving the feel of him, the sound of his moans as her caresses had him biting his lip to stay silent. Though she sat with all her weight on his hips, he was so strong that he effortlessly lifted her, continuing to rock into her as she held his gaze.

If she could convince him that she loved him, and needed him to fight harder to save himself, she believed he might be persuadable. But Charlie needed to be convinced, so Cynthia studied the man she loved and pondered how best to prove something he was afraid to believe. How best to teach a man he's loved without words? She feared it was beyond her. But she had to try. She had to fight her shyness, and a lifetime's habit of protecting her pride.

Twisted in the sheets, his body undulating beneath her, moonlight from her bedroom windows created stark shadows against his corrugated stomach. It glinted off his now heavy-lidded blue eyes that stared back at her. If he saw her struggles, he hid that knowledge in the shadows that cut into his face, framing the hard line of his jaw, the flare of his nostrils. Charlie's face reminded her of Michelangelo's *David*: hard and perfect. But his body was a Rodin. *The Vanquished One*. A man seen through the prism of black bronze, clawed into existence, scarred, and strong, more beautiful for his imperfections.

Charlie was like that. More beautiful for his imperfections. She drew her fingers over the scars along his wide ribs, his abdomen, and chest. So many scars. All badges of courage, earned daily as he pushed through chronic pain, practicing a stoicism beyond most people.

"I'm yours," she said, leaning forward, allowing her nipples to tease his chest as his strokes increased in speed. She felt herself spiraling toward a climax, and he knew it. His intense gaze told her he reveled in it. Moonlight bathed their skin, so he could see her eyes, could see her truth. "All you have to do is take me, Charlie."

His hips stilled as he sat, his fingers burying themselves in her blond waves, gripping her head, controlling her as he covered her mouth with the most mind-clouding kiss she'd ever experienced. Her knees hitched up to keep their bodies close, and then she was wrapping her legs around his waist, holding on as Charlie twisted, throwing her onto her back and thrusting inside her while his mouth gave her a master's class in heaven on earth.

She tipped over the edge, where arousal promised release, and opened her eyes, looking at him. "Charlie!"

She wanted to shout, "Don't leave me!" but a remnant of pride caught the words before they escaped, and then Charlie left no room for pride, for nothing but him as he took her mouth back, dominating her with his kiss, and she climaxed.

"I got you," he whispered, as something inside her shattered into a million pieces.

Her tears surprised her, welling against her lashes, but she was too busy riding her orgasm to worry they'd be seen. Then she was suspended in a place so free of worry and pain, it lured her to stay. She felt Charlie shudder above her, following her down the rabbit hole to satiation, arching against her, moving inside her as his release lengthened her aftershocks. Then she floated, gently, down to reality and felt calm, if buffeted. Her every defense was gone.

Charlie collapsed on her, his lips against her neck, his chest a bellows as he caught his breath. She trembled, her palms flat on his muscular back.

"We're running tomorrow," she whispered. "It's arranged. I've never asked you for anything, Charlie, ever. Do this for me. Do it for your parents." He propped his weight onto his elbows, and her hands fell to her sides, lost in the tangle of sheets as he studied her face, frowning.

"I'm on borrowed time...since forever. This was inevitable," he whispered.

She shook her head. "Promise, Charlie. Give it to me."

His jaw muscles flexed, and his gaze hardened. "I couldn't save your brother, Cynthia. I'll be damned if I don't save you." It was the worst thing he could have said, because it validated her fears. Charlie dropped a kiss on her lips. "Let me do this. Let me...save you," he said.

"But will it ever be enough?"

"Huh?" He blinked, his confusion clear.

"Will sacrificing your career, your good name, maybe your life, finally square us? Will it be payment enough?"

He shook his head, clearly baffled. "Payment? What the hell are you talking about?"

"Terrance drank himself stupid, Charlie. He got behind the wheel, and he died. *You couldn't have stopped him.* You've paid enough. *You don't owe me a thing.*" In a perfect world, she'd be yelling, not sobbing. Well, Cynthia was *ugly* sobbing, and she'd earned every moment of it.

"It's not like that, Cynthia." Charlie squeezed her tightly, kissing her tears. "But, yes, I do owe you," he said. "More than you could ever know."

"Run away with me," she sobbed. "Please, Charlie." She saw the truth in his eyes. He'd do no such thing.

He was hopeless. *She* was hopeless. As much as they'd changed, they'd stayed the same. Charlie was determined to save her, and Cynthia was unable to save Charlie. Once again, she would be on the sidelines, watching him hurt, fearing he wouldn't survive. Well, she couldn't live through that again.

Running wasn't a great plan. Becoming a fugitive never was, but it was a plan, and if Charlie continued to fight her on this in the morning, she'd cuff him to the bed until she convinced him. No, she'd hire muscle to shuttle him to the plane. She couldn't lose him.

"Shh," he said, rolling to the side, rubbing her back as she continued to clutch him close. "Let's talk about this tomorrow. Try to sleep."

Soon he was spooning her, and she felt safe in his arms—and *loved.* Cynthia fell asleep assuring herself that the morning would make things better. He'd be more persuadable. She was tired now, and couldn't bring herself to leave the heaven of his arms to dig her handcuffs from her pocketbook, but tomorrow would come soon enough, and then she'd find a way...or she'd use the damn cuffs.

Chapter Fourteen

Charlie woke to a phone ringing, but the noise stopped in time to allow lingering in the sweet spot between sleep and consciousness. His usual aches and pains weren't noticeable, despite not working out or stretching these last few days, and he supposed the sleeping hundred-and-something pound heating pad draped across his body, breathing on his neck, had a lot to do with it. He smiled, and his arms tightened around Cynthia as memories of last night swamped him. They'd slept, but off and on, waking to a caress, or a kiss that ended with making love. Last night was amazing.

Now, her breasts mashed against him, her fists pressed to his ribs, he couldn't help but note that, even sleeping, Cynthia was prepared for a fight. He liked that about her, wanted her again, ached with it, and despite the new day and the million things he needed to do, Charlie wanted to back burner everything to hear her moan his name once more. He wanted her begging him to linger as he kissed her breasts, to gasp once again as he buried himself inside her, making them one, moving in concert. His body stirred just thinking about it.

The phone rang again. Cynthia's phone. From the looks of her, she wasn't waking soon. His smiled faded. Neither of them had slept much last night, but the night had passed, his decision was made, and it was time to do the right thing. He lifted the phone, saw Benton's name on its screen, and chose "accept," rather than "ignore."

"Charlie Foulkes here," he whispered. A glance told him Cynthia remained asleep.

"Charlie." Benton paused, and for a moment, Charlie wasn't sure if he would continue speaking. It was Cynthia's phone. Maybe the task force leader had nothing to say to Charlie. "She with you?" Benton said.

"Sleeping," he said. "What do you need?"

"You." The word was clipped. "Face to face."

Charlie revisited all the planted evidence in the case and wondered what had changed. Maybe Coppola complained and Benton got a call from the FPC. "What happened?" he said.

"An abandoned van happened." When Charlie didn't respond, Benton sighed. "Rented with your credit card. Your prints are all over it."

Charlie had rented a Camry in Florida. He glanced at his pants on the floor, where he kept his wallet. "A van?"

"Yes. Rented with the credit card you say doesn't exist. You know, the credit card that bought your gun. We found your wallet, too. In the van with your prints all over it," Benton said.

Shit. More manufactured evidence. Someone wasn't taking any chances. "I'm coming in," Charlie said. "It's time we talked." A glance at Cynthia had him studying the dark circles under her eyes, and making the decision he didn't have the heart to wake her for such bad news. "Don't call Cynthia again, though. She's had a…rough night."

"Oh, right. How was Florida?" Definite snark. Yup. Benton was pissed, despite his calm tone.

"We got in late. Listen." He glanced at the bedside clock. "It's six AM. I'll meet you—"

"It's gone beyond that," Benton said. "We're outside."

We. Charlie didn't know why he was surprised. "Ten minutes?"

Benton cleared his throat. "Modena is at the back door, and I'm at the front. In eleven minutes, you'll be forcing us to break in."

"Understood." Charlie hung up, pressing a kiss to Cynthia's forehead.

When she woke, her protective streak would kick in. He might be dumb as a stump when it came to people, but he knew what Cynthia would do. She'd allow nothing to stand between her and Charlie. Not the task force, not Internal Affairs, not even her self-interest. She'd sacrifice her career, even her freedom, if she thought that was the price to protect him. Knowing that gave him the strength he needed to disengage from her embrace and leave the bed.

Leave her.

He told himself that if he'd been a good friend he never would have given in to his desire and made love to her. Hell, their marriage was supposed to protect her, not put her at greater risk. Now, to divert attention from her being at the crime scene and destroying evidence at the safe house, he was in the unenviable position of allowing himself to be framed for murder. Benton's discovered van and fake credit card sealed his fate, and when Cynthia woke, she'd lash out. Any negotiations between him and the task force would need to happen before then...before Cynthia did something rash.

Ten minutes later, changed, Socks fed, he quietly left, still wet from his shower. As promised, Benton greeted him out front. The team leader surprised Charlie by extending a Dunkin Donuts coffee in a paper cup. Benton seemed watchful, not derisive, and made Charlie think he was reserving judgment. It was more than he'd expected.

Special Agent Modena closed Charlie's backyard gate, stepping onto the sidewalk. He sipped from a Dunkin Donuts coffee cup as his eyes narrowed, contemplating Charlie. Benton signaled his cherry red Dodge Charger with a tilt of his head, and they all walked toward it, casual, controlled, all by the book.

Charlie couldn't help but wonder if that would change once he'd confessed.

* * * *

Two hours later, the interrogation room door flew open, and in stormed a Cynthia that Charlie hadn't seen before. Wearing yesterday's rumpled suit, her usually coiffed hair fell in tangles around her face. Her makeup, usually impeccable, was smeared around her eyes. That is, the makeup that hadn't rubbed off on his sheets last night. Her pink pocketbook swung on her arm like a weapon as she scanned the room, and with laser focus, she glared at her supervisor.

"Benton!" she said.

"Now, Deming—" Modena left his seat at the interrogation table, palms up, and approached Cynthia.

"*Sit down*, Modena," she snapped, not bothering to even look at the special agent. "Benton, this is crazy, and you know it. Charlie couldn't kill a fly, never mind execute six hardened criminals!"

"Stop." Charlie could see where this was going, and knew it was a waste of time. Hands cuffed, linked to the metal loop at the table's center, Charlie had already been processed, searched, fingerprinted, and suited up in a bright orange jumpsuit. "I've told them everything."

"Everything?" She shook her head, exchanging looks with Benton and Modena, as if Charlie wasn't making any sense. A uniformed officer poked his head in the room, eyeballing Benton, who waved him off. After an annoyed glance at Cynthia, the grizzled officer left, closing the door behind him.

"Sit, Deming. Just—" Benton pointed to the chair next to him. "Sit." Modena stepped to the corner of the room, his eyes leveled on Charlie, as if he was attempting to read his mind.

When Cynthia reluctantly sat, Charlie sighed, knowing that her sitting next to him wasn't a good thing. The optics sucked, making her look culpable on an equal level, and *hello*. He was in an orange jumpsuit. This interview, from now on, had to be about separating Cynthia from his actions. Real or not.

"I gave them access to my bank account," Charlie said.

Other than a widening of her eyes, she gave no other indication that she'd heard him. That was a good thing, because they both knew his habit of keeping his computer on sleep mode and his login information on autofill meant anyone who had access to his computer could have arranged that deposit. Benton would know that, too, and being the phenomenal investigator that he was, he'd throw a wide net for suspects. Cynthia had access to Charlie's laptop. She'd be in that suspect pool.

"We found the million dollars and, as expected, it traced back to that Coppola syndicate shell company's account," Modena said. "Stone Industries. It establishes Charlie's motive." Charlie saw it a bit differently. Whoever had access to the million in his account had motive. If it was easy enough to manipulate deposits, how difficult would it be for the culprit to withdraw? Once again, how big the suspect pool was remained unknowable, but Cynthia was in it.

"I told them about the evidence I found in my trunk," Charlie said. Once again, Cynthia thankfully remained quiet. Talking about a mysterious blond presence in his driveway that night would only shift questions toward Cynthia.

"They're a match," Benton said, "to the hoods, duct tape, and zip ties found on the victims."

"The *victims*." Cynthia narrowed her eyes at Benton. "You mean the contract killers. Let's not pretend these men were victims."

"The tests I ordered came through," Charlie said, needing to interrupt Cynthia before she got on a roll. He knew from experience that once she began defending him, things could get out of control. "My hair was found on the victims' clothing," he continued. "And..." Now was the test. If Cynthia had lost her mind and decided to torch her life, she'd do it now. She'd speak up. He narrowed his eyes, doing his best to signal he needed her to stay silent. "I have no alibi for the murders." Cynthia opened her mouth as if to speak, and he saw her eyes turn wild. He shook his head, helpless to control her.

"We found a van," Benton said. Cynthia closed her mouth with a snap, glaring at the task force team leader. "Inside, we found the victims' prints, along with Charlie's. There's plenty of DNA samples there, but the prints are enough. It puts Charlie in the van with the six vics. Evidence points to him transporting them to the crime scene."

Cynthia was breathing heavy, looking only barely tethered to calm. "This is stupid." She turned to Charlie. "You coming here. Saying what you've said. This van—" She caught Benton's gaze. "You're saying Charlie went on a scavenger hunt? Picking up the victims, gathering them together, lining them up neatly in a row after putting hoods on their heads and binding them? There are a million what-the-fucks in that supposition alone."

Charlie knew he had no proof to support his innocence, but sharing his thoughts on the case would point fingers at Cynthia. A lot of planning had gone into these murders and framing Charlie, so he had to be smart to counteract the killer's ambitions. Otherwise, the life he'd meticulously built, and Cynthia's life, would be ruined.

"Why don't you tell us what happened?" Modena said, his eyes narrowed, focused on her face.

"Charlie didn't do it," Cynthia said.

"You keep saying that, Deming." Modena took off his suit jacket, rolling up his shirt sleeves, then he rubbed his sniper tattoo on his forearm as if it irritated him. Brows lifted, he seemed merely curious, but his green eyes revealed an intensity his expression otherwise belied. "Why isn't Charlie saying that?"

Cynthia's jaw dropped. "He did last time you brought him in!" Her head snapped toward Charlie. "Right? Tell them again! Tell them!" He couldn't. The moment the team stopped looking at Charlie as the unsub, they'd discover she was the most likely prime suspect.

And Cynthia knew that. He saw her frustration, her lips compressing, the violent emotions she barely held in check. He wasn't surprised when she slapped her palm against the table, glaring at him. It had him focusing on her left hand, his grandmother's emerald and diamond rings. Grammy Foulkes never could have imagined they'd be worn in an interrogation room, but here they were, sparkling under the fluorescent lights.

He and Cynthia were married. He loved her. With all his heart. He'd loved her since she sucker punched that woman at MIT. Her knuckles had bruised and split that day. Her family paid thousands of dollars in reparations, but she'd earned Charlie's devotion for life. Love came in fits and spurts, until it was painful to think about, so over the years, he'd learned to pretend it was something else.

He couldn't pretend anymore. He loved her.

"No," Charlie said. He wouldn't proclaim his innocence, not now, not when he had no proof. Not when his silence gave her time to find the real culprit, and keep her reputation intact, save her career. "You know what you have to do, Cynthia."

"*Bullshit.*" She glared.

He shook his head. "Stop. Just…stop." If she spilled her guts to Benton, this sacrifice would be for nothing. She had to know that.

"There is more evidence against me than Charlie," she said.

Modena folded his arms over his chest and rolled his eyes. Benton grimaced and made a slicing motion to his throat while looking at the security camera. The red light winked out, and taping stopped.

"You have to feed my cat," Charlie said. "So don't do anything stupid."

"Your cat?" Cynthia squealed her response, then shifted in her seat, facing Benton. "Remember my head injury?"

"Something to keep in mind when she explains herself," Charlie said. It would discredit whatever story she shared.

Cynthia narrowed her eyes at Charlie before turning back to Benton. "The night of the murders, I left the gym, and the next thing I knew, I was waking up in bed at the Chinatown safe house."

"The one near the crime scene?" Benton said.

"Yes," she said. "I woke with my gun drawn, recently shot, its magazine missing six rounds."

"Making yourself look like an accomplice helps no one, Deming," Modena said.

"I blacked out. Lost my memory." She glanced at Modena. "I don't remember everything, but between me and Charlie, we've pieced most of it together."

"Ah," Modena said, grimacing. "Between you and Charlie, you remembered you were at the safe house. I'm sure you have proof." Modena's skepticism annoyed Cynthia, but calmed Charlie's fears.

Cynthia shook her head. "No, you're not hearing me. I called Charlie at ten that night."

Benton arched a brow. "Witnesses reported hearing the gunshots at ten."

"Yes." She licked her lips, and Charlie saw that sweat had beaded on her upper lip. From where Charlie sat, she didn't seem like a credible witness. She acted desperate. "I later found my phone in my car. It was dead. I'm thinking at ten PM I called Charlie for some reason, phone went dead, I heard gunshots, and investigated."

"Thinking? But you don't know for sure?" Benton said.

"Mostly sure." She shook her head. "My number must be listed on Charlie's phone log, under recent calls. Ten PM on the nose, he said."

Benton pressed his lips closed, exchanging weighted glances with Modena. Charlie wished he had a large dose of Cynthia's voodoo so he could read what the investigators were thinking.

"She blacked out that night," Charlie said. "We can only guess what really happened."

Cynthia shook her head. "The flash drive—"

"Is gone," Charlie said. Cynthia glared at him. "So, drop it, Cynthia. It's gone."

He'd hidden it under a floorboard in his living room, thinking he might need it at some point. He didn't destroy it, because it was evidence, and that would be illegal. Charlie still had hope things could work out, and maybe, if he played it right, he'd get his life back, but that could only happen if he didn't break the law.

"What flash drive?" Benton said.

She shook her head, squirming on her seat. "Forget it." Charlie could see her frustration and confusion. "But I *was* at the safe house that night. You could dust it for fingerprints."

"You've been in and out of that place for the last few months," Modena said.

Cynthia bit her lip. "Check the dumpster. I threw up in a waste bin, and the sheets have my blood on them." She touched her healing injury.

"And if the dumpster has been emptied in the last few days?" Benton tilted his head to the side.

"Find area security cameras," she snapped, turning in her seat to glare at Charlie, as if this was all his fault. He supposed in a way it was. "ATMs on the block."

"Why bother?" Modena shook his head. "If you were in the safe house, there'd be proof. It has a twenty-four seven digital security monitor. The surveillance—"

She shook her head. "The video got deleted. I turned off the machine."

Benton groaned. "Dammit, Deming. You'd think by now you'd know enough not to touch technology."

Charlie couldn't help but be surprised that Benton immediately jumped to the right conclusion. Charlie's relief had him slouching in his chair. Cynthia noticed and scowled at him before turning back to Benton.

"Charlie saw me in his driveway the night before," she said.

"I saw a blonde," Charlie said. "Ask her if she remembers being there."

"I don't," she amended reluctantly, nibbling on her thumbnail, "but there's a chance I went into his house, took his gun from his gun safe—"

"What?" Modena said, looking confused.

"I know, right?" Charlie shook his head. "She was at the gym, and they log in members' comings and goings. She's confused. Knock to the head, remember?"

Cynthia slapped Charlie's arm, not bothering to look at him while she kept her attention on Benton. "I'm the only other person who has the code for his gun safe. I have a key to his house. I have access to his DNA, his fingerprints," Cynthia said. "He keeps his online banking login information *autofilled*." She did send Charlie a particularly virulent glare then, before turning back to the two other agents. "It would give me access to his bank accounts, and, having access to all Coppola syndicate files, I could have found an account number from one of the many Coppola shell companies." She shrugged. "Done some magic."

Modena laughed. "'Cause you're so good with computers?" Cynthia glowered at her teammate.

"She hasn't balanced a checkbook successfully since she opened one in college," Charlie said.

"Neither have you," she said. "We have accountants. Stop trying to make me seem crazy."

Benton grimaced. "Deming, you know you've been known to fry technology simply by turning it on. How can we believe you're capable of a sophisticated forensic accounting scheme? Because that's what happened."

"Huh?" She glanced at Modena. "Well, I'm connected to the Coppola syndicate case. More so than Charlie," she said. Everyone in the interrogation room was connected to the case. It wasn't saying much. "I was at the scene during the kills. Didn't you find my DNA at the scene?"

"No." Benton frowned, shaking his head. Charlie tensed, opening his mouth to change the subject, but then Benton scowled at Cynthia. "*You're pushing reasonable doubt*. But I am not a jury! I get to decide what is a lead in my cases!"

"You know her, Benton," Charlie said. "She's not a killer."

Cynthia's expression hardened as she sat back in her chair, arms folded over her chest. "I know myself. There's no way in hell I killed anyone. Not in cold blood. And I know Charlie. He couldn't do it either."

"You're not helping Charlie." Modena folded his arms, frowning. "Any prosecutor worth their salt will just build a conspiracy case against you two, and I have to be honest, Deming, you're making their case for them."

"And it has to stop," Benton said. "We understand that you love Charlie—" Cynthia stood so quickly that her chair screeched against the tile floor. Charlie caught her looking at him, her face flushed, her behavior showing all the earmarks of a wild animal caught in a trap.

"Deming?" Modena said in a quiet voice, looking as if he were poised at the truth. Charlie feared he'd piece it together. "You love him, right?"

"Charlie." Her eyes begged him to help her, to deny all their accusations, to claim the one thing he couldn't say without allowing her to be put under the spotlight. He couldn't claim his innocence without implicating her.

"Deming," Benton said, "we know people do a lot of strange things for people they love. I suggest you do as Charlie says. Take a step back from this case, and allow us to proceed. He's complying with the investigation. It will look good to the judge."

She shook her head vehemently. "He didn't do it, Benton. Modena, you have to believe me!" Modena and Benton looked everywhere but at Cynthia. That's when he knew he'd succeeded in protecting her. They believed him, not her, most likely because they wanted to, because they loved her, too. "Charlie, tell them or I'll—"

He panicked, fearing she'd confess to a murder she didn't commit. "I'm guilty," Charlie said. *Guilty of loving her.*

A feeling of peace settled on him, even though tears welled in Cynthia's eyes, because his confession stopped her potential confession from having legitimacy. For now, anyway. He hadn't given up on the investigation clearing his name. He'd only given up on Cynthia's ability to keep herself out of trouble.

Cynthia's jaw dropped, her shock evident. "What have you done?"

"Paid a debt," Charlie whispered. He couldn't save Terrance, but he could save his little sister. Cynthia blanched, and her eyes glazed over. For a moment, the room was silent as Cynthia swayed, looking moments from fainting. He reached for her, but his cuffs stopped him from leaving the table. "Catch her, Modena," Charlie snapped.

"Damn." Modena reached for Cynthia, but she slapped his hand away, stepping back, inhaling sharply. Modena turned to Benton. "The cameras were off. We don't have that on tape."

Cynthia locked eyes with Charlie. He winked, because he'd known that when he'd spoken. She glared the moment she recognized his strategy, and then she lunged at him, grabbed his jumpsuit's lapel, and gave him a fierce tug, her face inches in front of his.

"No more games," she growled. "You hear me? You shut up. Just keep your damn mouth shut while I figure this out."

He was counting on it, so he winked again, and then lifted his cuffed wrists. "Until then, I'm indisposed, so I'd appreciate it if you'd hurry it up, please."

Cynthia's chin quivered as she searched his eyes, and then she covered his mouth with a long, lingering kiss. Charlie allowed himself to enjoy it, to linger with her, and forced Cynthia to be the one to break their kiss.

"I... I..." She looked as if she wanted to say something to him, but held back for some reason. "Just don't say anything."

"Deming, outside," Modena said. When Cynthia didn't move, but just held Charlie's jumpsuit by the collar, fists bunched in the orange material, Modena cleared his throat. "Charlie?" Modena said quietly. "Will you tell your wife I'm about to throw her over my shoulder if she doesn't leave the room on her own steam?"

Charlie's cheek kicked up, his gaze still locked with his wife's. "Cynthia, if Modena lays a hand on you, I promise I'll knock him flat."

Modena sighed, hands on his hips. "Well, that's not productive."

Cynthia sniffed, nodded, and then left the room without saying another word.

The red light was soon lit on the security camera, and Charlie knew they wanted him to play his greatest hits, like confessing to a massacre he didn't commit, but Cynthia asked for time, so time is what he'd give her. Now it was the only thing he had to give.

He smiled at the special agents. "She loves me," Charlie said. Benton nodded. Modena's frown deepened. "Hey," Charlie said. "I was wondering. Does your team have any evidence that I didn't give you, or couldn't have been planted by your industrious anonymous source?" Benton and Modena exchanged disgruntled frowns. "Yeah," Charlie said. "I didn't think so. Doesn't that seem odd?"

As one, the two special agents nodded. Then Benton turned to the security camera and drew his finger across his neck again. The red light blinked out. "About that," Benton said. "Modena and I have a theory we'd like to run by you."

Charlie studied the two agents' expressions, and for the first time since he'd become entangled in the Chinatown Massacre, he felt as if things were going his way.

Chapter Fifteen

Cynthia's head was pounding as she rushed down the hall, pushing through the incident room's door. Though she'd had a headache to some degree since she'd woken in the safe house, it had turned into a raging headache. Too much going on, and not enough time to process. The door slammed against the wall as she scanned the room and saw Vivian O'Grady and Special Agent Gilroy standing around the monitor, watching the interview continue between Charlie and the other team members. Their heads had swiveled toward her when the door bounced off the wall.

"They shut off the monitor, then turned it back on, and then shut it off again," Vivian said. "Do you know why?"

Vivian's brown hair was pulled back into a chignon, and her brow was furrowed. She dressed like a librarian from the fifties. All buttoned up, bow at the neck, pearls at her throat. Vivian smoothed her palms over her tweed skirt, making Cynthia think she was wiping nervous sweat. Cynthia sympathized. She couldn't remember the last time she was this stressed. Gilroy was scowling, studying Cynthia as if the monitor glitch had been her fault.

"Don't look at me. Ask Benton," she said, hurrying to her desk, dropping her handbag onto the neat surface. "He's running the show."

Gilroy tilted his head toward the monitor. "Charlie going mute Benton's idea, too? Or was that yours?"

"He's my husband," Cynthia said. "What do you think, Gilroy?" She turned to the IT specialist. "Vivian, do you have Tylenol? My head is killing me, and I used the last in my bag." She sat, pulling desk drawers open, searching for a medicine bottle. Instead, her eye alit upon a comb, which she used to tug through her messy hair. "I rolled out of bed and didn't take the time to look at a mirror." Cynthia saw a pack of gum in the back, grabbed it, and popped the peppermint gum into her mouth. "My head hurts." How was she supposed to save Charlie when she couldn't even hold a thought in her head? "Tylenol, Vivian?"

"Yes." The IT tech hurried toward the back wall, where her desk was situated.

The incident room's door opened, and she expected to see Modena or Benton, ready to ream her out. Instead, she saw one of the forensic techs. "Kevin." Cynthia saw a file in his hand. "Now isn't a good time."

"I printed additional crime scene photos and stuff," Kevin said, walking toward her, his blond hair slicked back as if he'd just had a shower. "Autopsy photos, crowd shots. I've got the updated evidence list, with accompanying photos. Everything is logged, with descriptions." He handed Cynthia the manila file. "And I printed out the photos I took at Charlie's house. They're new." He pursed his lips, lifting his brows. "So…how is Charlie?"

"What?" Cynthia said. "Why? I mean, *why* were you at Charlie's house?"

"More importantly, when?" Gilroy said. "And who authorized it?"

"Benton's warrant was signed last night," Kevin said. "The search is still going on. I just got back, printed the photos, and came directly here, hoping someone would tell me what's going on." Kevin shifted between his feet, glancing at the door as if he feared someone might overhear. "We have his computer in the lab, his gun safe, and all his files in the evidence locker. Anyone want to tell me why?"

"Charlie is prime suspect," Gilroy said. "Keep that to yourself, if you know what's good for you." Kevin didn't seem surprised, and why would he be? Cynthia figured being sent to scour a man's home, with the man in question in custody rather than dead, kind of tipped a person off.

"Of course." Kevin seemed disgruntled rather than curious. Cynthia suspected, like her, Kevin saw this deviation in the investigation as a huge mistake.

"Who logged in the evidence?" Cynthia said. Vivian handed Cynthia a paper cup of water and two Tylenols. Cynthia swallowed them without taking her eyes off Kevin. "You?"

"No. That's Teresa's job." Kevin glanced at his watch. "She's downstairs, finishing up the paperwork. We drove to the precinct together, so right about now she'll be wondering where I am."

Cynthia frowned at the folder sitting atop the other photos, and suddenly realized she and Kevin must have just missed each other this morning. Did he take pictures of rumpled bed sheets, evidence of her and Charlie's night of passion? And were they in this folder? Cynthia nudged it with her acrylic nail, equal parts curious and wary to see her personal life in a case file folder.

"I better go," Kevin said. "Teresa might be waiting for me in the garage, and I have her keys. An interim M.E. is stepping in for Charlie until this misunderstanding is cleared up, and she's arriving in the next hour." He glanced at Cynthia. "Socks, Charlie's cat, is still in the house. I thought it best to leave him there, rather than disrupt his life. He's got plenty of food in his dish, and water, and I told the detectives to make sure they don't let him escape when they leave." His expression told her he had questions, but he kept them to himself.

"Thank you." Cynthia nodded, feeling a little weepy at the mention of Socks, and Kevin's kindness, but it didn't make her any less cautious about bringing him into her circle of confidants. Someone who knew Charlie, and had access to his stuff, was framing him. That was the only way to explain the overwhelming amount of planted evidence. They had access to his house, his computer, his gun, and they wanted him blamed for these murders. That meant she and Charlie knew who was doing this to him. They trusted this person, and that trust led them to this moment, with Cynthia's head pounding, feeling helpless, and once again unable to protect Charlie from someone else's disastrous decisions. It might not be the accident all over again, but it felt like it was inexorably heading there.

The incident room door slammed against the wall again. Teresa, this time. Blue eyes wide, her mouth open as if she'd surprised herself with the force she'd used to open the door. "Sorry," Teresa said. "Don't know my own strength. Ah, Kevin? You have my keys."

"I think the door's hinge is broken," Vivian said, "because it just slammed that way for Cynthia."

Gilroy took Kevin's folder, and some of the photos slipped out onto the desk, landing in front of Cynthia. She squinted, afraid of what she'd see, but it was just a photo of the kitchen counter. Her heart settled as she took a deep breath, forcing herself to focus on the details. On a kitchen that had always been a refuge from the world, but was now being treated as a crime scene. The same kitchen where Charlie had bent a knee and slipped his grandmother's rings on her finger in front of his parents. 'Til death do us part.

"Are those the photos?" Teresa's lips compressed, her gaze locked on the file. Kevin shrugged. "I told Kevin I wanted—" She cut off her sentence with a shake of her head. "Never mind. Doesn't matter." She tucked a blond lock behind her ear, and hesitated at the door. Cynthia supposed the tech was equally upset about Charlie being a suspect, and probably wanted to look at all the evidence to find something to clear him. If Cynthia were kind and empathetic rather than desperate and jealous, she'd say something calming about Charlie's chances of coming out of this unscathed, but she didn't have it in her. Instead, Cynthia pressed a hand to her pounding forehead and focused on Teresa, trying not to hate her for crushing on Charlie.

He was sexy, loveable; who wouldn't crush on him? Cynthia needed to grow up. She would grow up. Figuring Teresa would be one more set of eyes on the photos, she waved her forward. They needed all the help they could get.

"Come in," Cynthia said. Teresa approached with obvious reluctance, and Cynthia couldn't blame her. If their places were switched, Cynthia would resent the hell out of Teresa.

"Yes?" Teresa said.

Cynthia splayed the photos on her desk, side by side. The bedroom with rumpled sheets. Charlie's office, neat, and organized. The kitchen counter, with Sock's plunder pile of odds and ends. Everything was familiar, and nothing stood out. She glanced at the other eyes looking at the photos. Gilroy's expression was neutral. No surprise there. Cynthia suspected the only person that could make him move a facial muscle was his girlfriend, Vivian, and she was poring over the photos, her expression a mask of worry. Kevin was grimacing, shaking his head, and Teresa was looking everywhere but at the photos.

"What are we looking for?" Kevin said.

"Something that catches your eye that might help Charlie," Cynthia said. What she wanted to say was, "Do you see anything the killer might have planted that could cause Charlie problems?" but she couldn't do that. The killer knew Charlie. If he wasn't in Charlie's small circle of friends, he was friends with one of Charlie's friends. Any one of them in this room could have been unwitting sources for the killer. She refused to think they would help willingly.

Teresa glanced at the photos, then caught Cynthia's gaze. "Is Charlie… okay?"

"No," Gilroy said, not elaborating. In this instance, it was Charlie's fault. Cynthia had a plane on standby. But where was Charlie? In custody.

Her eyes dropped to her desk, onto the photo of Sock's plunder. They'd have to arrange for someone to care for the cat. Just the idea of it broke Cynthia's heart. Socks was a stray, and now they were about to orphan him again. Who knew what kind of behavioral issues would layer onto the ones he already had, hoarding things the cat thought important enough to steal? Cynthia's finger dragged the picture of the kitchen counter toward her, and looked again at the magic marker, the purple leather heart charm. The silver and purple flower charm and a dirty sock. Cynthia supposed Charlie's scent was on these items, and that's why the cat was forever stealing Charlie's socks.

Vivian narrowed her eyes at Gilroy, who seemed clueless about why his girlfriend was disgruntled with him. "Teresa," Vivian said, "we don't really know what's going on with Charlie." Then she glanced at Cynthia, as if she might have answers. She didn't.

Teresa nodded, and then caught Kevin's gaze. "Well, I have a doctor's appointment and you have my keys, Kevin."

Kevin pulled out a set of keys from his pants pocket, and then handed it to Teresa. Something shiny fell from Kevin's pocket. Cynthia's eye tracked it, but it bounced out of sight, under her desk.

"You coming or staying?" Teresa lifted her brows at Kevin, but didn't wait to hear his answer. He waved goodbye to the special agents and then hurried after the tech.

"You dropped something, Kevin." Cynthia bent at the waist, looking for the shiny object.

"Huh?" Kevin looked in the direction that Cynthia pointed, then joined her in the search. Cynthia found a small, rectangular silver object. It was metal and had the letters "NYU" inscribed on it. She picked it up, her head still under the desk, hidden from view. Knowing that, she had a moment of weakness, and she lost her composure. The sky was falling. If she couldn't solve this case within the next few hours, Charlie would be formally charged with six counts of murder. When she could no longer stay under the desk without comment, Cynthia schooled her features and inhaled slowly. She pulled her head out from under the desk and sat, handing the tech what she'd found: a silver and purple charm. Kevin frowned, cupping it in his hand.

"Must have fallen off Teresa's keychain," he said. He held it by its small, broken metal loop. "She went to NYU."

"Yeah. I remember seeing a photo on her desk," Cynthia said. "Sorority girls."

Cynthia's headache pounded from sitting up so quickly, but as it abated she was able to blink through the pain. She picked up the photo of Sock's plunder as Kevin reached the incident room's door. Teresa's keychain charm had the same color scheme as the purple heart charm, and the purple and white flower in Sock's plunder pile.

"Kevin, wait," Cynthia said.

Kevin slipped the charm into his pocket. "I have to go before Teresa leaves me behind."

"*Wait.*" Her tone broached no argument. She waved him toward her. "Give me that charm."

"What?" Gilroy said.

"I know that look," Vivian said. "She's thought of something."

Kevin paused, exchanging glances with Gilroy and Vivian, but they were both looking at Cynthia. He stepped forward, reached into his pocket, and retrieved the charm for her. Cynthia placed it on the photo.

"Tell me I'm not imagining this." Cynthia could hear the breathiness of her voice and told herself to keep her cool. "Does this charm match what is in the picture?"

"I don't know," Kevin said. "I think so." Cynthia thought it matched.

Gilroy shrugged. Vivian nodded enthusiastically.

It begged the question: Why the hell had Teresa been in Charlie's house? Or was there another explanation?

Charlie wouldn't have lied to Cynthia. He said no woman, other than her and his mother, had ever been in his house. Unless Charlie was lying to spare her feelings? Images of Charlie and Teresa having a secret affair flooded her brain, and Cynthia immediately rejected the thought. Though that scenario would explain Teresa's hurt, it required Charlie to be cast as a liar, and that was too farfetched for Cynthia to buy. Charlie was a rule follower, unless it came to protecting Cynthia. Then she was positive he'd lie up a storm. *As he'd just done in the interrogation room, telling Benton he was guilty.*

But she couldn't see how the lie of Charlie having an affair with Teresa would benefit Cynthia. It didn't make sense, so Charlie didn't lie. He didn't knowingly have more than her or his mother in his house. That left one option: Teresa was in his house without Charlie knowing about it. Or, rather, Teresa's charm keychain was in Charlie's house. Kevin had easy access to it. Socks found the charms as they fell from the defective keychain. It's the only thing that made sense.

Kevin stared at the picture. Gilroy stepped to his side, scowling at the evidence.

"Harris, honey?" Vivian glanced at Special Agent Gilroy. "What am I missing?"

Gilroy knew. He locked gazes with Cynthia. "The colors match. They're charms. What do you want to do?"

"Kevin, sit. If you're involved in this, so help me—" Cynthia said, so upset she could barely speak.

"Involved?" He lifted his hands, horrified, shaking his head so hard his blond hair fell in his face. "No no, tell me what you want."

"Sit. And don't move." Kevin found the nearest chair, sat, and kept his hands up, as if she had a gun pointed at him. Cynthia tilted her head to the incident room's door. "Bring Teresa back here, Gilroy. Put them both into interrogation room 1."

Gilroy shook his head. "Charlie is in interrogation room 1."

She stood so quickly her chair rolled back and hit the desk behind hers. "Then interrogation room 2, Gilroy, just get her before she leaves!" Gilroy nodded and hustled out the door. "Vivian, I need you to pull up everything we have on Teresa Johnson and Kevin...Kevin, what's your last name?"

"Hilliard," he said, turning toward Vivian. "That's H-I-L-L-I-A-R-D."

Cynthia blinked, momentarily distracted by Kevin's compliance. "Do background checks, social media, who they're related to, who Teresa is dating. Call their landlords."

"We own. Me and my wife," Kevin said, shrugging when she glared at him.

Cynthia dismissed him with a glance. "Vivian, I want to know what they had for breakfast. We clear?" Vivian nodded and hurried to her desk.

"Bagel with a schmear," Kevin said, talking to Vivian.

Cynthia wanted to trust Kevin, but he worked closely with Teresa. She had no idea if he was a player on the chessboard or a pawn. All she knew was Charlie was in more danger than she'd thought. "Vivian, call Benton and tell him I have information I need to share with him and Modena. Ask them to come here *immediately*, please." Vivian nodded and lifted her phone's receiver from its cradle. She dialed as Cynthia locked the incriminating photo into her desk.

"You stay!" she said to Kevin.

Then she ran from the room, down the hall, in the opposite direction than she knew Benton and Modena would be coming from. Interrogation room 1. Once she'd turned the first corner, she did her best to look casual as she waited, peeking, until she saw Modena and Benton leave the room and enter the incident room. Then Cynthia bolted down the hall, uncaring of who might witness her strange behavior. Then she burst into interrogation room 1.

Cynthia hurried to Charlie, grabbing his cuffs, unlocking them from the table, and then from around his wrists. Unable to help herself, she grabbed his lapels and pulled him into a kiss. Charlie's mouth opened automatically, and though she felt all kinds of urges to linger, she broke it off.

"I'm brilliant!" she said.

He smiled. "I know."

"We've got a break in the case," she said. "But you're not safe in police custody. We have to go."

"What is this break?"

"Teresa and Kevin," she said. "Your techs. I'll explain later. It's just a lead. I have no proof, but I'm not taking any chances with your safety. We were right. This is looking like an inside job, Charlie. Come on." She hurried to the door and opened it, peeking into the hall. Coast was clear. "Now." She waved him to hurry up and follow her.

Charlie shook his head, rubbing his wrists. "I'm not going anywhere. And what's this about my techs?"

"Oh yes, you are." She hurried to his side and grabbed his hand, tugging. "Come on. We're running out of time."

"Talk, Cynthia." He shook her off and folded his arms over his chest.

Cynthia glared. "Listen, I can't prove anything, but I know one of them is guilty. They were in your house. Those charms Socks found? Remember? The purple heart and silver flower? They came from Teresa's keychain, which Kevin uses a lot, so he could just as likely be the culprit."

"I don't believe it." Charlie shook his head, frowning. "What keychain is this?"

"Charlie, just—" She shook her head. "Just trust me on this."

"Not when you want me to become a fugitive when things are finally going our way. I need an explanation," he said.

Cynthia pressed her palms to her pounding head. "I have no idea how deep in the department this goes. I trust my team, but we're surrounded by hundreds of people I don't know from Adam. Your techs work for the BPD. You're probably being framed by your own forensics department! What if it goes deeper than the techs? What if she's only following orders? No matter what happens today, you'll end up in holding, and what if there's an "accident"? You'll die as a prime suspect with a shit ton of evidence pointing to you. I won't allow it, Charlie. I can't! So…" She grabbed his sleeve, tugging, but he wouldn't budge.

Charlie grabbed her hand and tugged back, until she was firmly wrapped in his embrace. "You're not thinking clearly. Where are Teresa and Kevin?"

"Gilroy is bringing them to interrogation room 2." She hugged him quickly, then reached up, cupping his cheeks. "Listen to me. They'll come back any moment. I have a plane on standby. Money. A place to stay. We'll figure this out, but you can't stay here, Charlie. Please, Charlie. *Please.*" She could tell from his gaze that he was thinking about it. "They're blond, right? It could have been either of them in your driveway that night. The charms place one of them, or *both* in your house at some point. Think of that...maybe it's *both*. We don't have motive, but Vivian is working on that, and Gilroy is interviewing them now. I need you safe." She buried her face against his chest, holding him tightly. "I can't lose you."

He kissed her temple, and then nudged her chin up, forcing her to meet his gaze. "Because you love me. You never would have kissed me months ago if you weren't in love with me."

True. He sounded so sure. "Why'd you let me stay away so long?"

His gaze grew somber. "I thought you were fighting it, that you didn't want to love me. And I didn't want to force myself on you." He pressed a kiss to her lips. "Doesn't mean I didn't want to go to you every day, every hour, and demand for you to want me, too. I did. My parents were haranguing me every day to do just that, but call me crazy, I wanted you to want to love me."

"You know I do. I love you, Charlie." She pulled out of their embrace. "Which is why we need to go now. Please, trust me on this." She tugged his arm again.

"Fine," he said, no longer resisting. "But once we're gone, you need to call Benton and explain what you're doing." She opened the door and made sure the coast was clear. "What's the escape plan?" He held his arms out, looking huge. "I'm a redheaded man in an orange jumpsuit." He was right. Winging it wouldn't work, and they had to leave now, before one of the agents came back.

"We could cuff you again." She hurried back to the table, grabbing the discarded handcuffs. "We avoid as many people as we can, at least the people with authority to stop me, and then maybe we'll have a shot at escaping through the garage." She secured his wrists with cuffs. "Sorry about this, but I don't see any other choice."

Charlie's eyes crinkled with amusement. "When this is resolved, I want these handcuffs as a souvenir."

She narrowed her eyes. "Take this more seriously, please."

Charlie nodded, donning a frown. "Sorry. Proceed."

Cynthia opened the door, peered into the hall, and then grabbed his arm. She led him down the hall, avoiding eye contact with all who passed, and brought him to the back elevators, where the cleaning crew transported their carts from floor to floor. Neither said a word, and since they knew security on every floor was videotaping them, neither spoke as they stepped onto the elevator.

She patted her pocketbook hanging over her other arm, assuring herself that she had her phone, it was charged, and once she was in the car, she'd call Benton. The elevator binged when it arrived at the garage level. She reached for Charlie's elbow, needing to continue to pretend he was her prisoner until they reached his car. Then she'd uncuff him and head for the airport.

"Cynthia, did you drive?" he said.

"No. My car is at my apartment. I caught a cab."

He lifted his brows and tightened his lips. "They have my keys with the rest of my personal items." Charlie's tone was conversational. "I'm not even wearing my own underwear."

"Damn." They had no wheels. The elevator door opened, and suddenly their transport problem was no longer their worst problem.

Angelina Modelli Coppola stood, backlit by the garage's fluorescent lights, pointing a HK handgun at Charlie's center mass.

Chapter Sixteen

Charlie had a wire taped to his chest, and Benton and Modena wore earbuds, allowing them to receive audio of whatever was going on around Charlie. "Angelina Modelli," Charlie said, hoping the agents were paying attention. "Pointing a gun at me in the garage. And I thought my day couldn't get worse."

When Cynthia had left the interrogation room, the agents told Charlie about an Internal Affairs case they'd initiated after receiving the first "anonymous source" evidence. It quickly turned up Teresa Johnson's real last name: Pinnella. She was Joseph "Fingers" Pinnella's daughter. Fingers was a known contract killer for the syndicate.

"Coppola," Modelli said. "My name is Mrs. Dante Coppola." She wore her signature black suit and white open-collar shirt, the syndicate's contract killer uniform. It didn't bode well for him and Cynthia, because Modelli wasn't looking happy. In fact, she seemed as upset as Cynthia, who'd yet to uncuff him, so Charlie wasn't feeling all that happy either. "Get in." Modelli tilted her head to her right, indicating a black van idling with its side door open. Teresa Johnson, aka Pinnella, was in the driver's seat.

Cynthia held onto Charlie's arm as they walked to the van. She released him only when she crawled inside, kneeling, as Charlie followed suit, his handcuffs jangling. Up front, Teresa clutched the wheel, and Charlie could see her tears reflected in the rearview mirror. It was small comfort to know Teresa, too, was unhappy.

"I'm sorry," his tech whispered, her gaze still aimed out the front windshield. "She...she says she'll kill my family if I don't do what she says." Modelli climbed in, her gun aimed at Charlie.

"Shut up, Teresa, and drive." Modelli slammed the van door, and then knelt between the two bucket seats up front, her back to the windshield, gun steady and trained on him.

Then the gun drifted toward Cynthia.

Charlie pushed Cynthia behind him, forcing Modelli's gun to be trained only on him. Cynthia shoved him back, grabbing his arm so she could kneel beside him. His cuffs made it difficult to force the issue, though he would have if the van didn't peel out, sending them both to the floor.

"What is this about, Modelli?" Cynthia said, struggling to regain her balance and sit up. "Where are you bringing us?"

"Does it matter?" Modelli said, holding onto the back of Teresa's seat for balance. She waved her gun, indicating something behind them. Charlie glanced back and saw duct tape, zip ties, and brown cotton pieces of material he recognized. His stomach dropped as he realized what she had planned for them. "Put the hood on, Special Agent Deming. Then, Dr. Foulkes, you're going to duct tape it around her neck and zip tie her hands behind her back. Don't worry about DNA contamination. When they find your body, I'll make sure there's no doubt you're the killer, just like with the other six." Charlie's eyes remained focused on Modelli's gun as she explained how he and Cynthia would end.

"No." He might die today, but not like that. He'd make sure of it.

Modelli compressed her lips. "I can kill you now or later. Your choice." Her aim never faltered. "Get the hood. The tape. Now."

Cynthia reached for the items, her hands trembling. "Don't shoot him. I'm doing it. See? Look. I'm doing it." Grabbing the tape, zip ties, and a hood, she fumbled with them, having a hard time finding the hood's opening. "But I want something in return." Modelli shook her head, her eyes narrowing, and then glanced at Teresa.

"Drive faster," Modelli said. The van jerked forward as its speed increased, throwing Charlie against the van's interior wall. Cynthia hit the floor hard, wincing on impact and dropping the tape.

"Tell me why," Cynthia said, righting herself and picking up the tape again. "Why are you doing this?"

"I'd heard you got married." Modelli tilted her chin at Charlie. "I just want what you have."

Charlie had no idea what she was talking about. What he had was a gun aimed at his chest and the possibility of two taps to the skull—and his wife executed. "Excuse me?"

"I want my husband," Modelli said, and she said it with such emotion a sob cut her last word short. She cleared her throat, glancing at Cynthia. "I want my husband."

Cynthia shook her head. "How does killing us get you Coppola?"

"Not us," Charlie said. He had no idea what was going on in Modelli's head, but it was clear, even to him, her goals had little to do with him and Cynthia.

Modelli nodded, her focus on Cynthia. "One dead syndicate contract killer wouldn't make the news. I needed a massacre big enough to create a scandal to discredit your husband. Those men were connected to him by the syndicate case, and they were available." Modelli shrugged. "Simple as that. Nothing personal. I knew where they were, and they were gullible. I told them I had a scheme to fuck with the FBI and that Dante sanctioned it."

"Did he?" Charlie said for the benefit of his wire.

Modelli glanced at him, but then turned her glare back on Cynthia. It made him think maybe some of this was personal. Maybe Modelli hated Cynthia enough to make it personal. "They came without question, because they love my husband. The rest was easy." She became thoughtful. "I did wonder if dying for love would be different, but it looked the same to me on this side of the gun. They just died, like everyone else. Am I right, Special Agent Deming? You were there." Again, Modelli's eyes narrowed, as if she wanted to hurt Cynthia.

"This was about discrediting me," Charlie said. The crime lord could file suit, request a mistrial, and maybe have the evidence Charlie touched turned inadmissible.

Cynthia crawled to Charlie's side, holding his forearm, as if she feared Charlie might jump Modelli. With a gun pointed at them? Not likely.

"You're beyond discredited, Foulkes," Modelli said, smiling. "You're screwed." She glanced at Teresa. "I had help, of course." Charlie met Teresa's gaze in the rearview mirror and felt his anger flare. Modelli saw and shook her head. "Don't be angry at Teresa. Your wife would be dead without her. When she'd arrived, gun drawn, looking to ruin all my carefully laid out plans, I was about to take the shot, but Teresa knocked her over the head first. She went down like a stone." Modelli chuckled. "And when I was about to put one in her temple, Teresa stopped me. Told me to use her. Isn't that right, Teresa? She said 'Use the Fed. Frame the Fed.'" Modelli's smile widened. "She didn't know the plan, of course. It had to be you. *Dr. Charlie Foulkes*. But it did get me thinking: Implicating Special Agent Deming in the murders would create a nice distraction. It distracted you," she said, her gazed locked with Charlie's.

"You used my gun," Cynthia said, "but not on the vics."

Modelli's smirk was derisive. "You won't find my prints on the gun, if that's what you're hoping for."

"Was this Dante's idea?" Cynthia said. "You're going to kill us. Why not admit it? Why keep that a secret?"

"No," Modelli said, her smile fading. "Dante doesn't know."

It was on tape, Charlie realized. The pertinent facts, anyway. *This was all Modelli.* No matter what happened from here on, live or die, Modelli's crimes would be provable. This case would close. Charlie found it little consolation as he stared at the wrong end of Modelli's gun. She gripped the driver's seat, steadying herself as Teresa seemed to hit every bump in the road, and then aimed her gun at Cynthia. They were fish in a barrel. Handcuffed, five feet from a cold-blooded killer, any attempt to wrestle the gun from Modelli would land Charlie shot, maybe dead, and then who would save Cynthia?

"When Dante's free, I'll tell him what I did for him, and then he'll realize—" Modelli bit her lower lip. "My lawyer assures me when you're implicated in the murders, all your cases will be up for review. They'll be thrown out by a judge. They'll have to release Dante on bail, at the least, and then we'll run. We'll run so far no one will ever find us."

"I get it." Cynthia climbed to her knees, the hood still gripped in her hands. "You love him, but doesn't it bother you that he doesn't love you?" Cynthia's tone dripped with sympathy.

"It doesn't matter."

"Of course it matters!" Cynthia snapped. "Dante Coppola doesn't love anyone but himself."

"I know," Modelli said, acting as if Cynthia was being difficult. "I'm not like you. I don't need that. I need Dante." Charlie couldn't help noticing that Cynthia seemed to be taking this conversation personally, too, and couldn't understand why. Sure, her profiler voodoo was important, but they had a gun trained on them. He thought that a more pressing concern.

"There's a reason why I never suspected you," Cynthia said. She seemed poised, but for what? Charlie grabbed her hand, in case she decided to lunge at the woman.

"Yeah?" Modelli smiled.

"I was convinced that you knew once Coppola gained his freedom, he'd leave you, or kill you. Either way, you had to know you wouldn't have him. You need him incarcerated, Modelli, to *keep* him."

Modelli narrowed her eyes. "You're wrong. He needs me." She glanced out the van's windshield, as did Charlie. Teresa had driven them to the original crime scene, where the Chinatown Massacre occurred.

"Why are we at the crime scene?" Charlie said, for the benefit of any special agents listening in.

"Pull over there," Modelli said to Teresa. "Next to that wall." Then she waved the gun at Cynthia. "Hurry up. Put on the hood, the zip ties. Now. You,"—she waved her gun at Charlie—"duct tape the hood on her neck." Charlie shook his head. He couldn't do that. "Do it," Modelli said, her tone low, determined as she straightened her arm, aiming the gun at his chest. Charlie thought being shot dead preferable to putting that damn hood on the love of his life's head. He wouldn't do it. "I can shoot you now and stage your body later," Modelli said.

Cynthia held her palms up, between Modelli and Charlie. "No. Don't shoot. I said I'd do it!" With trembling hands, she picked up the hood and the duct tape and swallowed hard. "I'll do it," she whispered, as if to herself, dredging up the courage. "Just...Charlie?" She lifted her chin, locking gazes. Her eyes welled with tears, breaking his heart. Was this how it would end for them? "Live, Charlie. Okay? Just...*live*." Then she pulled the hood over her head, and the ripping sound of her pulling a length of duct tape echoed in the van.

"*Fuck this.*" Charlie tugged off her hood and looped his handcuffed wrists over Cynthia's head, trapping her to his chest. Then he threw them to the van's floor, taking the impact on his shoulder before rolling on top of her. He tensed as he waited for a bullet to rip through his body as he protected every inch of Cynthia, shielding her with his body. The back? Knee? Hip? His mind scrolled through Anatomy 101, and decided a bullet to the sciatic nerve would be excruciating. Cynthia struggled beneath him, but forehead to forehead, he held her panicked gaze. If he was dying now, he wanted Cynthia's eyes to be the last thing he saw, *her* breath the last air he breathed, her *body* the last thing he felt.

"Get up, for shit's sake," Modelli said.

"We choose," he whispered. "And I choose you." Charlie heard Modelli pull back the slide and chamber a bullet. Cynthia's palms were pinned against his chest.

"I love you," Cynthia whispered as her fingers curled, digging into his chest.

"Lina, no!" Teresa shouted.

A gun discharged and echoed in the cabin. Blinding pain had Charlie's body arching. Cynthia screamed. A screech of braking tires. He became weightless, and within a heartbeat, everything rushed to the front of the van. Cynthia slammed into him, still wrangled by the loop of his cuffed wrists, and knocked the air from his lungs as he impacted with the seats.

The windshield shattered. Air bags deployed. *Pop-pop.* One after the other, and then there was ringing in Charlie's ears and Cynthia's hands patting him down. He felt pressure on his leg. Sirens screamed in the distance and broke his shock. He sat, eyes wide, as air inflated his lungs and shattered glass rained off him. Cynthia was talking to him, but he couldn't process her words.

"I'm okay. Are you okay?" Nauseous, his focus dropped to his leg. He noted the blood, the burning. He was losing blood, but there was no spurting, so no major arteries were hit. He ripped his jumpsuit's pant leg, hindered by the cuffs. "What did we hit?"

"The brick wall. Modelli flew through the windshield. I don't know if she's alive," Cynthia said, her eyes on his leg. "Is it bad?"

The bullet seemed to be a through-and-through. "Well, this sucks."

"Charlie! *Is it bad?*" Tears ran down her cheeks, but you wouldn't know it from her fierce expression and pugilistic posture. Her hands were poised to put pressure on his wound.

"Uncuff me." He held out his wrists, noting the blood dripping from his fingertips. It took a few tries, but Cynthia retrieved the key from her pocket, and once free he sniffed the air. Smoke free. "Do you smell gas?" He didn't. Cynthia shook her head. "It might not last. Let's get the hell out."

"First, your leg." She found the duct tape roll and wrapped its length around his wound until Charlie nodded, sure it would hinder bleeding without cutting his circulation.

"Check on Teresa." He grabbed the sliding side door and it opened easily as Cynthia crawled up front.

"Teresa?" She gripped the seat, peering at the tech's face, and then legs.

"Benton," Charlie spoke into the microphone taped to his chest. "I hope you got all that."

"Huh?" Cynthia turned her head in time to see Charlie open the top buttons on his jumpsuit and reveal wires taped to his chest. "Benton," Cynthia snarled, "if you're listening, I'm going to *kill* you." Charlie heard sobs coming from Teresa. Cynthia turned back to the driver. "Broken nose. Legs pinned." She pulled the deflated air bag off Teresa and grimaced when she got a good look at the tech's legs.

"Benton, we need an ambulance," he said. "Teresa's pinned in the van. Hurry, please." His leg wound was burning.

"Teresa, for all I know this van is about to blow up, so don't dick around. Tell me how you were involved." Glass fell off Cynthia's hair and shoulders as she tugged at the tech's seat belt, releasing her strap.

Cynthia wasn't wrong. The van's stability seemed iffy at best, and if Teresa was pinned, they didn't have much time to free her. As much as he wanted to hear explanations, he wanted Cynthia as far away from this van as possible while he heard them.

"Cynthia. Outside." He didn't wait for Cynthia's agreement, but instead grabbed her around the waist and dragged her from the van. Not an easy task while hobbled by a GSW to the thigh. When Cynthia's feet hit tarmac, she pivoted to the van's door, tugging on the handle. It didn't move. Charlie nudged her hand aside and tried. The metal was bent. That door wasn't opening without heavy equipment. "How you doing in there?" Charlie said. Teresa was dabbing at her bloody, broken nose with her fingertips.

"I'm pinned." Teresa didn't meet his gaze. "Kind of numb. That's probably not a good sign." She glanced at Charlie. "Thanks for asking. You...you were always nice to me."

Hopping onto the footstep with his good leg, he allowed his other to hang as he squeezed his upper body in through the window. Grabbing the dashboard that now pinned Teresa's thighs, he used all his strength to lift it. Gained merely an inch, but Teresa grew pale and gasped from the pain. He saw his attempts were making her bleed faster, so he released his grip and stepped back. They'd have to wait for the fire department.

Cynthia had climbed on the van's hood, using the brick wall to stabilize her balance. She pressed two fingers to Modelli's neck. "She's alive."

"Get down from there," Charlie said, the buzzing in his ears growing louder; a combination of blood loss and his initial adrenaline rush after the crash fading.

"So, Teresa, why'd you frame Charlie for murder?" Cynthia hopped down, and somehow didn't break an ankle in her heels.

"I never wanted to..." Teresa shook her head, dropping her gaze to her lap, now covered with shattered, bloody glass. "When my father turned state's evidence," Teresa said, her voice faint, "Lina promised not to kill him if I helped her. I refused, because my father was in WITSEC. I figured he was safe. Then she threatened to kill my whole family. So I had no choice. I said yes."

"You could have asked for help. Instead, you put other people in danger." Cynthia paced next to the van, staring down the road, watching the progress of the first responders driving toward them, sirens growing louder. "Charlie? Sit down before you fall down."

Teresa caught Charlie's attention. "I'm bleeding." She smiled through her pain. "I think I nicked an artery."

"No. You're just sitting up, so it seems like a lot. The weight of the dash should be enough pressure to keep you safe until they can get you out of there." Charlie glanced at Modelli. Her gun was nowhere in sight, but he didn't want to take any chances. "Where's the gun, Cynthia?"

"In the van," Cynthia said, compressing her lips. "She's out cold, and I think she broke her neck."

"Shit." That meant he had to climb up to Modelli. With Cynthia hemming and hawing the whole time, he managed to do that, dragging his left leg behind him as he triaged the contract killer. "If it's broken, I can't tell from palpation," he said, "but she's likely suffering internal injuries, broken bones." He carefully slid off the front of the van and took a moment to breathe through his pain and dizziness. Cynthia wrapped his arm around her shoulder. "Sit down!" she shouted. He did, lowering with one leg as he propped his back against the driver's side running board, under the window.

"Did *you* kill anyone, Teresa?" Charlie asked as soon as he adjusted his bad leg. With a head injury, it was important to keep her talking. And that seemed a good a question as any.

"No," Teresa said. Her voice was quiet, but seemed strong enough considering her circumstances. The fire truck arrived, and the ambulances and police cruisers, skidding to a stop. Relief scratched at his worry.

Cynthia leaned a hand on the van's door, peering at Teresa. "Did you know the WITSEC witnesses would be killed?"

Charlie licked his lips, deciding a whiskey neat would be in his future.

"No. I didn't," he heard Teresa say above him. "I arrived when she'd lined them up against the wall. You arrived. I panicked, knocked you out, and then Lina shot everyone. Just…just shot everyone. I thought she was going to shoot me, too. I convinced her not to kill you. Don't believe her about me wanting to frame Charlie or you. I said whatever I could think of to stop her from killing you." Doors opened and slammed as sirens were silenced and uniformed police and firemen rushed toward them.

Cynthia nodded. "What *did* you say? I mean, to convince her not to kill me?" Charlie was interested to hear the answer, so he leaned and looked up, but could only see Cynthia's face.

"I told her," Teresa said, "that Charlie was in love with you." Teresa's bloody hand rested on the broken driver's side window frame, causing shattered glass to fall on Charlie's head. "Lina had me falsify evidence, but I kept anything connecting you back. Dug out the slugs from the shots she took. Discarded the blood samples I knew were yours."

Charlie watched Cynthia's face twist with confusion. "Why would you do that?"

"Because Charlie loves you," Teresa whispered. EMTs converged on them, and Charlie was lifted onto a gurney as Cynthia was hustled away from the van.

"Cooperate with the FBI, with the DA. Make a deal," Cynthia shouted to Teresa.

Charlie sighed as an IV needle was stuck into the crook of his left elbow and he was wheeled to the ambulance. Teresa had been extorted, threatened, but had been instrumental in saving Cynthia's life twice. Modelli's bullet hit Charlie's leg just as Teresa slammed on the brakes. A deal would happen. Charlie would make sure of it.

Firemen approached with heavy equipment, and Charlie knew they were set to cut Teresa from the van. He saw EMTs hovering over Modelli like flies. Cynthia was at his side, holding his hand. "Charlie, you're going to be the death of me." She sniffed, her chin quivering as they rolled his gurney into the ambulance. He decided to give her something else to think about other than his leg.

"We've got Angelina Modelli Coppola on tape confessing to six counts of murder," he said. "Money laundering, transferring funds out of the country, conspiracy to fraudulently implicate me, conspiracy to—"

"Murder is enough," Cynthia said. "That might take some of the pressure off the DA to hit Teresa with accessory charges." Police sirens heralded a phalanx of additional black and white cruisers.

Whatever they'd put in Charlie's IV had him comfortable quickly, and feeling lazy. It wasn't long before Teresa was being wheeled past his view out the open ambulance back door, also hooked up to an IV. He shouted to her. "Teresa," he said, "how did you gain access to my gun safe? Only me and Cynthia had that code."

Teresa grimaced, turning her head toward him. "I eavesdropped when Special Agent Deming was criticizing you for using her birth date for your passwords." She raised her voice to be heard over the chaos. "You should have listened to her." Then Teresa's gurney was wheeled away.

"*I know*, right?" Cynthia scowled at him, but he was too distracted by the EMT cutting the duct tape off his leg to call her on it. It should have hurt, but the meds made him not notice. When he was bandaged, and Cynthia was still scowling, he grabbed her hand.

"Make a choice. Do you want to yell at me or be grateful we're okay?" Modelli's body was wheeled past them by an EMT accompanied by a uniformed officer. She was still unconscious.

"A choice, huh?" Cynthia scowl faded. "Like the choice you made in the van?"

He nodded. "I chose you. To die in your arms, if need be, rather than see you die."

"Oh, Charlie." Her chin quivered. "That's the most romantic thing I've ever heard."

"I will always choose you, Cynthia. You know that." He hugged her, straightening his leg to give the EMT more access to the wound. Charlie saw Benton's cherry red sports car park at the curb, beyond the cruisers and cops waving people back. He ran full tilt toward them.

"Everyone alive? We heard it all." We? Charlie saw Modena exit the car at a more comfortable pace and saunter past the cops putting up crime scene tape. This scene had only been released yesterday, and now it was a crime scene again. The area businesses were not going to be happy.

"We're alive." Charlie nodded to Modena as he approached. "Modelli was alive when last I saw her."

Cynthia scowled at her team. "It would have been nice to be brought into your plan. Might have saved me a ride in a van."

Modena shrugged. "You ran with a known fugitive. Don't blame us."

"We heard it all," Benton said. "Proof Charlie was targeted because of his connection to the Coppola case."

Modena nodded. "Modelli's plan would have worked, too."

"She had help. Teresa must have been the blonde in Charlie's driveway," Cynthia said.

"Sooner or later," Charlie said, "the forensic evidence would have proven I was innocent."

"Forensics takes time," Benton said. "The wire was a better idea."

"But why the wire?" Cynthia shook her head, obviously confused. "You couldn't have known I'd take Charlie. And he resisted at first."

"We knew Modelli was in the area," Modena said. "And before you pulled that stunt back at the precinct, we were minutes away from dangling Charlie as bait on a perp walk, hoping for the best."

Cynthia's eyes widened with fury. "You were going to put Charlie on an undercover op? *My* Charlie!"

"We were out of options," Charlie said. "But then you'd basically solved the case, so I thought your idea of running was probably the best." The EMT waved the agents away from the door. "How am I doing?" he asked his EMT. She was in her thirties, cool as a cucumber, short hair and almond-shaped brown eyes.

"You're going to live." She smiled. "But we need to bring you to the ER to irrigate the wound." She leaned toward the front. "I'm closing the door and then we're ready to go."

Modena and Benton waved and headed toward the crime scene as the EMT closed them inside the ambulance. Cynthia still held his hand, looking worried.

The trip to the hospital was uneventful, and other than a nurse waving scissors too close to his privates as she cut the jumpsuit off, his treatment progressed without a hitch. An hour later, hydrated with two bags of Lactated Ringers solution, antibiotics, and pain meds, Charlie was sewn up, with two more scars to add to his collection. Benton called twice, and Modena was two doors down interviewing Teresa as the doctors worked on her. Everyone waited for news of Modelli's prognosis.

Charlie didn't care about any of that. He just wanted to go home and be with Cynthia. She was worrying him, not meeting his gaze, though her hand was never far away, touching him, clasping his, patting his arm. Benton had Charlie's belongings driven to the hospital, so Cynthia drove him home in his own clothes rather than borrowed scrubs.

Socks greeted him, angry and hungry.

And it was there, standing in the kitchen, watching Socks demolish a can of Cat Chow, that Charlie finally said what he'd been wanting to say since the van. He turned to Cynthia, saw her distraction as she stared at his cat eating, her folded arms rumpling her suit jacket. Dark circles and blood smears were in sharp contrast to her pale complexion. She was a woman who had been through a lot, and he was sorry for it. The last couple of days had taken its toll, and she deserved to crash, thinking about manicures and long baths, and maybe takeout, but words were pressing at the back of his throat, begging to be said.

"Stay married to me, Cynthia." She didn't move, didn't even clench her jaw. But her eyes tracked up his body until they met his gaze. "I love you. I need…" He eased his weight onto the hospital-provided cane and limped toward her. "I need you with me, in my life, all the time, or I'll never be happy." He stepped in front of her, not touching her, because she seemed unmoved and walled off to him. "We are not friends with benefits. We're in love. Admit it. You're in love with me."

She unfolded her arms and stepped close, pressing her palms to his chest. Her right hand landed over his heart, which he knew was racing a mile a minute. It made Charlie wonder if this was part of her voodoo, measuring how fast she could make his heart race.

"I am," she said. "I am in love with you."

That's what he wanted to hear, yet she remained so still, as if she were waiting for something. "And you'll stay married to me?"

She nodded very solemnly. "I will."

"You love me." He covered her hands with his free one, and then pressed his forehead to hers, needing to lean to do it. "I need you to say it again," he whispered. "Tell me everything. Please."

"I love you, Charlie Foulkes. I love you so much sometimes it scares me to death, because..." She inhaled sharply, as if she were barely keeping her composure.

"I'm not dying anytime soon." Was that the problem? He was injured again and it must be bringing up all sorts of traumatic memories for her. Car accident. Terrance. Almost dying.

"You say that now," she laughed, blinking away tears. "In the van..." She shook her head. "When Modelli shot you, I nearly died from fright. I think my heart did stop. I can't do that again, Charlie. I lost Terrance—"

"We lost Terrance."

She nodded. "I can't lose you."

Now that was a problem he could live with. Charlie sighed, quite happy, as he dropped his cane, balanced on one leg, and wrapped her in his arms. "I'm here, and I love you," he said. "We can't change the past, but the future is ours. And Cynthia? I feel so incredibly *lucky* to spend it with you." He knew she was holding him tightly, in part to help him balance on one leg, and it hit him as funny. He blamed the meds. But the feeling of happiness that was filling all the nooks and crannies of his heart was all Cynthia.

He kissed her as the sting of the past died, and in its place was born a wonder and excitement for their future. He and Cynthia had a second chance, and this time he wouldn't screw it up. This time, he knew what he wanted from her, and he knew what he'd get.

Everything.

Epilogue

Three months later, Cynthia donned her favorite casual dress, a rose and pink Dolce and Gabbana number that never failed to make her husband smile, and stepped out onto the back porch of Charlie's house. Though, technically, it was their house now. They'd rejected his parents' demands for a redo on the wedding ceremony, and instead opted for a BBQ in lieu of a reception. Charlie's contribution to the event were the invitations, a photograph of Charlie on bended knee on the sidewalk outside of the crime scene. Somehow, the photographer captured a moment of surprise and delight on Cynthia's face, though she only remembered being embarrassed and horrified. It was a great picture.

The weather couldn't have been more sublime, and the company was perfect. The whole gang was there. Charlie's parents, Delia and Paul, were assembling a fruit trifle on the table on the porch, while Charlie manned the grill, turning steaks, wearing an apron with the graphic design of a tuxedo on it. Benton and his pregnant wife, Hannah, admired their baby daughter, Ellen, who sat on the grass, clapping her hands. Gilroy was feeding Vivian O'Grady crudités dipped in ranch dressing by the picnic table on the lawn, and Modena was sipping beer, staring longingly into the eyes of Charlotte, aka Avery Toner Coppola, an engineering student from the University of Massachusetts. Charlotte's sister, Brittany, aka, Millie Toner, a blond, beautiful teen, was looking bored as she scrolled on her iPhone while sitting on the porch's back stairs.

"Everyone grab a beer," Cynthia said. "It's time for a toast."

"Not you," Charlotte said to Brittany, who rolled her eyes and then went back to scrolling on her phone. "If you're thirsty, I'll get you a cup of punch."

"Is it that time?" Charlie pulled the steaks off the grill and put down the tongs.

"I think so," Cynthia said. It had been hard enough keeping the secret this long, she couldn't wait another moment longer. "If you're grabbing a punch for Brittany, could you get me one too, Charlotte?" She saw Charlotte's eyes widen, and Hannah started laughing, resting her palms on her pregnant belly.

"We have an announcement." Charlie stepped to her side, taking a beer from Gilroy, who delivered open bottles to all without a drink, then he slipped his arm around Cynthia's waist, giving her a "Go for it" wink.

"I'm pregnant!" Cynthia shouted, throwing her hands in the air. Everyone applauded and stepped forward, throwing questions at them. Then Charlie's parents took turns hugging them, and wiping Cynthia's happy tears.

"Do you have any names chosen?" Delia said. Her husband put his arm around her waist, smiling.

"Yes, mom." Charlie gave Cynthia a squeeze. "Terrance," he said.

"If it's a boy," Cynthia said. "And Terry if it's a girl."

"He brought us together. It's only fitting," Charlie said, catching Cynthia's gaze. "I owe him so much." He gave her a squeeze, dropping a kiss on her lips. "I love you, Cynthia," he whispered.

There'd been a time where Cynthia would have dreaded hearing Charlie say things like "owe" and "debt." They were words that felt like shackles she'd never escape. Now, she understood, and appreciated what Charlie had been trying to tell her all these years.

"I love you, too," she whispered back.

Terrance's death was a tragedy. It wasn't fair that he'd died and Charlie lived, that he didn't get a tomorrow. Sure, life wasn't fair, but it was important to acknowledge what Terrance lost, and what they'd gained. From their shared deadly past, a love grew, a debt was owed, and she'd happily pay it every day by honoring her brother's memory.

Charlie's arm tugged her close as he looked at the smiling faces surrounding them at their wedding reception BBQ. Today, life was good, and she'd learned to grab those days when they came. Charlie was hers, she had his baby in her belly, and she had hope that happiness would be their new normal. She sniffed, feeling weepy.

"You okay?" Charlie said, ignoring all the congratulatory chatter around them and focusing on her.

She nodded. She was. "I'm happy." Then she kissed him to prove it.

And knew he was convinced.

If you enjoyed *Deadly Past*

by Kris Rafferty,

make sure you read the first book

in the

Secret Agents series:

CAUGHT BY YOU

available at your favorite e-tailer

Turn the page for a quick peek!

Chapter 1

"Deming? Are you insane?" Special Agent Vincent Modena was in the back of the FBI's surveillance van, kneeling knee to knee with Special Agent Cynthia Deming, the task force's profiler. It wasn't Deming who was the problem; it was the five-pound flounder she held by the gills. It was staring at him, and smelled hideous.

"Your cover is a week-long fishing trip. You're too clean." Deming narrowed her blue eyes, and then slapped the fish against Vincent's chest.

"Stop!" He grabbed her wrist, processing the moment. Rich, blond, gorgeous Cynthia Deming, in a black Dolce & Gabbana suit and heels, was on her knees swinging a fish. Nope. He was living it and still didn't believe his eyes. Meanwhile, the flounder hung limp in the air between them. "I'm supposed to keep Avery Coppola *in* the diner, Deming. Hit me with that again, and the smell will chase her *out*." She broke his grip, seemingly teetering between agreeing and having another go at him with the fish.

Special Agent Jack Benton, FBI task force team leader, jumped from the van's passenger seat into the back. "What the hell?" He grimaced, glaring at the profiler and Vincent, as if Vincent had anything to do with the fish. He didn't.

"Exactly," Vincent said. "What the hell, Deming?"

"What's with the fish?" Benton's black hair hung in his face, obscuring the intensity in his blue-eyed gaze. His year-long deep embed with Dante Coppola's syndicate crashed and burned yesterday, requiring the task force to extract him. His split lip hinted at the bruises and abrasions hidden beneath his conservative black suit and tie, but it was the banked rage that made his team nervous. Benton hadn't taken time off to shake his role of gunrunner, and some deep embeds needed more recovery time than others, but he'd escaped with a lead, so Benton wasn't going anywhere. The lead was, Coppola hired contract killers to find and kill his ex-wife and her little sister. Rumor had it, when she'd divorced him three years ago, the ex-wife left with incriminating files. Now, Coppola knew where the ex-wife was, and so did Benton. It appeared as if the task force lucked out and got here first.

"The fish is necessary for authenticity," Deming said. "Modena's too..." She waved a hand at him. "Handsome."

"Hey, Benton." Vincent held Deming gaze and then winked. "Deming thinks I'm handsome."

She shook her head, barely paying attention to Vincent. "Maybe *clean* is a better word. After a week of backcountry camping, he wouldn't be this clean." She used the back of her wrist to nudge a blond lock off her cheek. "No one sleeps outside for a week, lives off fresh catch of the day, and doesn't suffer from puffy face and bad hair. Avery's clever and distrustful. She's had to be to escape detection for three years with a sister in tow. With contract killers on her scent, she'll smell a rat if Modena doesn't commit to his backstory."

"She'll smell something." Special Agent Harris Gilroy was the task force's official driver. Blond hair cropped to his head, brown eyes, mid-thirties, he looked like an Irish bare-knuckle fighter, crooked nose and all.

"His backpack is enough of a prop," Benton said. "Get rid of the fish, Deming."

"Fine." She tossed it into a Styrofoam cooler, and then stripped off her latex gloves, throwing them inside, too. She seemed on edge. Yesterday's violent extraction of Benton had notably rattled her, rattled them all, as did the dead bodies the team left behind. And when Deming was rattled, she distracted herself with details—like Vincent's backstory and a fish—so Vincent tried not to take the fish assault personally.

"Our warrant is to surveil Avery Coppola's apartment," Benton said. "Unfortunately, I couldn't convince the judge that rumored files containing alleged evidence is grounds for a search warrant, so we watch and wait for Coppola's men to make their move. If the files are in her apartment, she either surrenders them, or we need probable cause to take them. If Coppola's men find her, maybe make a move on her at the apartment, we've got them and our probable cause, so cross your fingers. Modena, you keep an eye on her at the diner while we set up the cameras outside of her apartment. I want any potential attack on video. Let a judge and jury see who these monsters are, and if we're forced to bust into her apartment to save her, and happen to find evidence, they'll be forced to make our findings admissible in court. Time is short, folks. We have no idea when Coppola's men will show, but this isn't rocket science. If she has files, which my contact assured me she does, it's probably hidden in her apartment. Coppola's men have to know that."

"Yeah, about that, Benton," Deming said. "I think I should go in the diner instead of Modena. Look at him. He looks dangerous. She'll think he's a contract killer, maybe run, and ruin the whole operation. We can think of a different backstory for me."

"Deming, you'd be walking into a backwoods diner wearing Dolce & Gabbana," Vincent said. "Do you really think you'll get anywhere near her without making her suspicious? And Benton knows I have advantages you don't have." He allowed a slow smile to crack his lips. "Leave the ex-wife to me."

She shook her head, still not convinced. "But—"

"I know. I know. I'm handsome, clean, *and* dangerous." Vincent winked, trying not to enjoy Deming's annoyance too much. Being on the sidelines was twisting her in knots. She wanted in on the action, and he didn't blame her, but he'd waited too long to meet Avery Coppola to just give this moment away. "I think you're crushing on me."

"Blow me, Modena." She turned toward Benton, waiting for his decision.

"We stick with the plan," Benton said. "Modena, go."

Gilroy reached into a console between the two front seats and produced a bottle of Febreze. He aimed it into the back of the van and sprayed with no concern for whom he doused. Between the fish smell, and being gassed by Gilroy, Vincent found it a relief to spill out into the parking lot, backpack slung over his shoulder.

As the task force sped off in the van, heading down the street toward Avery Coppola's apartment, Vincent walked toward the diner, passing a multitude of beat up SUVs and trucks, listening to his hiking boots crunch gravel underfoot. The chirping of birds, the breezes rustling through maple and oak leaves, it was a nice change from the city. August in the North Country of New Hampshire, mountainous. Vincent was enjoying himself, and the diner's aromas wafting through the air. His stomach growled as he approached the door, but his thoughts were all on the woman inside.

Avery Coppola. *Damn.* Her name had been popping up in the Coppola case for a year now, but Vincent had only actively studied her for the last few months. He was a little ashamed to be this excited about meeting her... Dante Coppola's one vulnerability. Avery was the crime lord's ex-wife, so probably poison, without conscience. Totally his type. Vincent's ex-wife taught him a thing or two about women like that. On his second tour in Afghanistan, she'd sent him a Dear John letter paper clipped to divorce papers. It had a way of changing a man's paradigm real quick. It certainly forced Vincent to see things more clearly. Women were mercurial at best, self-serving at worst. It was weird to know he had something in common with a murderous crime lord. Both he and Coppola married women who'd betrayed them.

He'd memorized Avery's pictures. She had the look of an innocent, red-headed imp, and seemed younger than her years. She certainly didn't look like someone who could inspired an ex-husband to hire contract killers to off her. Not a sterling personal recommendation, and yet, the contradiction tickled Vincent's curiosity. What would she be like? Or rather, how best to bend her to his will?

Benton wanted to try and flip her, see if they could convince her to give up the goods on her ex, rather than make the Feds slog for the evidence, but they didn't have enough intel to know how best to approach her. Deming, the task force's profiler, suggested they feel her out with some casual conversation. Benton had tapped Vincent, and he'd report back to the team after they'd finished installing security cameras around her apartment.

Just meeting her would probably answer most of the questions his team had. Then, if all went as planned, they'd find the leverage they needed to flip her, and she'd help break open the task force's RICO case against her ex-husband. If *that* went south, she'd either face jail time or risk a bullet between the eyes. Dante Coppola wasn't pulling his hit on her anytime soon, and now that he knew where she was, she had a target on her back. The FBI would offer her protection, if she was willing to deal, but they couldn't make her accept their help. No, that would take persuasion. And that was where Vincent came in.

He smiled as he opened the diner's door. A bell chimed overhead, announcing his arrival. It was old-fashioned and kitschy, and he liked it. As he stepped inside, he finally admitted to himself that he'd been anticipating this meeting with Avery Coppola since he'd first seen her photo nearly a year ago. He was excited, and when his gaze zeroed in on her behind the diner's counter, his chest tightened because he knew... This was going to be fun. Lots and lots of fun.

About the Author

Kris Rafferty was born in Cambridge, Massachusetts. After earning a Bachelor's in Arts from the University of Massachusetts/Boston, she married her college sweetheart, traveled the country and wrote books. Three children and a Pomeranian/Shih Tzu mutt later, she spends her days devoting her life to her family and her craft.

Printed in the United States
by Baker & Taylor Publisher Services